Blood and Gold

Also by Joseph A. West
in Large Print:

Ralph Compton: Doomsday Rider
Ralph Compton: Showdown at
   Two-Bit Creek

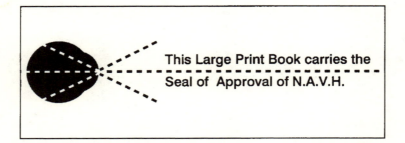

This Large Print Book carries the
Seal of Approval of N.A.V.H.

Ralph Compton
Blood and Gold

A Ralph Compton Novel

Joseph A. West

Thorndike Press • Waterville, Maine

Copyright © The Estate of Ralph Compton, 2004

Published in 2005 by arrangement with NAL Signet, a division of Penguin Group (USA) Inc.

Thorndike Press® Large Print Western.

The tree indicium is a trademark of Thorndike Press.

The text of this Large Print edition is unabridged. Other aspects of the book may vary from the original edition.

Set in 16 pt. Plantin by Elena Picard.

Printed in the United States on permanent paper.

Library of Congress Cataloging-in-Publication Data

West, Joseph A.
    Blood and gold : a Ralph Compton novel /
by Joseph A. West.
        p. cm. — (Thorndike press large print westerns.)
    ISBN 0-7862-7603-7 (lg. print : hc : alk. paper)
    1. Cowboys — Fiction. 2. Travelers — Fiction. 3. Red River Valley (Tex.-La.) — Fiction. 4. Large type books.
I. Title: Ralph Compton. II. Compton, Ralph. III. Title.
IV. Thorndike Press large print Western series
PS3573.E8224B58 2005
    813'.54—dc22   2005003436

Blood and Gold

As the Founder/CEO of NAVH, the only national health agency solely devoted to those who, although not totally blind, have an eye disease which could lead to serious visual impairment, I am pleased to recognize Thorndike Press★ as one of the leading publishers in the large print field.

Founded in 1954 in San Francisco to prepare large print textbooks for partially seeing children, NAVH became the pioneer and standard setting agency in the preparation of large type.

Today, those publishers who meet our standards carry the prestigious "Seal of Approval" indicating high quality large print. We are delighted that Thorndike Press is one of the publishers whose titles meet these standards. We are also pleased to recognize the significant contribution Thorndike Press is making in this important and growing field.

Lorraine H. Marchi, L.H.D.
Founder/CEO
NAVH

★ Thorndike Press encompasses the following imprints: Thorndike, Wheeler, Walker and Large Print Press.

The Immortal Cowboy

This is respectfully dedicated to the "American Cowboy." His was the saga sparked by the turmoil that followed the Civil War, and the passing of more than a century has by no means diminished the flame.

True, the old days and the old ways are but treasured memories, and the old trails have grown dim with the ravages of time, but the spirit of the cowboy lives on.

In my travels — to Texas, Oklahoma, Kansas, Nebraska, Colorado, Wyoming, New Mexico, and Arizona — I always find something that reminds me of the Old West. While I am walking these plains and mountains for the first time, there is this feeling that a part of me is eternal, that I have known these old trails before. I believe it is the undying spirit of the frontier calling, allowing me, through the mind's eye, to step back into time. What is the appeal of the Old West of the American frontier?

It has been epitomized by some as the dark and bloody period in American history. Its heroes — Crockett, Bowie, Hickok, Earp — have been reviled and criticized. Yet the Old West lives on, larger than life.

It has become a symbol of freedom, when there was always another mountain to climb and another river to cross; when a dispute between two men was settled not with expensive lawyers, but with fists, knives, or guns. Barbaric? Maybe. But some things never change. When the cowboy rode into the pages of American history, he left behind a legacy that lives within the hearts of us all.

— Ralph Compton

Chapter 1

I had thirty thousand dollars in paper money and gold coin in my saddlebags and now the rain had settled the dust on my back trail that had been nagging at me for the past two days.

Maybe the dust meant nothing.

It could have been kicked up by a puncher like me, heading back to Texas broke and hungover, vowing never to come up the trail again and wishing mightily he'd steered well clear of the bright lights and easy sin of Dodge.

But dust could mean something else.

It could mean I was dancing with the devil and they were playing his tune.

Me, I was eighteen years old that summer of 1880 and still kind of green, even though I'd been up the trail three times. I had twice tangled with Comanche and once, the spring before, had shot it out with three rustlers south of the Washita.

After the smoke cleared, big Bob Collins, the trail boss, had slapped me on the back and said I'd done good, though I doubted that I'd hit anybody, being no great shakes with the long gun, though I'm a fair to middling hand with the Colt.

But that was then, and this was now.

Since I'd crossed the Cimarron and ridden into the Indian territory, I'd tried not to pay any mind to the dust. I'd been a-singing to my pony, mostly sappy love songs that I'd heard in Dodge and a dozen other cow towns. The paint didn't like my singing none, shaking his head, his bit jangling, every time I murdered a high note.

But having such a disapproving audience didn't bother me, on account I knew I'd soon be seeing my best gal again. Sally Coleman, with her blond hair and blue eyes, lived on her pa's ranch about a hundred miles south of the Red. A gal as pretty as Sally had her choice of men, but it was in my mind that I'd marry her someday and raise up a passel of kids with her.

Hanging on my saddle horn, covered up by my slicker, was a straw bonnet, all tied around with blue ribbons, that I'd bought for Sally in Dodge. That bonnet cost me a week's wages, but I reckoned just to see her wear it would be worth the money, and then some.

Before the rain started, I could tell that the dust behind me was a ways off and not getting any closer.

But now there was nothing to see and I was fast becoming uneasy.

It was no secret in Dodge that I'd ridden out of town with thirty thousand dollars. That was money enough to tempt a man, especially the shifty border trash, gamblers, dance hall loungers, goldbrick artists and the like, who migrated north with the herds every spring to Dodge and Caldwell and Wichita, eager to separate a drover from his hard-earned wages.

And there were others, much more dangerous, dry, hard-eyed men who wore their guns like they were born to them, lean riders who haunted moon-shadowed trails and never looked at a thing directly, but saw everything. When such men went to the gun, they were almighty sudden and certain and I wanted no part of them.

Was it men like those who rode behind me?

When you're eighteen, you figure you can't be killed. I'd seen plenty of dying on the Western Trail: punchers trampled in stampedes, drowned in river crossings, snakebit, dragged by runaway ponies. But death always chose some other poor feller

11

and seemed content to tiptoe around me.

But now I couldn't shake the feeling that danger was dogging my trail and maybe, just maybe, I wasn't as immortal as I thought. Being eighteen doesn't make a man bulletproof, and, looking back, I realize them's words of wisdom.

The rain had started that morning just after sunup, driven by a gusting south wind that hammered cold drops against my slicker and drummed on my hat.

I was riding through the Gypsum Hills country west of the Red Bed Plains, a series of rolling hills, buttes and red mesas some 150 to two hundred feet high, all cut through by narrow gullies. The hills are capped by fifteen- to twenty-foot layers of gypsum that sparkle in the sun — the reason the Indians called them the Glass Hills.

Here and there grew stands of red cedar, blackjack and post oak, some of them lightning-blasted and dead, and under my horse's feet primroses, black-eyed Susans and tiny violets peeped out from among the grama grass.

I kept turning my head, checking behind me, and saw nothing but the rain-lashed landscape, iron gray clouds so low I reckoned I could reach up and grab a handful and I figured it would be like clutching at wood smoke.

I rode on, heading due south. A hundred or so miles to my west lay the majestic Black Mesa and directly in front of me, but still a long ways off, rose the weathered crags of the Wichita and Arbuckle mountains.

There was no letup in the rain, a steady, hissing downpour that ran off my hat brim like a waterfall and beat steadily on the shoulders of my slicker.

It was getting close to noon and I was becoming needful of coffee and a smoke. I'd tried to roll a cigarette earlier, but the rain had battered tobacco and paper from my fingers, scattering brown shreds over the front of my slicker. I'd given vent to a few choice cuss words, I can tell you, even though I knew if Sally heard me she'd be real annoyed. That little gal was dead set against cussing and she'd made that plain to me a time or two.

Reining in the paint, I glanced around, looking for a likely spot to hole up for an hour. If the riders behind me were honest men, they'd likely be sheltering from the downpour, and outlaws don't much care for getting wet either, come to that.

It seemed to me, I could stop and brew

up some coffee and then be on my way again, and nobody the wiser.

Like I said, that was how it seemed to me. But as things turned out, I was about to lead my ducks to the wrong pond.

About a hundred yards ahead of where I sat my horse, the gypsum crowning one of the hills slanted sharply downward to about thirty feet above the level. A narrow creek ran along the bottom of the hill under the gypsum shelf and the slope had been undercut, eroded away by wind and floodwaters, forming a natural, shallow cave about ten feet deep, twice that much high and maybe forty or fifty feet long.

A few stunted juniper grew higher up the hillside, where there might be fallen branches, at least enough to boil up some coffee.

I kneed the paint forward and rode up to the cave. Now I was closer, it was pretty much as I've described and I saw traces of previous fires, built small, the way Indians do. A goodly supply of dry wood, mostly pine and hickory branches, was scattered around and I was glad I didn't have to depend on the wet, slow-burning juniper.

I swung out of the saddle, eased the girth on the paint and led him to a patch of good grass close enough to the overhang that he'd be out of the worst of the rain.

The saddlebags I took with me back to the cave. When a man you regard as a friend as well as a boss gives that much money into your trust, you take care of it real well. That was what I thought anyway, and I believe I had the right of it.

I started a fire, and when it was burning good, I went to the creek and filled the coffeepot. Then I fetched Sally's bonnet and my sack of supplies back to the cave and laid them in a dry spot. That done, I threw a handful of coffee into the pot and set the pot on the coals to boil.

I shrugged out of my wet slicker and laid it on the ground, then adjusted the cartridge belt and holster around my hips. The faded blue shirt I wore was damp at the collar, and from the knees down, my brown canvas pants were soaked.

I was an inch above middle height that year, skinny as the shadow of a barbed wire fence, but most of the beef I did have was in my arms and shoulders, so that when I had a mind to push or pull something, it usually moved.

My hair was auburn, tinting red in places, and my eyes were gray. Bob Collins told me one time that when I was riled, my eyes shaded to the coldest gray he'd ever seen in all his born days.

Well, I didn't get riled often. If folks let me be, then I did the same for them. I was a peace-loving man with nothing to prove, and now I turned eighteen and was almost man grown, I didn't see much sense in fighting and feuding just for the hell of it.

Of course, as I stood there waiting for the coffee to boil, I'd no way of knowing that I'd soon be getting into plenty of both. And looking back, I think maybe that's just as well. A man needs a few quiet moments when he can be at peace with himself and the world. I reckon a wise man is never less alone than when he's alone.

I stepped to the mouth of the cave, looking out at the lashing rain, enjoying the solitude of that wild, beautiful country and the smell of boiling coffee and wood smoke and the sweet, fresh tang of wet grass and sage.

As was my habit recently, my fingers absently strayed to my top lip, where I hoped to grow a man's mustache. But to my disappointment, all I felt was downy fuzz, the same fuzz I'd been feeling every day since I'd left Texas close to four months before.

Back in Dodge, I'd envied Sheriff Bat Masterson his fine mustache and the way it set female hearts to fluttering when he tipped his hat and cut a dash. Me, I'd hoped to ride back to pretty Sally with a fine mustache of my own and cut a few dashes my ownself. But the way my whiskers were progressing, or rather how they weren't progressing, made that possibility more and more unlikely.

I sighed kind of deep and sad, dropped my hand and went back to the fire. I kneeled and picked up the coffeepot, ready to fill my cup. Then I froze real still when I heard a voice behind me.

"Rise up easy, Dusty Hannah, and when you turn, make sure the only damn thing in your hand is the coffeepot."

I recognized that voice, and I did what it told me.

"Howdy, Clem," I said, turning mighty careful, slow as molasses. "Thought you'd be across the Red by this time. That's what I thought."

Clem Kennedy shrugged his narrow shoulders. "You thought wrong, Dusty. You know how it is. Man stays in Dodge until his wages is gone. Trouble is, good whiskey and bad women don't come cheap."

"I don't know how it is, Clem," I said. "I still have my wages, at least most of them, in my pocket."

The man with Kennedy sneered and

spoke up for the first time. "Well, well, well, Clem, ain't he the reg'lar little do-gooder? Why, I reckon if'n he was a dog, somebody would've stolen him when he were just a pup."

"Let it go, Luke." Kennedy smiled. "This boy knows why we're here, so we'll get right to it." The smile slipped, then vanished into a tight-lipped grimace. "We want the money, Dusty."

I was conscious of the coffeepot in my right hand. If it came to gunplay, I'd have to drop it before I went for my Colt, and that would cost me time, more time than these two would allow.

I knew Clem Kennedy, a thin, sour man with hard blue eyes, a ragged, tobacco-stained mustache hanging under his nose like a dead rat. He'd come up the trail with us, and before we'd even reached the Red, he'd complained to Simon Prather, the owner of the herd, that he was a top hand and shouldn't be riding drag.

"Let the kid eat dust, Mr. Prather," Kennedy had whined. "He's still got plenty to learn."

Now Simon and Ma Prather had taken me in when I was a homeless youngster just fourteen years old, and I knew he considered me a top hand. But rather than be accused of favoritism, he'd asked me, head down, digging into the dirt with the toe of his boot the way he did when he was embarrassed, if I'd keep the peace and ride the drag.

Of course, I'd agreed, knowing what kind of fix Simon was in for experienced riders. And that was how come I'd eaten dust all the way from Doan's Crossing to Dodge, though Simon later paid me top hand wages.

The man called Luke I didn't know. But he looked hard and mean and the walnut handle of the Colt at his waist was plenty worn from hard use.

Slowly, I kneeled and set the coffeepot down, surprised that it had not occurred to either man that I'd done it to save time on the draw.

Were they that confident?

The way they looked at me, their eyes filled with amusement not unmixed with contempt, I reckoned they were. To these two, I was just a half-grown boy without a mustache and mighty green, and they didn't think I counted for much.

Kennedy had killed a man in El Paso and a drover in Wichita, and he was real slick with the Colt. Luke would be just as good and, on account of how he looked like a man who hard wintered, I figured maybe even a shade better.

I swallowed the lump in my throat and said, "Clem, the money belongs to Mr. Prather. He told me to give it to Ma."

Kennedy snorted. "Old lady Prather ain't my ma. Besides, we need that thirty thousand more than she does." The man's hand was very close to his gun, his slicker brushed back. "Now do you hand it over or do we just take it?"

I was cursing myself for letting these two get the sneak on me. They must have left their horses somewhere back in the hills and walked up on me quiet as thieves in a dark alley.

I played for time, trying to hold on to my hair a bit longer. "Clem, you know how much Mr. Prather needs that money. After the three bad years he's had, the boss is in hock to the banks up to his ears. The money will pay his way."

All this was true. Simon Prather didn't trust banks, but he'd borrowed heavily from them, and there was a twenty-five thousand dollar lien on the ranch. The thirty thousand dollars in my saddlebags represented his last chance of getting out from under all that debt and holding on to the SP Connected.

The man called Luke twisted his lips in a sneer. "Don't you worry none about Prather, boy," he said. "He's already a half-dead man. He's dead from" — his hand went to the middle of his chest and swept across to his left shoulder — "from here to here, an' his mouth is so twisted he can't even sup his soup." Luke's hand dropped to his gun again. "Don't you be worrying none about that half-dead man on account of how in a few weeks' time he'll be beyond caring about his ranch. Just hand over those damn saddlebags."

It came to me then that Kennedy and his companion were sure-thing killers and that was the only reason I was still alive. We were standing only a few feet apart, and they knew if lead started flying I could get a bullet into at least one of them before they dropped me.

I guessed they had figured the odds and had decided it was better to take the money without gunplay and put a bullet in my back later.

"Listen, boy," Kennedy said, his voice real soft and reasonable, "we can split the wampum in those saddlebags three ways. That's ten thousand for you, Dusty, more money than you could make in a lifetime punching cows." Kennedy turned to his companion. "Ain't that right, Luke, a three-way split, fair and honest as the day is long."

"Oh sure," Luke said, smiling real thin. "Share and share alike is what I always say." He stretched out his arm. "Here's my hand on it, boy, and I'll surely be offended if'n you don't take it, me trying my best to mend fences an' all."

Now I might have been born at night, but it wasn't last night. I knew if I took Luke's hand he'd pull me off-balance so Kennedy could get a bullet into me. I stood right where I was and shook my head. "I don't shake hands with thieving trash," I said.

Well, that tipped over the outhouse sure enough.

Luke's smile slipped and he said, "I'm sorely disappointed in you, boy."

And he went for his gun.

I don't remember drawing. But suddenly the Colt was in my hand and I realized with a jolt of surprise, I was faster, a lot faster, than Luke. I fired and saw my bullet take him square in the chest, his own shot following a split second later, but flying wild.

Kennedy had his gun out and we both fired at the same time. I felt his bullet burn across my left thigh, and I hit too high, taking him in the shoulder.

My ears ringing from the sound of gunfire, I stepped out of my own powder smoke and saw Luke lying on his back, the rain battering down on his face. He was dead as he was ever going to be.

Kennedy was half bent over, groaning. He was out of the fight, his shattered right shoulder a bloody mess, gun dangling loose from a scarlet-streaked hand.

The man's face was deathly white under his tan and he snarled a vile oath. "Damn you, boy, I never pegged you for a gunfighter."

"There's much you don't know about me, Clem," I replied, trying my hardest to make what I hoped was a grown man's reply. "You should have steered well clear of me." I nodded toward Luke's body. "Ride on out of here and take that with you."

"Hard talk, Dusty," Kennedy said. "Mighty mean and hard."

"You dealt the cards, Clem," I said. "I'm just playing out the hand you gave me."

"You think you being a gunfighter an' all will help you get that money to Texas?" Kennedy asked, his eyes ugly.

"Clem, I'm no gunfighter," I said. "Before today, I'd never killed a man and right now the fact that I have is troubling me plenty."

"Well, you practice with that Colt, boy. There will be others after me and they won't be near as trusting an' friendly as me and Luke was." Kennedy gasped in pain as he straightened. "No man should have thirty thousand dollars all to his ownself when poor folks are hurting."

"The money isn't mine," I said. "And it isn't yours either."

"You'll never make it back across the Red, Dusty," Kennedy said. "Luke Butler was a named man and he had friends."

I nodded. "Maybe so, but I reckon I'll take my chances."

Later, after he'd caught up his horses, I stood in the rain and watched Kennedy ride away, Luke Butler's body draped facedown across the saddle of his buckskin.

Kennedy glanced over his shoulder once, with eyes that burned hot with hate, like he wanted to remember me for all time. Then he turned back and I watched him go until he was swallowed up by the hills and the shifting steel curtain of the rain.

It was still not yet one, but the afternoon

had turned cheerless and dark. The clouds and hills had merged into a gloomy, uniform gray, so there was no telling where the land ended and the sky began. Off to my left, a jay fluttered among the branches of a cedar growing at the base of a low mesa, sending down a shower of water. The branches shook again for a few moments as the bird sought a new perch and then the tree returned to stillness.

The bullet that had burned across my thigh had not broken the skin, but my leg felt numb and sore as I scouted the area for a few minutes, saw no one and returned to the shelter of the cave. I teased the fire into flame and put the coffee back on to heat.

When I sat and rolled a smoke I was surprised that my hands were steady. I lit the cigarette with a brand from the fire and set to studying on what had happened.

Clem Kennedy had called me a gunfighter and that was a label I did not want to wear. Back in Dodge, I'd seen the named shootist Buck Fletcher kill a man in the Long Branch. After the smoke cleared, I'd looked into Fletcher's eyes and seen only despair and something else . . . hopelessness maybe, like he knew he was a man caught in a trap of his own making and there was no way out.

I didn't want to end up like that. I wanted a place of my own with a wife and kids, smoke from our cabin tying bows in the air, the white laundry fluttering on the wash line and an ugly spotted dog sleeping on the stoop.

Gunfighter.

I'd killed Luke Butler, a gunman of reputation, and where Western men gathered, that was a fact that would be noted and talked about.

Clem had been right. Others would come. Most would be motivated by the lure of easy money, but there would be a few with a completely different agenda. Those would be wild ones and they'd test me with their own lives to see how I stacked up, how I ranked in the gunfighter hierarchy.

I poured coffee into my cup and drank it strong and scalding hot.

My heart was heavy as lead, my spirits troubled, and beyond the shelter of the cave roof the raking rain rattled relentlessly as it continued to fall.

Then I heard the flat boom of a rifle shot. And another.

Chapter 2

I'd no way of knowing what those shots meant, but I didn't want to just sit there and let trouble come to me a second time.

Rising, I tightened the girth on the paint, then swung into the saddle. I'd forgotten the saddlebags!

I stepped down, threw them onto the back of the saddle and mounted again.

An eighteen year old makes his share of mistakes, and as things turned out, I'd sure roped the wrong steer by taking along those saddlebags. But that was something I wouldn't discover until later, when it was way too late.

The shots had come from the north, and I swung around the base of the hill and rode up a wide gully, splashing across a deep, swift-running creek with tall cotton-woods the color of smoke growing on both its banks.

After I cleared the creek, the gully widened out, hemmed in by a series of low red sandstone mesas, their bases thick with cedar and juniper.

I followed the gully for a couple miles, riding tense and alert, my .44.40 Winchester across the saddle horn. There was no sound but the rustle of the wind through the grass and the steady, hissing counterpoint of the driving rain.

The day had gotten grayer still, and I saw no sign of life anywhere.

But when a man rides wild country, it's wise for him to pay attention to his horse. As I rode into a grassy valley dotted here and there with cedar and clumps of sagebrush and bunch grass, the paint's ears pricked forward and his head came up real fast. He snorted, and the bit in his mouth jangled.

I leaned over and patted the paint's neck, whispering to him to take it easy. This seemed to calm him down some, but he was still up on his toes, dancing nervously to his left, his head tossing, not liking what he smelled in the wind.

I fought the horse for a few moments and finally got him turned and urged him deeper into the valley. About half a mile ahead, a steep-sided bluff jutted like a red-brick wall into the valley floor and from where I was I couldn't see what lay beyond.

My hat did little to shield my face from the rain, and water kept running into my eyes. I wiped the oilskin sleeve of my slicker across my face and peered ahead.

Nothing moved.

The land was empty and bleak and it seemed whoever had fired those two shots was long gone.

A hunter, I thought, trying to convince myself that was the case. But who would hunt in a pounding rain when all the animals were taking shelter?

I had no answer for that and decided to let it go. It was time I got back to the cave, picked up my bits and pieces and hit the trail south, away from these silent, threatening hills.

All things considered, I'd be real glad when I got back to Texas and handed Ma Prather her money. After that, I could live a normal life again and start seriously courting pretty Sally Coleman with an eye to making her my wife.

I was in the act of swinging my horse around when something caught my eye, just a flicker of movement at the base of the bluff. I stood in the stirrups and studied the area — and saw a horse walk slowly from the bluff then stop and begin to graze.

It was a big, rangy buckskin and it could only be Luke Butler's horse. But where was the bandit's body?

Curiosity has always been one of my failings, and now like a complete fool I gave in to it.

I rode toward the horse, keeping my rifle close to hand. For the first time I saw where the wet grass had been trampled flat by the passage of Kennedy's mount and the dead man's buckskin. As far as I could make out, the tracks led to the edge of the bluff, then swung wide around its slanting base.

The rain was even heavier now, fair hammering down, and I reckoned the creeks that cut between the hills would soon flood their banks. The branches of the red cedars were heavy with water, drooping forlornly almost to the ground, and fast-running rivulets poured down the rusty sides of the surrounding buttes and mesas, bringing with them white streaks of gypsum.

The buckskin raised his head when he saw me coming, studied me for a few moments, then, unconcerned, went back to his grazing.

Where was Butler's body? And where was Clem Kennedy?

That second question was soon answered.

Kennedy lay half-hidden in the grass about fifty yards from the bluff. He was lying on his back, his eyes wide-open, a soundless scream frozen on his gaping mouth, teeth long and yellow against the stark gray of his face.

I swung out of the saddle and kneeled beside the man's body. Kennedy had been shot three times, once by me, and twice more by a person — or persons — unknown. One shot had merely grazed his neck, but the second, deadlier bullet had crashed smack into the middle of his forehead.

I stood and looked around. There was no sign of Kennedy's horse or anything else for that matter, just the grazing buckskin, the hills and the gray clouds and the streaming rain.

Clem Kennedy was an ill-natured man who had made his share of enemies. But why kill him all the way out here, in the middle of nowhere in a pounding rainstorm?

Unless . . .

Had his killer heard the gunshots from back at the cave and believed Kennedy had already robbed me of the money I was carrying? That was a real possibility. And since the bushwhacker hadn't found the saddlebags on Kennedy's horse, he must know I still had them.

I held my Winchester in both hands at the high port as I prepared to walk back to my paint, the hairs at the back of my neck rising.

Was the killer still here? And was I already in his sights?

I had no time to answer that question . . . because I'd not taken three steps when the sky fell on me.

Chapter 3

I didn't hear the report of the rifle, but I felt the smashing impact of the heavy bullet that crashed against my head and felled me to the ground.

I lay there stunned, unable to move. The shot had paralyzed me. I couldn't feel my arms and legs but I tasted the smoky tang of blood mixed with rain as blood ran down my face and into my mouth.

My eyes were just half-open slits, but they were open wide enough for me to see four men leave the base of the bluff and walk toward me. As they got closer, I saw a tall man, long yellow hair spilling over his shoulders from under his hat, leave the others and sprint toward me.

"Yee-ha!" the man yelled, grinning from ear to ear, punching into the air. "Lookee here, boys! I nailed him right through the head."

Despite the scarlet haze of blood pouring into my eyes, I made out the .50-90 Sharps rifle the man was carrying, some kind of brass telescopic sight running the entire length of the barrel.

"Lafe, does he have the money?" another man asked.

"Hell, he wouldn't be carrying it on him," the yellow-haired man said. "Search them saddlebags on the paint."

There was a few moments' silence; then I heard a man's exultant yell: "It's here, Lafe! Every damn cent of it."

"Lemme see that," Lafe said.

Through stinging eyes that I could barely hold open, I saw the four men gather around the saddlebags.

"Hell," Lafe whispered, "I ain't seen that much money in all my born days." He threw the saddlebags over his shoulder. "Right, let's get out of here. And I want that paint. Hell, he must go sixteen hands if he's an inch."

Only money, a lot of it, would have brought these men into the wild hill country. So far the trail I had taken from Dodge had led to blood and death . . . and unless they killed me, I vowed this wouldn't be the end of it.

Footsteps swished through the wet grass as the bandits walked away. But then the man called Lafe came back and kicked me viciously, his boot thudding into my ribs

34

once . . . twice . . . three times. . . . Then the shocking, blinding pain made me lose count.

"Hey, Lafe, how come you're kicking a dead man?" somebody yelled.

I heard Lafe laugh, a loud, cruel bellow. "For making me stay out here in the damn rain," he yelled. "That's how come."

And he giggled and kicked me again.

Then I knew nothing but darkness and with it came a merciful end to pain.

I woke to a throbbing agony in my head and each gasping breath raked my chest like a red-hot knife blade.

Rain battered at my upturned face and from somewhere far off I heard the angry rumble of thunder. I clenched and unclenched my fists, and to my relief, the feeling slowly returned to my fingers. After a few minutes I was able to move my legs, and I struggled into a sitting position.

My horse was gone, and with it the saddlebags and Simon Prather's money.

But I had no time to contemplate the disaster that had befallen me. I had to get to the buckskin and go after those robbers.

The rain was still painting the sides of the surrounding buttes and mesas bloodred, and the sentinel trees stood soaked and silent. The wind had dropped some, but the rumble of thunder was much closer and every now and then as the sky banged and flashed white, the buckskin raised his head and stood stiff-legged in alarm.

The horse was getting spooked and I was in no shape to be chasing him down.

I couldn't tell how badly hurt I was. My head ached and when I put fingers to the right side of my scalp they came away stained with blood.

The men who had bushwhacked me had taken my horse, but they'd left my guns, and I figured, with the arrogance of youth, that they'd made a big mistake.

That I was too sore wounded to follow them never even entered my head. And that was my mistake.

Slowly I fetched up to my feet, and immediately the land around me spun like a weather vane in a whirlwind, then lurched right and left, so that I figured the mesas were standing on end and the trees were dancing. Nauseous, I sank to my knees and was violently sick, retching up all the coffee I'd drunk a short time before.

I didn't need anybody to tell me right then that I was as weak as a two-day-old kittlin' and in a whole heap of trouble.

Off to my left, a lean coyote stepped out of the trees again and looked at me with keen interest, every now and then tossing his head as he licked his chops. To him, I was just a poor, wounded creature that might die pretty soon and provide an easy meal or three.

I directed all my pent-up anger and despair at that coyote, yelling at him to stay the hell away from me and go find himself a rabbit to kill.

Of course, all my hooting and hollering did nothing to ease the mind of the buckskin and he trotted maybe fifty yards closer to the base of the bluff, stirrups bouncing, figuring me for a crazy man.

I guess the coyote studied on things some and reckoned I was still mighty spry because he slipped back into the trees and was gone like a puff of smoke.

Desperately I tried to concentrate, summoning up whatever little strength I still possessed.

Somehow, I had to make it to the buckskin.

Fury drove me. I swore to myself that when I caught up with the long-haired man called Lafe, there would be a new face in hell for breakfast in the morning.

Slowly, painfully, I crawled on my hands

and knees toward the grazing buckskin.

As I inched closer, he'd raise his head now and then to look at me, trot away a couple of steps to maintain the same distance between us, then go back to his grazing.

Thunder rolled across the iron sky and lightning forked among the hills around me, plunging again and again into the wet earth with skeletal fingers. A lone cedar growing on the gradual slope of a hill just beyond the bluff suddenly took a direct hit. A deafening crack, accompanied by a searing flash of light, and the tree seemed to explode, branches scattering into the air every which way. Fire spurted as the blasted cedar lurched on its side, the flames dying immediately in the teeming rain.

All this was way too much for the jittery buckskin.

The horse turned in my direction, arched his back, then took off, galloping across the distance between us. Neck stretched out, his eyes rolling white, the buckskin pounded past, his kicking hooves beating on the wet grass like the cadenced thump of a muffled drum.

"Hold up there, boy!" I yelled, in a totally futile effort.

The buckskin was gone, splitting the wind and skinning the ground, and soon he was lost to sight among the crowding grayness of the rain-lashed hills.

Me, I knew I had to go after the horse.

I rose to my feet, staggered a few steps, then stumbled, stretching my length on the grass. I rose again, fell again, got to my knees and looked around.

The land was spinning wildly and the pain in my head was a living thing, eating all the life out of me. I tried to struggle to my feet, crashed hard onto my back and mercifully knew no more.

I woke to a dark face bisected by a huge walrus mustache looking down into mine. Guttering firelight revealed concern and a hint of amusement in the black eyes, and I saw the flash of white teeth as the face split into a smile.

"Ah," the man said, "young Lazarus awakes."

Another robber!

I grabbed for my Colt but it wasn't there. The black man had followed my movement and now his smile widened. "Is that how you thank a man who just saved your life? Gun him?"

Then, reading the panic in my eyes, he

said, "Your Colt is close by, young feller, and so is your rifle. And I brung in your horse."

I opened my mouth to speak, failed, then tried again. "My paint?"

The man shook his head. "Big buckskin. I found him out there in the hills. I whistled an' he came to me, nice as you please." My rescuer frowned. "Here, are you telling me he ain't your bronc?"

I shook my head slightly, a movement that caused me considerable pain. "My horse was stole."

Right then I didn't know if I could trust this man, and I guess it showed in my eyes because he pulled his yellow slicker aside, flashed the badge pinned to his coat and said: "Name's Bass Reeves. I'm a deputy U.S. marshal for Judge Isaac Parker out of Fort Smith with jurisdiction over the Indian territory." He smiled. "Does that set your mind at ease, boy?"

"What . . . what are you doing out here?" I asked, understanding nothing.

Bass Reeves shrugged. "Hell, boy, out here is where the desperadoes be."

I glanced around me. The rain had stopped and I was back in the shallow cave at the base of the gypsum hill. Beyond Reeves' wide shoulder the cobalt blue sky was streaked with bands of gold, lilac-colored clouds building high above the horizon. The fire crackled and I smelled wood smoke and bubbling coffee.

I struggled to rise, but Reeves pushed me back with a firm but gentle hand. "Best you lay there still for a spell, boy," he said. "I think maybe your head might be broke."

Gingerly, I reached up to feel my wound, but my fingers touched only a thick bandage.

"Spare shirt I found in your blanket roll," Reeves said. "I tore it up for bandages. Used it on your ribs too. Figure they might be broke as well."

That shirt was brand-new. It had cost me three dollars in Dodge and I'd expected to wear it and cut a dash when I met Sally and commenced to courting her. That Reeves had ripped it apart chapped my butt, but I didn't think it polite to tell that to a man who'd saved my life.

Instead, I said, "How did you find me?"

The lawman jerked a thumb over his shoulder. "Found three men out there. Two of them dead, all shot to pieces, one half-dead." Without even a hint of a smile, he added, "The half-dead one was you, of course." Reeves sat back on his haunches and rolled a cigarette. "You smoke, boy?"

41

"Name's Dusty Hannah," I said. "And, yes, I smoke."

Reeves nodded. "Smoking is bad for a young feller, Dusty. Stunts his growth and takes his wind." He lit his cigarette with a brand from the fire, the scarlet flame casting bronze shadows under his eyes and in the hollows of his cheeks. "Want to tell me about it?" he asked.

"Are you asking me in your capacity as my savior or as a deputy U.S. marshal with jurisdiction over the Indian territory?"

Reeves nodded. "A little of both, Dusty. A little of both, I'd say."

I was irritated that Reeves was so obviously enjoying his smoke and hadn't thought to share, but I fought that down and in as few words as possible told the lawman the story of how I came by thirty thousand dollars only to lose it to bushwhackers.

Reeves listened in silence, and when I quit talking he nodded and said, "The man who shot you is Lafe Wingo. He's a sure-thing killer for hire and he'll gun any man, woman or child for fifty dollars. Ol' Lafe now, he has maybe twenty killings under his belt and he's trying real hard for more. Mostly he carries a scoped Sharps, but he's fast enough with the Colt when put to it."

Reeves took off his hat, revealing sparse curly hair, wiped off the band and settled the hat back on his head. "Last I heard Lafe was running with the three Owens brothers, Hank, Charlie and Ezra. Of the three, I'd say the oldest, Ezra, is the meanest, but that don't mean the other two are any kind of bargain. All three of them can shoot and they've killed their share." Reeves thought that through for a spell, then added, "More than their share."

A silence stretched between us; then the lawman said, "How did you get tied up with this Simon Prather feller?"

I fetched up on one elbow and this time Reeves didn't stop me. "I were just a younker when the cholera took my folks," I said. "I was taken in by my pa's brother, Ben, who has him a tumbleweed ranch down on the Neuces River country.

"Uncle Ben was all right I guess, but he had a son four years older than me by the name of Wiley, and me and him used to go at it with our fists, buck, tooth and hang-nail.

"Over the years, Wiley beat me 173 times and I beat him once — the last time."

"You mean you kept count?"

"Uh-huh. Scratched each time we fought

on the inside of the barn wall with a nail, and when I'd make ten, I'd put a line through them lines and start all over again."

My hand strayed to my shirt pocket for the makings, but Reeves threw me his own, an act that made him rise considerably in my esteem.

I rolled a smoke, lit it, then said: "Maybe it was my last fight with Wiley that helped Uncle Ben make up his mind. That night he drew me aside and said real thoughtful that he couldn't afford to feed me no more on account of how I could eat my weight in groceries. And besides, he said, the ranch would go to Wiley one day and there would be no place for me.

"Then he said: 'Dusty, I got two daughters and I'll have to find dowries for them both, so you see how things are with me.'

"Well, I said I did and then I said on account of how I'd finally pummeled Wiley, there sure didn't seem much point of me staying around anymore.

"As it turned out, Uncle Ben did all right by me. He gave me five dollars, his third best pony, a .44.40 Winchester and a new Colt. And even Wiley came through. He said I'd given him a black eye and his nose was broke but he had no hard feelings and he gave me his lucky rabbit's foot and fifty cents he'd saved."

Reeves nodded. "Rabbit's foot can bring a man luck, if he's real careful and steps light around trouble."

"Maybe so, but up until now, that's sure not been the case with me."

"So how old were you when you signed on with Prather down to the Red River country?"

"Fourteen," I replied. "And since then, I've been up the trail three times."

Reeves let that pass without comment and asked, "How do you feel?"

"How do you think I feel? My head's busted and I think my ribs are busted. I feel like hell."

The lawman smiled. "You were lucky, boy. If ol' Lafe's bullet had hit another inch to the left, you'd have been a goner for sure."

He hesitated a few moments and asked: "How come Prather didn't carry the money back to Texas his ownself?"

I was rapidly getting too tired to talk, but I lay back and made the effort. "In Dodge, after he sold the herd, something broke inside Simon's chest. He woke up one morning with his left side paralyzed and his face all twisted. Later that day he called me into his hotel room, where a doctor was attending him, and asked me to take the thirty thousand back to Ma. He said I was like a son to him and Ma and I was the only one of his riders he could trust. That's what he said, and I figured he meant it too."

"Hell, he should have just stuck his money in the bank," Reeves said.

I shook my head, very slightly. "Simon don't trust banks. He said all banks do is try to cheat a man. That is, when they ain't being robbed or getting caught on fire. He don't trust the boxcars either. He told me there's no place to run when you're riding the cars and I'd lose the money to train robbers for sure."

I shrugged. "Mr. Prather made it plain to me that he set store by his money and that's how it happened I was heading back the way I come, down the Western Trail. And I already told you," I added, a bitter taste in my mouth, "how I let Simon's money be took from me."

Bass Reeves pondered this doleful intelligence for a few moments, then said: "Judging by the tracks I saw, Lafe and the Owens boys are trailing south, back into Texas, where they can spend the money on women and whiskey at their leisure."

"And I'm going after them," I said.

The lawman shook his head. "You ain't fit, boy. You're all broke to pieces and the bullet that creased your head has addled your brain" — Reeves shrugged — "unless, of course, you wasn't too smart to begin with."

"I'm riding at first light," I said, stepping around that last remark as I tried to sound a lot braver and more determined than I felt right at that moment.

"Well," Reeves said, taking his makings back from me, "there's another complication that's muddying up the water."

"What's that?" I asked, knowing the news I was about to hear would be bad.

The lawman lit his smoke. "The Warm Springs Apaches are out and they're playing hob. The warriors are led by a young war chief by the name of Victorio and he's mean as a curly wolf. Since you've been gone he's been killing, burning and looting all over west Texas."

Reeves shook his head and smiled. "That Indian sure hates the white man."

I felt a sudden pang of fear. The SP Connected was southwest of the Red, and if what Reeves was telling me was correct, the ranch was right in the Apaches' path. Ma was there with the cook and a couple of stove-up old hands, good enough men, but too few and too stiff to stand off a Mescalero war party.

I sat up and when my head stopped swimming I asked: "Where are the soldiers?"

Reeves shrugged. "The Ninth and Tenth Cavalry with their Navaho and Apache scouts are out after them. Buffalo soldiers" — he said this last without noticeable pride — "but they won't catch Victorio. He's way too smart for horse sod'jers."

"Ma Prather and the SP Connected are in west Texas," I said, giving voice to my fears.

"Then she's in a hell of a fix, ain't she, boy?" Bass Reeves said.

Chapter 4

Only when Reeves stood did I realize how big he was. He was well over six feet and I guessed he weighed about two hundred pounds. He was big in the chest and shoulders with muscular arms and long, powerful legs and he had the Western rider's narrow waist and hips. His knuckles were large and knotted, scarred all over from dozens of rough-and-tumble fistfights, and his nose had been broke more than once.

I was told later that Bass Reeves could whip any two men in a bare-knuckle fight, and by the time I met him, he'd already killed twelve outlaws in the line of duty, either with his .38.40 Colt or his same caliber Winchester.

Now he looked down at me and asked: "Hungry, boy?"

To my surprise I found I was. I nodded and said: "I could eat."

Reeves nodded toward my sack of supplies. "What you got in your poke?"

"Bacon," I said. "And some corn bread."

The big lawman nodded. "I got me a slab of salt pork and a few three-day-old sourdough biscuits, so we'll have ourselves a feast." He smiled. "Good for you, boy. Build up your strength."

After we'd eaten I did feel better, though I was still very weak and my head was pounding.

Reeves said he'd ride with me as far as the Red, but that was where his jurisdiction ended and he would go no farther.

"Maybe we'll catch up with Lafe Wingo and the others by then," he said. "Maybe not. But we'll give it our best shot."

At first light we saddled up and headed south.

It was raining again.

Reeves' big red stud was a sight to see. Montana-bred, he went more than eighteen hands and had a right pretty white blaze. The horse's powerful legs with their four white stockings stepped high, his long, rangy stride eating up distance. But the buckskin was game and kept right along with him.

I was still very weak and dizzy and couldn't wear my hat because of the fat bandage on my head. But after the rain soaked that bandage through, I tossed it away, replacing it with my hat, even though the tight leather band threatened to punish me for days to come.

Bass Reeves was a personable man and I enjoyed his company. In the past, I had ridden with a number of black punchers and they did their work well. They were uncomplaining, even riding the drag, and I never had any problem with them.

There was a stillness in the big lawman — a kind of serenity, I guess — and when he reached for a thing his hand did not tremble. He pointed out things of interest along the trail that I'd never paid no mind to before. Maybe he was trying to keep my spirits up, because right then I was mighty glum, worrying about Simon Prather's money and how I'd get it back.

Reeves showed me the deep holes of the little burrowing owls, the only owls that eat fruits and seeds as part of their diet, mainly gathered from the tesajilla and prickly pear cactus. He pointed out where rutting elk had rubbed their antlers against trees, stripping the velvet as they prepared for combat. He said to listen close because their challenging bugles could echo for miles through the gulches between the bluffs and mesas.

Reeves could put a name to just about

every bird and plant we saw and he told me about a cave to the east of us where millions of bats roosted during the day, then took off in a spiraling funnel cloud that filled the sky at nightfall.

"I reckon it takes maybe thirty minutes for all them bats to leave their cave," he said. "Dusty, pretty soon the sky is full of them, filled with flapping black dots as far as a man can see. Some college feller told me one time the bats eat ten tons of insects every night, and that's how come the sodbusters love them so much."

Bass Reeves taught me a lot of things during those days we rode together.

When I happened to let it drop that I was no great shakes with the rifle, he showed me how to hold the sights of my Winchester real still on the target, told me when to inhale and when to hold my breath and how to get a clean break on the trigger so I didn't jerk the gun.

"Rifle shooting is all in the mind," Reeves said, "and that's why it takes every bit of your concentration. It's like when you tie a line to a fishhook, you direct all your focus on the knot. Dusty, you should use the same amount of concentration when you fire a rifle. It's an all-or-nothing proposition."

Keeping in mind what the lawman told me, I was hitting every target I shot at pretty soon, and then he made me work on my speed, cranking and firing the Winchester from the shoulder so fast that I sounded like a one-man army.

Once I dropped a whitetail buck with a shot from my rifle at a distance of two hundred yards and that night, as we broiled venison steaks, Reeves said I could unravel a Winchester bullet as well as any man and maybe a shade better than most.

The big lawman was impressed with the speed of my draw from the holster and he said he'd seen maybe just two or three faster, including his ownself, but it was an uncertain thing and not one he'd care to put to the test.

"In any case, we'll leave it alone, Dusty," he said. "When it comes to the Colt's gun you don't need any advice from me."

Maybe so, but very soon I was to see Bass Reeves use his Colt and I realized then that the black lawman could teach me plenty about shooting a short gun, and then some.

Reeves and me cleared the Gypsum Hills and crossed the Canadian. The riverbed was about six hundred yards wide but there was only about forty feet of water not more than a foot deep. We splashed through a shallow elbow of the Washita, then headed south again in the direction of the Antelope Hills across high tableland dotted here and there with post oak, stands of tall timber growing in the deep ravines.

Although we could see far across miles of country, there was no sign of Lafe Wingo and the others.

Reeves led the way as we rode on across rolling country, here and there rugged, flat-topped mesas rising dramatically more than two thousand feet above the level. Numerous small creeks, cottonwoods and willows growing along their banks, cut through the land around us, and the grass was good and plentiful. Juniper, pine and hickory crowned most of the hills, and here and there spires and parapets of weathered red sandstone jutted from their slopes.

Now the rain had stopped, we stowed our slickers behind our saddles. The days had become hot and still, and often the only sounds were the muffled fall of our horses' hooves and the hum of bees among the wildflowers.

Four days after my first meeting with Bass Reeves, we camped for the night at a bend of Cottonwood Creek, a fair-sized stream with many twists and turns, the leaves of nearby tall trees reflecting dark green in the millpond water over which even greener dragonflies hovered.

I broiled up the last of the salt pork and venison steak, and not much of either, and we washed down this meager fare with a half cup of thrice-boiled coffee and were wishful of more.

At times Reeves was a deep-thinking man, and we sat in silence and smoked, each occupied with his own thoughts, as the darkness gathered around us and an owl questioned the night from somewhere deep in the hills.

The big lawman, with ears long attuned to even the smallest sound that could signal danger, suddenly sat straight up, his body tense.

I opened my mouth to question him, but he held a finger to his lips, motioning me into silence. Reeves rose to his feet in one graceful, athletic motion, his gun coming up fast.

From out in the darkness I heard a faint, rhythmic creak . . . creak . . . creak. As my eyes finally penetrated the gloom, I made out the pale glow of a yellowish-orange light bobbing toward us.

I was never one to be afraid of the

boogerman and ha'nts and such, but I felt the hairs on the back of my neck stand on end as the creaking grew louder, now joined by the noisy clank of metal, and the light bobbed ever closer.

I drew my own Colt and was aware of Reeves fading like a ghost back into the shadows.

The creaking and clanking suddenly stopped and the light bobbed to a standstill.

The silence around me grew and out in the darkness I heard a horse stomp the ground and blow through its nose.

"Hello the camp!"

I looked around and found Reeves at my elbow.

"Come on in real slow, and keep your hand well away from your gun," he yelled.

"A gun?" echoed the voice from the gloom. "Is my name not Amos Rosenberg and am I not a harmless peddler? What do I know from a gun?"

But Reeves would not be moved. "Then ride in easy and keep your mitts up in the air where I can see them."

"Ride in, he says. Am I not riding in already?"

The creaking and clanking started up again and the bobbing light was gradually transformed into a guttering oil lamp fixed to the side of a small two-wheeled wagon drawn by a swaybacked, mouse-colored mustang. Pots, pans and ladles clanked on the outside of the wagon and the whole rig creaked and groaned like an old man getting up from his seat at the fire.

The driver up on the box was short and thin, a battered, flat-crowned hat on his head, a black beard, shot with plenty of gray, falling over his narrow chest. As he got closer, I saw dark eyes, bright as those of a bird, peering at us from under a pair of shaggy eyebrows, taking in everything, missing nothing. He looked to be about sixty years old.

"Hold up, Rosie," the man said, hauling on the reins, stopping just beyond the circle of the firelight. He looked around him. "How did I find your camp?" he asked finally. "Did I not smell your coffee from a long ways off?"

"Coffee's all gone," I said. I felt no threat from the peddler and decided to be friendly. "Sorry."

Rosenberg nodded. "No need for sorrow. I have coffee. Arbuckle coffee, fresh in the sack. Got sugar too, if that's to your taste."

Beside me, I saw Reeves think this through. Then he made up his mind as I had done earlier and holstered his Colt. "Peddler, I guess you've come to the right camp because we're fresh out of everything. That is, if your prices are honest."

"Honest?" Rosenberg asked. "And why would my prices not be honest?"

Reeves' smile was thin. "Out here, where there ain't a general store for miles around, a man could get to thinking he can get mighty rich mighty quick."

"Rich, he says," the peddler snorted, "out here in this wilderness where a man hears nothing but the howl of the wild beasts. Look at me. Am I not a poor man? Those most in need have no money to buy, and those with money have no need. Who then gets rich?"

Reeves' smile widened. "Well maybe so. Unhitch that pony and show us what you have in your poke."

I helped Rosenberg put up his horse, liking the way the man's quick movements were practiced and precise as he undid the traces, with no wasted effort.

The little man was a Child of the Book, one of hundreds of Jewish peddlers who wandered the West selling their wares, mostly dry goods like needles and thread, calico cloth, pots, pans and ladles. Most carried packs on their backs, trudging for miles across the prairie to isolated ranches and farms, but a few, like Amos Rosenberg, were successful enough to afford horses and wagons.

Peddlers also traded with the Indians and one I met had spent six years living with the Cheyenne and had him an Indian wife.

Most ranch and farm women warmly welcomed the peddler, not only for his goods, but because of the news he brought from the cities. I reckoned if put to it, Rosenberg could tell us how the women of fashion in Cheyenne were wearing their bonnets and how big were the bustles of the Abilene belles and how sheer their fine silk stockings.

The pioneer woman isolated amid an empty sea of grass for months and years at a time did not know or care that the latest fashion in Abilene was already a year old back in the East and two years out of date in Paris. It was all new and exciting to them, so no wonder the visit of the peddler was a welcome thing, eagerly anticipated.

Rosenberg seemed to be a shade more prosperous than the rest, because in addition to his dry goods, he carried a small supply of bacon, salt pork, flour and coffee. Arranged around the floor of his wagon, crammed beside bales of calico and muslin, were small kegs of vinegar, sugar and molasses. He had a glass jar of pink candy sticks and another of black-and-white-striped peppermint balls. To my joy he also carried sacks of tobacco and a supply of .44.40 shells in boxes, enough to replenish the ones I'd fired off so freely on the trail.

Between us, me and Reeves spent close to fifteen dollars on what the peddler had to sell. My major purchase was a new cotton shirt, but it seemed my free-spending ways did little to impress Amos Rosenberg. He glanced at the coins and crumpled paper money in his hand, shook his head and muttered: "And now you know why I am a poor man. It's because I buy dear and sell cheap." He shook his head again. "Oy, I fear you have taken advantage of me."

I doubted that very much, figuring he'd made a more than fair profit, but I held my tongue. I was well aware of how merchants loved to complain. Like sodbusters, they were quick to plead poverty while all the time having sacks of money stashed under their beds.

I filled our pot at the creek and soon had coffee boiling. Having a young man's appetite and still being mighty hungry, I fried up some bacon and pan bread and me and Reeves finally ate our fill. Rosenberg would have no part of the bacon, but ate a couple of strips of his own antelope jerky, which he washed down with coffee, strong and boiling from the pot, sweetened with molasses.

After we ate and got to smoking, the little peddler brought out a battered pipe and lit it with a brand from the fire. Every now and then, he'd stretch out his left hand, contemplate his pinkie finger and let out with a deep sigh, usually followed with a shake of the head and a muttered: "Oy, oy, oy."

"Finger broke?" Reeves asked with scant interest.

"Why would my finger be broke?" Rosenberg asked. "Who has a broken finger?"

The lawman shrugged. "Just asking."

"Oy vey," Rosenberg said again, looking at his pinkie, his head shaking even more.

Since the little peddler tended to answer a question with one of his own, I tried to trap him. "Tell us what's troubling you, Mr. Rosenberg."

"What is there to tell? Who needs to know?"

I shrugged. "You keep looking at your hand. Maybe it pains you."

Rosenberg nodded, his black eyes glittering in the firelight. "Ah yes, there is pain. But not in the finger." He placed a hand on the chest. "The pain is here."

I was right sensitive about pain in the chest after what had happened to Simon Prather, so I asked: "Is it in your pump?"

"Ah, is it in my pump? Boy, you hit the penny nail right on the head. It's in the heart sure enough. Oy, my poor heart is broke."

"How come?" I asked, then wished I hadn't. But Rosenberg surprised me. He answered the question straight as a fire poker.

"I had a ring," the peddler said. "I wore it right there on my little finger. It was a silver ring given to me by my wife." Rosenberg sighed. "She's no longer with me, took by the cholera this five years past."

"You lose it?" Reeves asked. He was idly rolling a smoke and didn't look up.

"Lose it? Why would I lose it? It was took from me."

"Who took it?" I asked.

"Brigands. Black-hearted brigands."

Now Reeves was all attention. His unlit cigarette drooping from the corner of his mouth, he asked: "Was one of them a man with long yeller hair? Carries a big Sharps with a fancy brass scope on the top? Goes by the name of Wingo?"

The peddler shook his head. "That man wasn't among them. There were six of them, and I heard the name of one of them spoken but it wasn't that name."

"Oh?" Reeves asked, his interest quickly fading as he lit his smoke.

Rosenberg nodded. "Their leader was a man named Yates and afterward I remembered that I'd seen him before."

Reeves' head snapped around. "Bully Yates? Big feller" — he traced a finger down his left cheek — "has a bowie knife scar right here."

"How should I know what gave him the scar?" the peddler replied. "But scar he has. Like I already told you, later I remembered him. I saw him use a scattergun to kill a man outside a saloon in Abilene three summers ago. Should I forget a thing like that?"

Reeves drew deep on his cigarette and shook his head. "Well, well, well, Bully Yates as ever was."

"You know him, Bass?" I asked.

"I should think I do," the lawman said. "I have a warrant for his arrest, signed by

Judge Parker. Yates is wanted for bank robbery and murder and any number of other
crimes, including the part scalping of a
loose woman he took up with for a spell."
He looked across the fire at Rosenberg.
"Did you recognize any of the others?"

The peddler shrugged. "The others I did
not know. But they were all hard men and
weighed down by guns."

"Well, I have a stack of John Does for the
others, so that doesn't make no difference." Reeves rose to his feet. "Can you
recollect where was you robbed, peddler?"

"Why should I not recollect? Was it not
me who was robbed?"

"Tell me straight now," Reeves said, his
face grim. "For I plan to start after those
men at first light."

Rosenberg nodded. "To the west of here,
maybe twenty miles. Maybe more."

"Over to the Salt Fork country?"

"Further west. By Sandy Creek."

Reeves thought that through, then said:
"That's wild, empty country to the west of
us. I'd guess Yates is holed up there, figuring to lay low until the heat over the
Lawton bank robbery dies down." The big
lawman threw his cigarette butt into the
fire. "Bully Yates was always a damn
careful man."

"He's not laying so low," Rosenberg pointed out, his face bleak. "He stole my ring and the seven dollars and eighty-three cents I had in my purse." The little peddler shrugged. "He also took some bacon, salt and flour and most of my coffee."

"I don't know about the money," Reeves told the peddler. "But when I get your ring back, I'll give it to the clerk of Judge Parker's court in Fort Smith. You can pick it up there."

Before Rosenberg could reply, I said: "Bass, you can't go after those men alone. Hell, man, there's six of them."

"And hard," the peddler said, shaking his head. "All of them hard."

"I don't have time to go back to Fort Smith and round up more marshals," Reeves said. "By the time we all got back here, Yates could have lit a shuck."

Reeves reached down and placed a hand on my shoulder, an unusually friendly gesture for a man as reserved as he was. "Dusty, you have your own trail to follow. I won't think any less of you if you don't follow mine."

Truth to tell, up until that moment I hadn't even considered going after Yates and his gang. But now, when I looked up into Reeves' eyes I saw a deal of shrewd speculation going on there. He was saying one thing, but thinking another, like he was determined to judge me as a friend and a man by what I said next.

I realized then that the cat that had my tongue was a wildcat and I sure had it by the tail.

So far we had seen neither hide nor hair of Lafe Wingo and the others. If I didn't catch up to them soon, Simon's money would be gone and his SP Connected doomed to foreclosure. Ma Prather would be thrown off the ranch and then what would become of her? I didn't even want to think about the answer to that question.

Yet how could I stand by and let Bass Reeves ride alone into a one-sided fight with six outlaws? Nobody needed to tell me that he'd saved my life and I owed him. Now that thought nagged at me, yammering to my conscience that I was an ungrateful wretch, giving me no peace.

Torn, I was about to speak when Amos Rosenberg's voice bridged the widening gulf of silence stretching awkwardly between me and the big lawman. "Marshal, I would ride with you, but I am too old and slow," he said. "I know of calico and cotton, pots and pans, but of tracking men and of guns and gunfighting I know nothing."

I rose to my feet, my mind made up. "I'll ride with you, Bass," I said, "if you'll have me."

The lawman stuck out his huge hand and I took it. "Proud to have you along, Dusty." He dropped my hand and slapped me on the back. "You'll do, boy. You made a man's decision here tonight, and by God, you'll do." He put his hand on my shoulder. "From this moment on, consider yourself a deputy of Judge Parker's court, duly sworn and appointed."

He turned to Rosenberg. "Thanks for the offer, peddler, but you best stick to the business you know."

Rosenberg shrugged. "Every man has his own business. You are right, Marshal. I'll stay with my own."

Absently my fingertips wandered to my top lip, touching only fuzz, and above me the bright moon lost itself behind a cloud and suddenly the land around me was shrouded in shadow, dark with foreboding.

Chapter 5

We rose before first light, drank coffee and ate some hastily broiled bacon; then we saddled the horses.

As Rosenberg hitched up his mustang, Reeves dug into his saddlebags and produced a thick sheaf of papers. "Thumb through these, Dusty," he said. "Make sure Bully Yates is there and pick me out five John Does."

I leafed through the warrants and sure enough found Yates. I passed the warrant to Reeves. "This is the one. Read for yourself."

The big lawman shook his head. "Never did learn to read or write or do my ciphers. I was born to slavery, Dusty, and my owner didn't see much need for a field hand to have book learning."

For me, reading was a pleasant way to while away idle hours and Simon Prather had an extensive library at the SP Connected, where I got acquainted with the works of Mr. Dickens and Sir Walter Scott, to name just a couple of the fine scribes who had opened up new worlds to me.

By not being able to read, Bass Reeves was missing out on a sight of adventure and excitement. But I didn't tell him that because I'm sure it was a thing he knew already. Besides, a man like Reeves made his own excitement and adventure, so maybe, after all was said and done, he didn't miss the books that much.

Reeves took the warrant for Yates and the John Does and stuffed them in the pocket of his coat, then walked away and started to tighten the girth on his horse.

I stepped beside him. "How do we play this when we catch up to them fellers?" I asked.

Reeves turned to me. "Well, I'll follow Judge Parker's instructions in these matters. I'll ride into their camp, identify myself as an officer and tell them I have warrants for their arrest."

"And suppose they don't want to be arrested?"

Reeves' face didn't change. "Then, boy, I reckon all hell will break loose and we'll have ourselves a Pecos promenade."

I felt my throat tighten. The odds were six against two and Yates and his outlaws would be no pilgrims. I found myself fervently wishing that Simon Prather had trusted banks because then I wouldn't be in this mess.

We made our farewells to Rosenberg, who gave each of us a little sack of peppermint candy and wished us luck, then took to the trail west.

The sky was brightening with the dawn, streaked with bands of scarlet, and a strong prairie wind was blowing, rippling the grass like waves on a vast green ocean.

The red light stained Reeves' face so he looked like a cigar store Indian and he was just as wooden and expressionless. I realized then that this man didn't know the meaning of fear. The big lawman would not take a backward step for any man, and he'd do his duty, no matter the cost.

From all this, I drew no comfort. I reckoned I was about to ride into a situation where I could easily get my fool head blown off and such thoughts do nothing to console a man.

We rode into rolling land cut through by numerous sandy creeks, none of them deep, and once we came across an old trail, probably made by Indians, that branched away from us to the north before disappearing between a pair of flat-topped mesas.

Reeves didn't push the pace, and by the middle of the brightening morning he insisted we camp by a narrow creek, just a shallow spring branch coming out of the hills, and boil up some coffee.

Sitting with his back against the trunk of a cottonwood, the lawman drank his coffee and then went to checking his guns, thumbing more loads into his Winchester.

Taking my cue from him, I did the same. I didn't feel much like talking. I tried to analyze why I had a knot in my belly and decided it wasn't fear, but something else. But what?

Then I understood what was eating at me — I was mighty worried that I would fail to play a man's part in whatever lay ahead. Had my gun battle with Clem Kennedy and Luke Butler proved that I could stand up, take my hits and go on fighting?

Maybe. Maybe not. That scrap had been almighty sudden and I'd had no time to think about it.

What I didn't want was to look into Bass Reeves' eyes when this was all over and see only contempt and accusation. There would be no living with myself after that.

As though reading my thoughts, Reeves looked over at me and smiled. "You're mighty quiet, Dusty. You scared?"

This was no time for lies and I answered his question straight up. "I don't know, Bass. I feel something, like crawling worms in my gut." I shrugged. "I don't reckon I'm scared, but maybe I am. Anyhow, that's what I think."

The lawman nodded. "It's all right to be scared. It's the ability to swallow fear and step up to the fight that makes a man."

"You scared, Bass?"

Reeves smiled. "Hell, boy, when I'm out here I'm scared all the time."

"I won't let you down, Bass," I said, knowing how lame that sounded.

"I know you won't, Dusty," the lawman said. "If it comes to a fight, I reckon you'll stand up just fine."

He tossed away the dregs from his cup and rose to his feet. "Let's ride, boy."

I glanced into Reeves' eyes at that moment . . . and saw with a shock they were guarded and wary. That look could have been caused by doubt, uncertainty, like he was having second thoughts about something . . . or somebody.

And that somebody could only be me.

We rode steadily west for a day and night, closing on Sandy Creek, where

Reeves hoped Bully Yates and his outlaws were still camped.

The days grew hot as the sun climbed into the sky and sweat trickled from under my hat brim into my eyes, the salt making them sting, and I felt rivulets ooze down my back.

The heat did not seem to affect Reeves and he rode erect and dry in the saddle, his careful black eyes probing the way ahead, restlessly studying every hill and timber-choked arroyo of that wild and beautiful country.

On the morning of the second day, as the Wichita Mountains loomed in the distance, he pointed to the ruin of a sod cabin a short way off the trail, all that remained of the structure a couple of walls and a sagging doorway covered by a ragged canvas tacked to the top of the jamb.

"Let's stop over there for a spell and get ready," Reeves said. "I reckon we're real close."

Whoever had built this cabin, probably a sodbuster, had given up and moved on, or it had been destroyed by Indians. Whatever had happened, the sad ruin provi
mute testimony t
now even the
people who h

gone from the place.

I swung out of the saddle, eased the girth on the buckskin, then squatted beside Reeves in the meager shade of a tumbled wall.

The lawman rolled a smoke and I did likewise, happy that my hands were not trembling.

"Dusty, we're going to ride right into Yates' camp," Reeves said. "Nothing fancy, just straight up and honest." He turned and looked at me, his eyes boring into mine. "You fine with that?"

I nodded. "I reckon."

Reeves nodded, drew deep on his cigarette and studied its glowing tip, his face thoughtful. "Now maybe Bully doesn't have the sand I think he has and will just throw up his hands. If that happens, though I doubt it will, the rest should be easy. But if he doesn't show the white flag, what happens next will be almighty sudden. I've seen Bully Yates work, and he'll make fancy moves and be powerful fast."

He turned to me again. "It will be a ___e-in business, so go to your Colt. Don't ___elo___ ___ won't have time. ___ding after your ___n go to your rifle. Don't try head shots. Aim low for the belly. A bullet in the brisket will drop even the toughest hard case nine times out of ten. Don't rush your fire, but even so, shoot just as quick as you can." His eyes probed mine, like he was looking for an answer to a question he had yet to ask. "If you're hit, don't drop out of the fight. Hit or no, you must stand on your two feet and keep getting in your work." Now he asked his question. "You understand what I'm telling you, boy?"

My mouth was suddenly parched and I took a quick swallow of coffee. Even then, my voice when I could finally form words was a feeble croak. "I understand what you're saying, Bass." I touched the side of my head. "I got it all wrote down in here."

The lawman smiled. "You'll do, Dusty." He nodded, but only to himself. "Damn right." He rose to his feet. "Now let's go and get her done."

We smelled wood smoke while we were still a fair ways from Yates' camp. Reeves, as was his habit when he embarked on any desperate venture, was humming softly to himself, a kind of tuneless, monotonous chant he made up as he went along.

We rode through a brush-covered gully

between two hills, our horses stepping carefully, and then into a narrow valley that doglegged off to our right. The slopes on either side of us were dotted here and there with post and shin oak and mesquite grew all over the flat.

The sun was directly above us, mercilessly hot, and the cloudless canopy of the sky was the color of washed-out blue denim. The legs of our horses made a swishing sound as they walked through the long grass and off to my left a bird called, called again, and then fell silent. My saddle creaked and the buckskin's bit jangled when he tossed his head at flies and I constantly wiped the sweaty palm of my right hand on my pants.

Ahead of me, I saw Reeves slip the rawhide thong off the hammer of his Colt and I did the same. We reached the dogleg and swung north with the valley. The scent of smoke was stronger now, and I smelled bacon frying.

The valley ended on the south bank of Sandy Creek, the shallow stream's entire length lined with cottonwoods and willows, a few scrubby elms raising their thin branches to the sky.

The wind was gusting, tossing the long grass, bringing with it the camp smells from somewhere off to our right.

Reeves turned in the saddle. "Close up, Dusty. I want you on my left if the shooting starts."

I nodded and kneed my horse beside the lawman's big sorrel. "I'll do the talking," Reeves said. "Bully Yates is a speechifying man, loves the sound of his own voice, so maybe I can sweet-talk him into surrendering." His smile was thin. "But I wouldn't count on it."

We rode right into their camp before the six outlaws were even aware of our presence.

A tall man in a black-and-white cow-skin vest and black hat saw us first. His jaw and the armful of wood he was carrying dropped at the same time. "Bully!" he yelled. "We got comp'ny."

Bully Yates was a huge man, big in the chest, shoulders and belly, and a cruel white scar stood out like a livid mark of Cain on his unshaven left cheek. The outlaw carefully set the pan of bacon he was frying away from the coals of the fire and rose slowly to his feet. He carried two guns, unusual at that time, worn butt forward in the holsters, their ivory handles yellowed with time and use.

The five other outlaws crowded close to

Yates and I could detect no sign of friendliness in their faces or fear in their cold eyes either. They were all hard cases, well-armed, and like Reeves there didn't seem to be any backup in them.

"Morning, Bully," Reeves said, sitting easy and relaxed in the saddle, his voice calm and conversational.

"It's gone morning," Yates answered, his voice sullen.

"Well, good afternoon then," Reeves said, smiling, as pleasant as you please.

"What do you want with us, Bass?" Yates asked, his eyes wary.

Reeves nodded. "That's the way, Bully. Get down to brass tacks right away and to hell with the pleasantries. I always say that my ownself." With his left hand he slapped the pocket of his coat. "You know me, Bully. I'm a duly sworn officer of the law and I've got me a warrant for your arrest on the charges of murder and robbery. And I've got five more just like it for you others. I plan to take all of you to Fort Smith, where you will get a fair trial and later be hanged at Judge Parker's convenience."

"Big talk for a black man with a half-grown boy at his side. Hell, there's six of us here."

Reeves waved a hand in my direction. "This boy is my deputy and he's already killed seven men in the line of duty. It would grieve me sore if'n you turned out to be number eight, Bully."

"In a pig's eye, he's killed seven men. That boy ain't hardly weaned yet." Yates' hard blue eyes found mine. "You ride on out of here now, boy. I got no quarrel with you."

I shook my head at him. "If it's all the same to you, Mr. Yates, I reckon I'll stick."

The outlaw shrugged. "Your funeral, boy."

Reeves kneed his horse a couple of steps closer to Yates. "Come now, Bully. Give it to me straight. Will you not drop those guns and surrender?"

"To hell with you!" Yates yelled. And his hands flashed to his Colts.

Reeves had been right. What happened next was almighty sudden.

I drew my Colt and fired at the man in the cow-skin vest, who was just then drawing a bead on me. My bullet hit him low in the chest and dead center and he screamed and dropped to his knees. I had no time to see what happened next because a bullet split the air inches from my ear and I caught the smoke and muzzle flash of a gun to my left. A tall redhead was thumbing back the hammer readying another shot, but I shot faster. My bullet hit the cylinder of the gun in his hand, bounced off and crashed into his chin. The man made a gurgling sound, rose up on his toes, then stretched his length on the ground.

I turned quickly and saw Yates lying facedown, his blood staining the grass around him bright scarlet.

Reeves was still shooting and one man went down to his gun, then another.

There was only one outlaw still standing. The man dropped his Colt and yelled: "No! Don't shoot, Bass! I'm out of it."

"Then step away from the fight!" Reeves hollered. "Back there by the tree." The outlaw quickly did as he was told, stark terror in his eyes, his mouth working.

I looked around me. The battle had taken less than ten seconds, but in that short time me and Reeves had played hob. Four men were dead and another lay by the fire, gut-shot, groaning his pain, his bootheels convulsively digging into the ground.

Gunsmoke drifted thick and gray like a mist among the surrounding trees and my ears were ringing from the concussion of the guns.

I felt sick to my stomach and my head ached. But I had no time to dwell on my miseries because the buckskin suddenly collapsed under me. I kicked free of the stirrups as the horse fell, and I sprawled flat on my back on the grass.

Reeves, bleeding where a bullet had burned across the thick muscle of his left shoulder, swung out of the saddle and gave me his hand. I grabbed it and he pulled me to my feet.

"The buckskin took a bullet early in the fight," he said. "I saw that. But he was game, stayed on his feet until the shooting was over."

The lawman slapped me on the back. "You did good, Dusty. When the chips were down you played the man's part."

I looked over at the two men I'd shot. "Are they both dead?" I asked.

Reeves nodded. "As dead as they'll ever be. You drilled 'em all right."

The green bile rose up into my throat and I turned away and retched convulsively for what seemed like an eternity until I started to figure there must be no limit to the contents of my stomach.

When I finally stopped and straightened up, I wiped a hand across my mouth and turned to Reeves. "I'm sorry," I said. "It just came on me sudden like."

Reeves, his black eyes unreadable, just smiled, kind of slight and slow and said: "I've seen worse." Now his eyes searched mine, carefully reading what he saw. "It ain't easy to kill a man, boy. And them as say it is, aren't men — they're animals" — he nodded toward Yates, who was staring sightlessly at the blue sky — "like him."

The wounded man by the fire groaned and kicked his legs and Reeves stepped over to him. "How you feeling, boy?" he asked.

The man raised his head, his face gray with pain and shock. "Bass Reeves," he gritted through bloodstained teeth, "you're a black son of a bitch."

Reeves kneeled and carefully set the frying pan back on the fire. He pulled his knife and one by one turned the bacon strips. Only then did he look at the wounded man. "You're gut-shot and dying and your time is short, boy," he said. "You ought not be cussin' like that when you're soon to meet your Maker."

"Damn you, Reeves," the man said. He clutched at his stomach and when he brought his hands away again they were stained bright scarlet with blood. "I'm dying hard," he whispered, "and I wish I'd never left Missouri."

"Do you have a ma, boy?" Reeves asked. "Somebody I can tell how you met your end?"

The outlaw, a freckled towhead who looked to be not much older than me, nodded. "I have a ma. She's back in Missouri but I don't want her to know I died like a dog. Best she never knows."

"Then so be it," Reeves said. He glanced over his shoulder at the outlaw who had quit the fight. "You," he yelled, anger edging his voice, "get the hell over here."

The man, fear camped out in his eyes, rushed over and stood beside the big lawman, his hands trembling. "Tend to this bacon," Reeves said. "And mind you don't burn it."

Immediately the outlaw dropped to one knee and shook the bacon in the pan, all the time looking at Reeves in horror, like he was a rattlesnake coiled to strike.

Reeves rose to his feet and began to feed shells into his Colt. "Dusty, I told you I'd ride with you as far as the Texas border," he said, reholstering his gun. "But that's changed now." He nodded to the outlaw who was frying bacon with a lot more careful attention than it warranted. "After we lay out the dead decent, I'm taking him back to Fort Smith."

"What about him?" I asked, pointing to the groaning young towhead.

"He'll be dead before nightfall," Reeves said. "I'd count it a favor if you stay with him until then. Even an outlaw shouldn't die alone."

I opened my mouth to object, then thought better of it. I'd now killed three men and their deaths lay heavy on me. Maybe if I stayed with the dying outlaw it might help even the score with my conscience, though I very much doubted it.

All I'd ever wanted was to get back to Texas with Simon Prather's thirty thousand dollars and then go to courting pretty Sally Coleman and give her the Dodge City straw bonnet.

Now I'd lost the money and been in two desperate gunfights and it was getting so that I could scarce bring Sally's face to mind, no matter how hard I tried.

The dream of marrying Sally that I'd kept alive through the heat and dust of the drive up the trail, the longing for her all bunched up in my throat, was fading fast, lost behind a haze of gunsmoke and the death cries of men. It was a worrisome thing and it was nagging at me, giving me no peace.

I vowed right there and then, as the

wounded man by the fire groaned and cursed at his own dying, that when I recovered Simon's money and got it back to the ranch I'd hang up my Colt and touch it no more.

I did not want the name of gunfighter. I'd no wish to end up like the men around me, gunmen dead in a lonely place, unmourned, with only the uncaring wind and the trees to whisper of their passing.

Nor did I want to kill ever again, though even as that realization dawned on me, I knew inevitably there must be more killing, more dying, before I got back my boss' money and once more crossed the Red and saw the familiar barns and corrals of the SP Connected.

Above me, a passing smear of thin cloud drew a brief veil across the sky and I heard a fish jump in the creek. Over by the cottonwoods, bees hummed among the wildflowers and at the fire the sizzling bacon in the pan spat and sputtered, filling the air with a down-homey smell that reminded me of cold Sunday mornings and Ma Prather in her gingham apron, round cheeks flushed, serving up hot buttermilk biscuits and coffee steaming from the old fire-blackened pot that stood day and night on the ranch house stove.

Would I ever sit at her table again?

It wasn't difficult to fire the odds facing me and come up with the answer, especially now that Bass Reeves was heading back to Arkansas with his prisoner.

It was Reeves' voice that interrupted my thoughts and brought me back to the stark realities of the present.

"Dusty, come over here and eat," he said. "It could be a while before you get the chance again."

I had no appetite, but I stepped round my dead horse and joined him at the fire. Reeves had taken the frying pan from the nervous outlaw and was holding it just above the flames. There was a half a loaf of stale sourdough bread among Bully Yates' supplies and this he cut into thick slices, laying each one on top of the bacon to absorb a goodly amount of fat. That done, he placed a few strips of bacon between two slices of bread and passed it to me.

"Eat, boy," he said. "It will settle your stomach."

Truth to tell, I had to force myself to bite into the sandwich, but I managed to chew it up some and gulped it down.

Reeves made a sandwich for himself and as the outlaw who had fried the bacon watched it disappear down the lawman's throat he asked: "What about me, Bass? You came on us so sudden, we hadn't et."

"What's your name?" Reeves asked the outlaw.

"It's Ellison, Jim Ellison," the man said. He took off his hat, uncovering a mane of wavy black hair. "There are them as call me Curly, on account of this."

Reeves nodded. "Heard of you. Heard you killed a man down on the Brazos a spell back."

"In a fair fight," Ellison said, bristling. "He was coming at me with his gun drawed."

"Maybe so," the lawman said. "But that's not the way I heard it."

"Then you heard wrong," Ellison said, jamming his hat back on his head.

"Well, Jim," said Reeves, nodding toward the frying pan, "There's a bait o' bacon left, so help yourself. But the bread is all gone."

"Here, take this," I said, offering my sandwich to the outlaw. "I don't have much of an appetite."

"Thought you looked a bit green around the gills, boy," Ellison said, eagerly taking the bread and bacon from me. He carefully peeled away some bread from where I'd bitten and threw it on the fire, then, his mouth full, added: "But you showed me something with the Colt's gun." He nodded toward the men I'd killed. "Sam and Lew were no pilgrims but you done for them both as nice as you please."

"They were coming at me with their guns drawed," I said.

Chapter 6

After Ellison had eaten, Reeves got a set of shackles from his saddlebags and roughly locked the outlaw's hands behind his back.

We had no way of burying the dead, having no shovels, so we laid them out as decent as we could, side by side, their arms crossed over their chests.

Reeves had stripped the men of their gun belts and these he hung over the horn of his saddle.

When he stepped beside me again, he looked down at the four dead men, then at me and asked: "Dusty, you got any words to say?"

I shook my head at him. "Bass, I don't have any words. When we buried a puncher on the trail, Mr. Prather always read from his Bible."

"Well, we don't have one of those," the lawman said. He turned to Ellison. "You, get on over here."

When the man stepped closer, Reeves

said: "You got anything to say over your hurting dead?"

Ellison shrugged. "We rode together but I never liked a one of them." He shook his head. "I got nothing to say."

"So be it." Reeves sighed. He raised his hat an inch off his head and said: "Ashes to ashes, dust to dust."

Then he turned on his heel and went back to where his horse stood.

It was little enough to say over dead men, but I reckoned it was a lot truer than most eulogies.

Wolves and coyotes would soon find the bodies and scatter the bones. In time, scorched by heat and frosted by snow, the bones themselves would become dust and blow away in the prairie wind until there was no trace of them remaining and of the four dead men nothing would be left . . . unless their restless spirits lingered on and haunted this place.

"Choose a horse for yourself, Dusty," Reeves told me. "The rest of them are now the property of Judge Parker's court."

I picked out a big black with a white blaze that looked like it could run and got my saddle out from under the dead buckskin.

Over by the fire, the wounded man had

90

been silent for a long time. Now he groaned, his knees jerking up as pain that was beyond bearing hammered at him.

Seeing this, Reeves nodded. "Seen that afore, how a gut-shot man kicks like that. It means his time is very short."

He put his hand on my shoulder. "Stay with him, Dusty. Then ride after Lafe Wingo and the others." He smiled. "I wish you all the luck in the world and I sure hope you get your money back."

I forced myself to smile. "I plan to get it back, Bass."

The lawman nodded. "Just be mighty careful. Wingo and the Owens brothers will be no pushovers. Every one of them is good with a gun and they've killed plenty of times before. And another thing" — his eyes were troubled — "when you get to Texas, don't tangle with Victorio if you can avoid it. Best you ride a hundred miles around Apaches than get in a fight with them because chances are you're going to lose your hair. If they catch you" — he nodded toward the dying outlaw — "you'll die like him and maybe a lot worse. However they kill you, the last thing you'll hear on this earth is your own scream. Remember that."

"All I want is to get Simon Prather's

money back," I said. "I don't plan on tangling with Apaches if they'll give me the road."

"That's the way, Dusty." Reeves grinned. "Although, when I come to study on it, I'd say Lafe Wingo and the Owens boys are a shade meaner than any Mescalero, including Victorio his ownself."

The afternoon was wearing on, but there still remained one thing to be done.

Reeves stepped over to the bodies and found Amos Rosenberg's ring on Bully Yates' little finger. He held up Yates' hand, removed the ring and slipped it into the pocket of his vest.

He walked back to his horse and tightened the girth, then helped the manacled Ellison into the saddle of his mustang.

Reeves gathered up the reins of his sorrel and walked toward me. He stuck out his hand and I took it. "Luck, Dusty," he said. "It sure was a pleasure to ride with you." He smiled, half-embarrassed. "You played the man's part and you helped save my skin today and that's a thing I won't forget."

The big lawman dropped his hand. "You know, young feller, if'n I was Lafe Wingo, I reckon I'd be right worried right about now if I knew you was on my trail."

Reeves had said it all and I didn't try to outjaw him. "Luck, Bass," I said. "It's a long ways to Fort Smith, so ride careful."

"Always do," the lawman said.

He swung into the saddle and caught up the reins of the outlaws' horses. He started to ride out, a dejected Ellison following behind. Reeves touched his hat as he went past me. *"Hasta luego,* Dusty Hannah."

I nodded. "See you around, Bass."

I watched Reeves and his prisoner ride through the valley, then disappear behind the hill that marked the dogleg where he would swing to the east.

The sun was lowering in the sky and the wind had picked up, rustling through the grass and trees and setting the creek to rippling. I stepped to the fire, fed it some more wood, stood there for a while watching the flames dance, then turned my attention to the dying outlaw.

He was looking at me, his eyes wild, whether from pain or hatred of me I couldn't guess.

"How are you feeling?" I asked, knowing how lame that sounded.

The outlaw didn't answer for a few moments, then said: "It hurts. It hurts real bad."

I kneeled beside him and looked at his

wound. His shirt and pants were black with congealed blood and when I lifted the shirt aside I saw the bullet wound in his belly, a gaping hole just below his navel.

There was no recovering from a wound like that. All this boy could do now was die.

"Do you smoke?" I asked.

The outlaw nodded and I rolled him a cigarette, lit it from the fire and placed it between his lips. Then I built one for myself.

"What's your name?" I asked.

The boy took the cigarette from his lips with a bloodstained hand. "Charlie Hunt," he said. "I was named for an uncle who fell at Chickamauga."

Pain slammed at him again and he gasped and quickly drew on the cigarette. "Oh God," he whispered. "I'm dying hard."

"Try to lie still," I said. "It will help."

The day slowly faded into night and a cold moon rose in the bright, star-scattered sky. The flickering firelight played on the bodies of the dead that lay around me, touching their pale faces with red. In the distance a coyote howled his hunger, a long, drawn-out wail that was carried far by the wind.

Mercifully, Charlie Hunt was now beyond pain and the blue death shadows were gathering under his eyes and in the gaunt hollows of his cheeks. He was no longer with me, but had traveled back to another time and place. He spoke to his ma and sister like they were right there by the fire and once he whispered the name of a girl he had known.

I guessed it was about midnight when his eyes flew open and he looked right at me. "I'm obliged to you for staying by me," he said. Then death rattled in his throat and he was gone.

As Reeves and me had done for the others, I now did for the man who was once Charlie Hunt. I closed the boy's eyes and straightened his legs and crossed his arms over his chest.

Then I saddled the black and rode away from that place of death, the glow of the moonlight painting the trail ahead, the grass, the hills and the pines the color of tarnished silver.

I rode through the night, the big black, well used to dark trails, moving out sure-footed and confident.

At first light I stopped in a grove of post oak and elm and made a fire. A narrow creek ran close by but only a trickle of water ran over its sandy bottom and it took me near five minutes to fill my coffeepot and the water was bitter at that.

Reeves and me had split what supplies we had, including those we found at the outlaw camp, and I made a meager breakfast of venison jerky washed down with weak coffee.

I eased the girth on the black and let him graze; then I spread my blankets and slept for a couple of hours.

The sun was climbing higher in the sky when I woke, drank the last of the coffee and swung into the saddle.

Doan's Crossing was a ways to the south of me, but I planned to reach it before nightfall.

By early afternoon I'd crossed two forks of the Red, the Salt and the North, both of them little more than sandy, shallow creeks lined with stunted cottonwoods. When I turned in the saddle, behind me the peaks of the Wichita Mountains were lost in haze and ahead lay a lush, grassy valley about four or five miles wide, brushy ravines on either side cutting deep into the surrounding hills.

I rode into the valley, the black walking knee-deep in grass and wildflowers. After an hour, the sky above me clouded over, and rain began to fall. I shrugged into my slicker and spread as much of it as I could over Sally's straw bonnet, which I gloomily realized was beginning to look the worse for wear.

The valley gradually widened until the surrounding hills were maybe six miles apart and mesquite began to appear. Here and there a few scrubby elms grew close to the bottoms of the slopes, their branches drooping as the rain fell heavier.

I studied the land around me. Had Lafe Wingo and the Owens brothers passed this way? And if they had, how long ago?

I had no answer to those questions and the valley seemed as empty of life as the canyons of the moon.

There was no trail where I rode, but once I saw where the grass had been trodden down by a small antelope herd that had passed this way.

The rain continued to fall and I was considering trying to find some shelter in one of the ravines when I heard a sudden rattle of gunfire. Then silence. A moment later another shot racketed through the valley, followed by another.

I reined in the black, trying to puzzle this out. This was a remote valley and as far as

I could tell, there was no sign of habitation.

Hunters maybe?

Or could it be Lafe Wingo and the Owens boys shooting at something or somebody?

This I doubted very much, but nonetheless I slid my Winchester from the boot, cranked a round into the chamber and rode forward again, the rifle ready across the saddle horn.

The gunfire seemed to have come from about a mile ahead and a ways to the north of where I rode, and I fretted that I might be riding into more trouble than I wanted or needed.

Catching my unease, the black's head was up, his ears pricked forward, his eyes on the valley ahead of us. Another shot split the quiet of the afternoon, echoing away into silence.

I rode on, wary now. Despite the slanting mesh of the falling rain, the air was clear and I could see for a good distance. The valley began to narrow again, then, to the north of me. I rode up on a wide saddleback between two high hills. The saddleback rose gradually for about a mile, rising to a height of three hundred feet, its crest studded by a ragged parapet of bare sandstone rock.

I reined in the black and stood there for a few minutes, studying the saddleback, wondering what lay beyond the crest.

A shot rang out, followed by another, and this time there could be no mistaking where they originated. Beyond the bench somebody was firing. But who? And at what?

My first instinct was to swing away from there and keep on riding. But I was always a curious young feller and now my prying nature got the better of me and like a dang fool I kneed the black forward and began to climb the rise.

I dismounted before I reached the crest and led the black into the rocks. Now I was there, I discovered that the summit of the saddleback was flat, about thirty yards wide, and the red sandstone rocks, each as tall as a man, were scattered everywhere around its entire length and width.

Leaving the horse, I crouched and sprinted to the edge of the rise, well hidden by the surrounding boulders, and looked down.

Below me, the saddleback sloped away to end in a wide, flat-bottomed box canyon surrounded on all sides by tall hills. A sod cabin, shaded by a huge oak, lay close to the base of the hill furthest away from me.

On one side of the cabin was a small timber barn, on the other a corral and, near that, a pigpen.

Corn shoots were greening a plowed-up piece of land to the front of the cabin and nearby ran a shallow creek, coming off one of the surrounding hills.

All this I saw in an instant, but what made my blood run cold were the Apaches hidden among rocks that must have tumbled down the rise in ancient times when the ground around here trembled.

From where I crouched I saw the backs of three of the Indians, but with Apaches, if you saw three there could be twice that number hidden.

And there were more of them. When I changed position to get a better angle on the cabin, I counted seven ponies tethered in a break in the hill to the right of the Apache position and there may have been others hidden from view.

Wooden shutters with narrow firing slits were drawn across the two small windows to the front of the cabin and from one I saw a puff of smoke followed by the bang of a rifle. A moment later a shot was fired from the other window and I heard the bullet whine off a rock near where an Apache crouched.

A warrior I hadn't noticed before suddenly rose and fired his Winchester at the cabin. Soon three more stood and began firing, their bullets thudding into the cabin's sod walls, a couple of shots splintering through the wood shutters.

The reason for all this firing became obvious when I noticed three Apaches run past the pigpen, then disappear from sight near the corral.

It wasn't hard to figure out what they were planning. They could reach the cabin from its blind side and then get up on the flimsy pole and sod roof, smash it apart and fire at the defenders inside.

I figured the sodbusters in the cabin had chosen to live in this canyon because it was well sheltered from the heat of summer and the snows of winter. But they had chosen unwisely, because now they were trapped like rats and it was only a matter of time before the Apaches wore them down.

On my first trip up the trail I'd seen what Comanches did to an Irish army scout and his Ute wife they'd captured. There was very little of the two left by the time we came across them, but it was obvious they'd taken a long, terrible time a-dying. Their last screams were still frozen on their gaping mouths and Simon Prather had to close their jaws with binding cloths so they'd look halfway decent for burying.

That was what the two firing from the cabin could expect, but I told myself it was no business of mine.

Bass Reeves had advised me to ride a hundred miles around Apaches and right now that seemed like mighty sound counsel. The sodbusters in the cabin meant nothing to me, and besides, I had to get back on the trail before Lafe Wingo slipped clean away.

But even as I did my best to justify it in my mind, I knew I couldn't leave. Down there in the cabin were probably a woman and maybe her young 'uns and the way the Mescaleros were riled up, what they would do to them didn't bear thinking about.

Cursing myself for a damned fool, I slid my rifle forward and sighted on the corral. Rain ran off the brim of my hat as the downpour grew heavier, scattering the slender plume of smoke that rose from the cabin chimney.

I waited. The *tap-tap* of rain hammered on my hat and I heard the drops hiss as they fell on the grass and bounced off the wet sandstone of the rocks around me. I drew my Colt and set it next to me, where it would be handy if subsequent events called for close work, though I fully planned to keep the Apaches at rifle range. Once I opened the ball, I didn't want those warriors swarming around me because the outcome of that would be a mighty uncertain thing.

Despite the freshness of the rain-cooled air, my mouth was dry and my quickening heartbeats thudded loud in my ears. I took a deep breath, as Bass Reeves had taught me, willing my heart rate to slow, the better to shoot the Winchester accurately when the time came.

And the time was now.

Down by the corral an Apache in a blue army shirt and white headband rose to his feet, looked around, then slowly moved toward the cabin on cat's feet. Another warrior, this one with a bright red band around his head, stepped after him.

I took a breath, held it and sighted on the broad chest of the first warrior. I took up the slack on the trigger and squeezed off a shot.

My bullet must have hit the man square because he threw up his arms, his rifle spiraling away from him, and crashed heavily onto his back. The racketing echo of my first shot had hardly died away when I fired at the other warrior. I didn't see the effect of my second shot because the Apache quickly disappeared from view.

But down among the rocks at the bottom of the hill, I'd sure stirred up a hornet's nest.

Three Apaches rose to their feet and turned in my direction, one of them pointing at the rocks where I lay hidden. I fired at this man, saw him fall, dusted another couple of quick shots down there and, crouching low, moved my position.

Rifles banged from the cabin and I saw another warrior go down, hit in the back.

The Apaches seemed confused, not liking the fact that they were caught in crossfire, and that moment of indecision cost them dear.

I fired again, nailing another squat, bandy-legged warrior, then quickly looked around for another target. There was none. The surviving Apaches had gone to ground, taking advantage of the cover of the long grass and rocks.

I reckoned four Apaches were down and maybe five, so there could only be a couple left. But even two Mescaleros were a handful to contend with.

Rifles banged again from the cabin, bullets whining off the rocks below, and I added my own fire, up on one knee, cranking and firing my Winchester from the shoulder as fast as I could. Roaring echoes crashed like tumbling boulders around the canyon and a cloud of gray gunsmoke shrouded the rocks around me.

The Apache is a practical, down-to-earth warrior. When he feels the deck is stacked against him, he has no qualms about running away and living to fight another day when the odds will be in his favor.

Three Mescaleros dashed from the break of the hill, crouched low across the necks of their ponies and hit the slope at a flat-out run.

One of the warriors was hit hard, blood staining the front of his shirt, and he seemed to be having difficulty staying on the back of his horse.

I rose to my feet, rifle to my shoulder, but let them pass. There had been enough killing already and I had no desire to further punish a beaten enemy.

The three warriors topped the rise about thirty feet from where I stood, one of them looking briefly in my direction with black eyes that burned with hate, then vanished down the slope and soon the thud of their ponies' hooves was lost in the incessant hiss of the streaming rain.

Me, I gathered up my horse, shoved the Winchester back into the boot, swung into the saddle and headed down the rise toward the cabin.

When I got closer, the door swung open — and two beaded, buckskinned Indians, rifles in hand, stepped out.

Chapter 7

Startled, I reined in the black, my hand instinctively going for the Colt at my hip.

But then I realized that the taller of the two Indians wasn't an Indian at all, but a white man with a red beard, hair of the same color spilling in tangles over his broad shoulders, and now he spoke to me.

"You came right in the nick of time, young feller," he said. "For a spell there, I reckoned we was done for."

Beside the man stood a pretty woman in a buckskin dress, her yellow hair in thick braids, a narrow beaded headband encircling her forehead.

"They attacked us just after sunup," she said, smiling, showing beautiful white teeth. "Our ammunition was running low and it was only a matter of time." Her dazzling smile widened. "Then you showed up."

A little girl, maybe four years old, walked out of the cabin and shyly stood behind the woman, looking at me now and then from behind her skirt.

I touched the brim of my hat. "Glad I could be of service, ma'am," I said. "I happened to be passing by and heard the shooting."

The man took a step toward me and said: "Name's Jacob Lawson and this here is my wife, Jen, and my daughter, Kate."

I nodded. "Dusty Hannah." And then, because I didn't want to share my troubles with them, I added: "Just a puncher headin' back to Texas."

"Well, Mr. Hannah," Lawson said, "ain't no point standing out here in the rain. Light and step into the cabin."

"Jacob," Jen said, her face suddenly clouded with concern. "Shouldn't we look at the fallen Apaches first? Some of them might only be wounded."

Jacob looked at me, as though for direction, like he was figuring me for some kind of expert on Indians. "There's one over there by the pigpen and maybe another," I said. "And three or four among the rocks back there."

"Then let's take a look," the man said.

I swung out of the saddle and led the black to the front of the cabin, where there was a hitching post. I looped the reins around the post and followed Jacob

Lawson and his wife, her daughter in her arms, to the corral.

The Apache I'd hit lay dead on his back, blood splashed on the front of his shirt. There was no sign of the other man I'd shot at.

We walked over to the rocks and found two dead Indians and a third who had been hit hard but was still breathing. The Apache was conscious and his obsidian eyes revealed only burning hate and defiance. His Henry lay where he'd dropped it and I kicked the rifle farther away from him.

Jen made to kneel beside the warrior, but I stopped her. "I wouldn't do that, ma'am," I told her. "He's still got a knife and for sure he'll stick you with it if he can."

"This man is hurt," the woman said. "We can't leave him out here in the rain."

"Yes, we can," I said. "If you take him inside, he won't thank you for it, ma'am, and he'll try to kill you first chance he gets." I glanced up the slope behind me. "Come nightfall, the Apaches will be back to carry off their dead. Just let him be until then."

"But . . . but that's inhuman," Jen protested, her blazing eyes searching my face.

I nodded. "Maybe so, ma'am, but this is a hard, unforgiving land and you do whatever it takes to survive." As the rain lashed down around me, I nodded toward the fallen Apache, looking into his wild, hate-filled eyes. "That warrior is like Comanche I've known, only a whole sight worse. You can't buy his friendship with kindness because he'll take that as a sign of weakness and he'll think you are afraid of him. Sure, you can carry him back to your cabin, nurse him back to health, but he'll reward you for it by killing you the very worst way he can." I looked at Jen, matching her anger with rising anger of my own. "You let him be," I said, "or kill him."

Jacob looked at me, a question in his eyes, as though trying to figure me out. "Y'know," he said finally, a smile touching his lips, "for a young feller, you talk old."

"I guess I've had some growing up to do in recent times," I said, matching his smile with one of my own. "Around these parts, just surviving makes a man grow old mighty fast."

Jacob turned to his wife, his voice making it clear that he'd brook no argument. "You heard what Mr. Hannah said, Jen. Leave this Apache be." Then, to take the sting out of it, he added: "Wife, he isn't one of those wounded little animals you're always finding. This is a fighting man and he's dangerous."

The woman looked at her husband, then at me, lifted her nose in the air and turned on her heel and stomped back to the cabin.

Jacob placed a big hand on my shoulder. "She'll calm down in a few minutes and realize that you have the right of it. Now please let me offer you the hospitality of our cabin. We don't have much, but what we have you can share."

My first instinct was to refuse and get back on the trail, but my growling stomach thought otherwise and I found myself nodding. "I'd be obliged," I said.

I glanced down at the wounded Apache and met his burning eyes. Summoning up the Spanish I could remember, I said: *"Todavia endecha. Usted es amigos estara detras para usted."*

The Mescalero glared at me for a few moments, then gathered what saliva he could find in his dry mouth and spat contemptuously in my direction.

"Hell, what did you tell him?" Jacob asked.

"I told him to lay still, that his friends would be back for him." I shrugged. "He didn't take kindly to it."

The Lawson cabin was clean but not well-appointed, though it had a wood floor, unusual for soddies at that time when most settlers made do with hard-packed dirt, occasionally whitewashed, but usually not.

I took off my hat and shrugged out of my wet slicker and Jacob directed me to a bench drawn up to a roughly made table. An Apache bullet had gouged a foot-long scar on the table's pine top and another had taken a chunk out of the arm of a rocking chair that stood by the fireplace.

As Jen, her back stiff, worked at the stove, Jacob opened the wood shutters and shook his head, his face gloomy, as he surveyed the broken glass panes in the windows.

Glass was hard to come by in the West, and until the panes could be replaced, he'd have to cover them over with wood, making the interior of the cabin even darker than it was now.

Despite the fact that it was still full daylight, Jacob lit the oil lamp that hung above the table and a pale orange glow spread through the small room, making the place seem less bleak. The wonderful smell of frying meat and boiling coffee wafted from the stove and I found my mouth watering, even as my empty stomach growled at me.

For a while no one spoke, my disagreement with Jen over the wounded Apache still frosting the air between us. Outside the rain continued to fall, hammering on the roof of the cabin, drops occasionally gusting through the broken windows. The wind was rising, whispering notions around the walls of the cabin, setting the lamp flame to dancing.

Jen finally turned from the stove, heaped platters in her hands, and laid them on the table with more of a thump than their weight merited. She returned with plates, silverware and chunks of cornbread, sniffed, then slammed each item on the table with not so much as a howdy-do.

Jacob gave his wife a long, warning glare, then turned to me and said: "Dig in, Mr. Hannah."

"Call me Dusty," I said without looking at him, all my attention riveted on the food.

Annoyed with me she might be, but Jen Lawson had set a handsome table.

One platter was piled high with fried antelope steaks, the other with boiled potatoes, and I helped myself liberally from both. Jen returned to the table and poured coffee for me and Jacob, then sat herself. Their daughter snuggled close beside Jen, who gave the child a small steak to chew on.

We ate hungrily, each pretending to be too busy with the food to notice the awkward silence stretching between us. But then I happened to turn my head to the left, my attention caught by a log crackling in the stove, and Jen exclaimed: "Why, Mr. Hannah, you're wounded!"

Absently my fingers went to my head, where Lafe Wingo's bullet had grazed me. I felt crusted blood, though the wound wasn't near as tender as it had been even a few days before.

"It's an old injury," I said, trying to make light of it. "I stepped into a stray bullet back to the Gypsum Hills country."

The woman's face was full of concern. "After you eat, I'm going to clean that wound for you." Her eyes softened as she touched the back of my hand. "You poor thing."

Embarrassed, I gave all my attention to my plate and Jacob laughed. "Dusty, better let Jen do as she pleases. She's forever nursing wounded critters back to health."

The air had cleared between us and Jen watched me with growing concern until I'd eaten my fill, sighed and pushed away from the table.

"That was an elegant meal, ma'am," I told her. "The first woman's cooking I've tasted in many a month."

Jen was looking at my wound intently, and to head her off, I dug into my shirt pocket, found my makings and asked: "May I beg your indulgence, ma'am?"

The woman nodded. "Please do. Jacob smokes a pipe and I'm well used to men and their need for tobacco."

Jacob stepped to the wood mantel above the fireplace and returned with a charred, battered pipe, which he proceeded to light.

I'd hoped our smoking would forestall his wife's attentions, but it was not to be. Jen left the table and came back with a pan of water and a cloth and began to bathe my wound.

Only now, as his wife fussed and fretted over me, did I mention to Jacob Lawson that I'd first taken Jen and him for Indians.

The big bearded man took that in stride. "Jen and me, our plan is to follow the way of the Indian and live as he does. That is why we dress as we do. Eventually, we hope to attract others to our valley who feel the same as we do."

As Jen dabbed at my head, she said: "We

wish to put away our guns and live as a community in perfect peace, love and harmony. When the Apaches came, Jacob tried to speak to them in friendship, but their only reply was a volley of gunfire that drove us into the cabin."

"They nearly done for us," Jacob said. "It was that close."

I nodded. "When the Apaches are on the war trail, as a general rule they ain't long on polite conversation."

"But even this won't deter us," Jen said, dabbing at my head with something that stung. "Our vision is to see this valley populated by hundreds of kindred spirits who wish to live as nature intended, close to the earth in the way of the native Red Man."

"It's a good way, Jen," I said, "but mighty hard. In the old days when an Indian ate, he filled his belly to bursting because he had no way of knowing when he'd eat again. In winter, when game and fuel were scarce, all the tribes suffered from hunger and cold. Even in good years a lot of them died, especially the old and the younkers like your little girl there.

"Now the buffalo are gone, things are even worse. To survive a bad winter, the Indian needs fat. The buffalo had plenty of fat, especially in his hump where he stored it, and in good years when the herds didn't drift too far south, that rich hump meat was easy to come by. Now the Sioux and the Cheyenne and the others must depend on antelope and deer and rabbit, and there's little fat on any of them. If they don't get government beef, and many of the wilder ones don't, they can fill their bellies with deer and jackrabbit in winter and still starve to death."

I rolled another smoke, thumbed a match into flame and lit it. "Like I said, it's a good way, but it's not an easy way."

"We'll teach the others who come to farm," Jen said. "Then our community need not depend on game to see us through the hard winters."

I dearly wanted to tell this starry-eyed pair that there was more to the Indian way than dressing up in beads and feathers and preaching peace and love. But I knew that nothing I could say would change their minds.

The Indian wasn't much on peace to begin with. Any warrior worth his salt would ride two hundred miles out of his way to get into a good fight, and as for love, well, maybe they loved their own tribe but outside of that everyone else was considered a potential enemy and treated as such.

Jen finished fussing over me and I touched the wound on my scalp. The dry blood was gone and the clean sting from the stuff she'd put on it felt good.

Outside the day was shading into night, and though I would dearly love to have taken up their offer of a bed for the night, I had to be on my way if I'd any hope of closing the distance between me and Lafe Wingo.

I rose from the table, thanked Jen again for her food and shrugged into my slicker. I'd left my horse at their barn where Jacob had given him a bait of corn, saddled him again and led him back to the cabin. As Jen and Jacob stepped outside I swung into the saddle.

"We whipped those Apaches pretty good today," I said, "but be sure of it, they'll come back for their dead. My advice is to stay in the cabin and keep your rifles close. The Apaches will hit and run, but they're mighty notional and they might just take it into their heads to renew the fight."

Jacob motioned to me with his pipe. "Thank you for all you did for us, Dusty," he said. "You saved our bacon and that's for sure."

"Glad I could help," I said, uncomfortable with his thanks.

"Come back and see us." Jen's white smile was bright. "And maybe next time you can stay a while and help us teach others the way."

"Till then," I said, touching my hat, knowing full well that I'd never visit this canyon again.

I swung the black around and cantered up the slope. The wounded Indian was gone from the rocks as I expected he would be and so were the bodies of the dead.

In this world no man stands alone, and others he meets leave their mark on him, no matter how passing or slight, adding in varying degree to the sum of his knowledge. Jen and Jacob Lawson were dreamers, but in their strange way they had shone a bright torch on the path I intended to take.

Soon I would wed pretty Sally Coleman and live with her happily ever after in a snug cabin of our own. I told myself love and peace we would have aplenty and there would be only a looking forward at happy events to come and not a single backward glance at what had passed before.

All this I thought as I rode under a wild, broken sky, the rain hammering at my face, the wind flapping the wet slicker around my legs.

That the wind blew unnaturally chill I did not notice, though I should have. There was a sharp, cold edge to its thin whisper that sighed of sundry perils to come.

But me, being young and in love, paid it no mind.

Chapter 8

I reached the Prairie Dog Town fork of the Red an hour before midnight and across the river lamps were still lit among the sprawling cabins, general store, hotel, cattle pens and corrals of Doan's Crossing.

The Red at this point was very wide, but mostly a series of broad sandbanks with only runnels of shallow water flowing sluggishly between them.

Though he was tired, the big black stepped across easily and I rode him into the settlement in a teeming rain.

That summer of 1880, Doan's Crossing was crowded with people, the Apache menace to the west and south bringing in punchers, ranchers, a few blanket Indians, soldiers, buffalo hunters, peddlers and itinerant preachers.

Jonathan Doan's general store, where there was a bar, was doing a brisk business and through the glass doors of the two-story hotel, men were constantly coming and going.

I had no desire for whiskey, but what I did need were supplies and news of Lafe Wingo and the Owens brothers.

Doan's nephew Corwin operated the livery store, and when I rode in, he recognized me, even though I was just one among the scores of punchers who had driven three hundred thousand head through the crossing that spring.

"You're late getting back, Dusty," Doan said as he took my horse and led him to a vacant stall.

Maybe Corwin Doan remembering me shouldn't have come as a surprise. He kept a record of every cow that crossed the Red at his place, the names of the trail bosses and who owned the herds. Simon Prather was one of the spring regulars, but the biggest herds by far were from the King Ranch, thirty thousand head every season.

I followed Doan and rubbed down the black with a piece of sacking before I thought it through and explained my late arrival. "Lingered too long in Dodge, Corwin," I said, not wishing to burden the man with my troubles. "Simon Prather took to feeling poorly and I stayed with him a spell."

"Right sorry to hear that," Doan said. He was a young man with serious hazel eyes, already balding, with a full black beard and mustache.

I watched him pour the black a good bait of oats and fork him some hay; then I walked back with him to the office.

"Planning to stay long?" Doan asked.

"Just tonight. I'll be moving out come daybreak."

Doan's face was suddenly troubled. "Is that wise, Dusty, a man riding alone? Yesterday Victorio and his Apaches ambushed a wagon train three miles south of here. Killed eight teamsters and there's another at the hotel who isn't expected to live."

"I've got no choice, Corwin," I said, deciding to tell a half-truth. "I'm overdue back at the SP Connected and Ma Prather will be some worried."

"Take my advice, Dusty," Doan said, "and stay here until this here Apache dustup blows over. Every troop of the Ninth Cavalry is out and they'll soon catch up to those damned renegades."

Changing the subject, I asked: "A lot of folks in town you don't know, Corwin?"

"Well I should say," the man answered. "Crossing's full of strangers since Victorio started to play hob."

"Thing is, I'm looking for a man by the name of Lafe Wingo," I said. "Him and three brothers who go by Hank, Charlie and Ezra Owens."

"Friends of yours?" Doan asked, a wary suspicion tingeing his voice. Corwin Doan had the Western man's ingrained reluctance to impart information about men who might be on the dodge, and me, I didn't have it in me to hold it against him none.

"Just acquaintances, Corwin," I said, trying to keep my face unreadable. "I'm a mite concerned about their whereabouts, what with the Apaches an' all."

Well, Doan thought about that some, then reached a decision. "Lafe Wingo and the Owens boys rode through three days ago," he said. "They put their horses up here for a couple of hours while they drank at the store. Then they left."

Three days. I was far behind them and the distance between us was widening fast.

Doan must have seen the disappointment in my face, because he said: "Dusty, the Apache troubles are flaring up worse and worse. I'm guessing those boys will ride careful and hole up somewheres until Victorio moves on or the army gets him. I'm sure you'll catch up with them, if that's your intention."

"It's something like that, Corwin," I replied. "As I said, they're only passing acquaintances."

"Strange though, Dusty, mighty strange."

"What's so strange?"

"That a nice young feller like you would be acquainted with Lafe Wingo and them. Those boys never done me no harm, mind, but Uncle Jonathan told me the whole passel of them are killers and outlaws."

"They are killers, Corwin. And Lafe Wingo is the worst of them, a sight deadlier with a gun than good ol' John Wesley or Clay Allison or any of them." I shrugged, forcing a smile, trying to make light of it. "And you're right, I guess I do tend to have some mighty unusual acquaintances."

I could tell that Doan figured I was keeping something back, but he decided not to push me further. He looked out at the lashing rain and the black sky and said: "Dusty, the hotel is full with so many folks coming in, but you can bed down here for the night. The barn is warm and dry and it will still only cost you two bits and I have good strong coffee here in the morning."

"I'm obliged, Corwin," I said. "I reckon I'll walk over to the store and get me a beer and see the sights, then head back this way."

"Step careful, Dusty," Doan warned as I made to walk into the rain and the gathering night. "There are some rough ones in town."

I waved a hand in acknowledgment and headed toward the general store, passing sprawling cattle pens, the blacksmith shop and the hotel.

When I reached the front of the store, a long, peaked-roofed adobe building, I kicked off clinging mud from my boots on the flagstone steps, then walked inside.

Doan's general store was a single room, with piled-up merchandise of all kinds at one end and a rough-hewn pine bar at the other.

The crowd had thinned out now the hour was growing late. A couple of tired-looking men in faded soldier blue gazed gloomily into the bottom of empty glasses and four punchers shared a bottle at one of the two tables in the place. A grizzled old-timer sat by the potbellied stove smoking a reeking pipe and Jonathan Doan, lord of all he surveyed, stood sentinel behind the bar.

I tarried for a while at the merchandise, wondering at the breathtaking luxury and plentitude of it all.

Spread before me were racks of gleaming

new Winchesters, stacked boxes of cartridges and wide-brimmed Stetson hats brought all the way from Wichita Falls. Shirts in every color of the rainbow were neatly folded row on row and among them boots and shoes with a notice that read: FOOTWEAR SOLD AT COST. From the rafters hung great slabs of sowbelly bacon, salt pork and smoked hams and arranged around the floor stood kegs and barrels of molasses, vinegar, flour and soda crackers. Rounds and thick wedges of yellow and white cheeses under glass domes competed for space on the counter with jars of spices, sugar, pink candy canes and black-striped peppermint balls.

The store smelled of plug tobacco, fragrant Virginia ham, the leather of boots and belts, fresh ground coffee, gun oil and the sweet, musty tang of calico and cotton cloth in bolts.

Me, I was so enthralled, counting through the round silver dollars in my pocket and mighty wishful for more, that it took me a few moments to realize Jonathan Doan was talking to me.

I turned and found him at my elbow. As his nephew Corwin had done, he said: "You're late getting back, Dusty."

And as I had told Corwin, I said I'd been

delayed in Dodge because of Simon Prather's illness. I made no mention of the thirty thousand dollars or Lafe Wingo.

"Well" — Doan sighed after I'd said my piece — "I take that news mighty hard. Simon Prather is a good man."

"Indeed he is," I said, letting it go at that.

Jonathan Doan was a small, bearded man with keenly intelligent, penetrating brown eyes and a gentle way about him. He was an Ohio Yankee but I didn't hold that against him, and he was a Quaker, and I didn't hold that against him either.

"So what can I do you for, Dusty?" Doan asked, smiling.

"I need supplies, Mr. Doan," I replied. "But I figure those can wait until morning. Right now I could use a beer."

Doan, not a drinking man himself, nodded. "Then step right up to the bar."

I crossed the room in a sudden silence, my spurs chiming. The reason for the stillness became apparent when I noticed one of the punchers at the table, a huge man with a thick mane of yellow hair, looking me up and down, with downright mean belligerence in his bloodshot eyes.

The others in the room, sensing as I did that the big puncher was on the prod and had sized me up as his victim, eyed me warily as I stepped to the bar.

"What will it be, Dusty?" Doan asked. There was a concerned edge to his voice and I guessed he was also aware of trouble brewing.

I ordered a Bass Ale, and while Doan bent down to find the bottle, I opened my slicker and moved it slowly away from my holstered Colt. I did it so casually I figured no one noticed, nor it seemed had they.

One of the soldiers caught my eye and his glance held a warning. He nodded slightly toward the door, telling me I should leave. I ignored the man and turned to the bar as Doan proffered me my beer.

"See any Apaches on your travels, young feller?" the old-timer by the stove asked, whether to break the tension or because he was blissfully unaware of what was happening I could not tell.

"Uh-huh, tangled with a passel of them north of here," I said, sampling the ale. It was cold and good.

The big puncher guffawed. "Yeah, sure you did. Why, you ain't old enough to have left your momma's teat. You didn't tangle with no Apaches. A passel o' them my ass."

Now a couple of things displeased me about this man. The first was that he'd called me a liar, the second that he sported a fine, sweeping dragoon mustache that put to shame the fuzzy growth on my top lip.

But I was in no mood for a fight, so I let it go. "Believe what you want," I said, shrugging. "Makes no never mind to me."

I turned back to the bar and said to Doan: "Beer is real good, Mr. Doan."

I felt a rough hand on my shoulder that half-turned me round and the huge puncher stuck his face into mine, whiskey heavy on his breath. "Doan," he said, "bring a bottle. I'm gonna teach this whippersnapper how to drink like a man."

"Let it be, Burt," Doan said. "This boy means you no harm."

The man called Burt grinned, his eyes bright and cruel. "Aw, Doan, I won't hurt him too bad. All I'm gonna do is pour some of your rotten whiskey down his throat."

I sized this man up as a mean drunk and a remorseless bully. He was huge, six inches taller than me and maybe sixty pounds heavier, the kind smaller men are all too willing to step around.

But now I was getting good and mad and maybe he saw something in my eyes because he took a single step back and his grin slipped a little.

"Mister, I don't want your whiskey," I said. "I'm wet and tired and I'm not here to borrow trouble, so let me be." I moved my slicker again, clearing my gun. "You've been duly notified. Let me be."

At heart this man was a coward used to knocking around men who were weaker and scared of him. But I wasn't afraid, and he knew it, because Burt dug deep, found no reserve of courage and retreated into bluster.

"When I say you drink with me, you'll drink with me," he yelled, turning to his grinning compadres at the table, seeking their support. The man knew he had gone way too far to back down, and though I'd given him an out, his pride wouldn't let him take it. He swung back to the bar. "Damn you, Doan, I told you to bring a bottle."

"Mister," I said again, "I don't want your whiskey. I'm not partial to it."

Burt jerked the bottle from Doan's hand, pulled the cork and held the whiskey high. "Open your trap," he said. "You're either gonna drink like a man or be carried out of here with two broken legs."

Me, I'd had enough. I was tired and wet and as far as I was concerned this hoedown was over.

Two things happened very fast. First, Burt grabbed the front of my shirt and pulled me toward him, the splashing bottle poised so he could ram it into my mouth. Second, I palmed my Colt and slammed the barrel hard against the side of his head.

For a moment the man just stood there, looking at me with glazed eyes that rolled like dice in his head. Then he collapsed to the floor with a crash that shook the building, as though an anvil had just dropped on his head.

I swung the Colt, covering the three punchers at the table, but not a one of them even twitched an eyelid. Three pairs of eyes regarded me in stunned horror, like I'd just scared them into salvation and Sunday school.

"Yee-hah!" The old man by the stove sprang to his feet, spry as you please, and threw his arms into the air. "Man, oh, man," he yelled, "I never seen nobody draw a Colt that fast. Boy," he hollered at me, "you're quick as double-geared lightning an' no mistake."

I ignored the oldster and spoke to the punchers at the table. "The man at my feet was duly notified," I said. "Any of you three have a problem with that?"

The youngest of the punchers, a boy

about my own age, shook his head. "We got no problem with you," and after a moment's hesitation, he added, "mister."

I nodded to the fallen Burt. "Then carry him out of here and let him sleep it off."

The three waddies rose as one and helped their limp, groaning compadre to his feet. I watched them carry Burt through the door before I turned back to the bar.

Jonathan Doan was looking hard at me, a strange expression that I found difficult to read in his eyes. "You've grown up, Dusty," he said finally. "I'd say you've grown up considerable since the spring."

He reached under the bar, found another bottle of Bass Ale and slid it across the bar.

"This one's on me, Mr. Hannah," he said.

Chapter 9

I rose at first light and brushed straw from my hair and clothes, stepped down the ladder from the hayloft, then checked on the black. The big horse seemed rested and looked like he was ready for the trail.

Corwin Doan was asleep in his office and I didn't wake him. I found a tin cup, quietly helped myself from the coffeepot on top of the stove and stepped to the door of the livery stable.

The rain had stopped for now, but a heavy mist hung over the Red, thick gray fingers spilling over its banks, probing among the buildings and corrals of the crossing so the cabins and fences looked like they were emerging from a cloud.

I set the cup at my feet, rolled a cigarette, picked up the cup again and smoked and drank, enjoying the sharp morning tang of tobacco and coffee and the quiet tranquillity of the breaking day.

Ten minutes later I saddled the black and rode to the general store. Jonathan

Doan was already up and doing and he told me Burt, nursing a hangover and a busted head, had ridden out an hour earlier. He said he didn't much care, on account of how he had no regard for the man, him being a bully and a no-account an' all.

I bought coffee, a little baking powder, cornmeal and flour. Bacon being expensive at that time and place, I settled for a slab of salt pork and my only extravagance was a small sack of the black-and-white peppermint balls I'd seen the night before.

Before he made up my meager order, Doan poured me a cup of coffee and told me to help myself to some soda crackers and cheese. Thus I made an excellent breakfast before I took to the trail again, riding through a gray mist under a grayer sky.

I figured I was due north of the SP Connected, but before I reached the ranch I must cross a hundred miles of broken, hilly country with two questions uppermost in my mind: Where were Lafe Wingo and the Owens brothers? And where were the Apaches?

For these I had no answers, neither question being calculated to set a man's mind at ease. When the rain began again, a steady downpour accompanied by the rumble of distant thunder, it only added to my gloom.

Ahead of me lay both forks of the Wichita and beyond that, down to the Cottonwood Creek country about twenty miles west of the dogleg of the Western Trail, was the SP Connected.

Before I reached the ranch, I had to catch up with Wingo and the others, dodge Victorio's Apaches and recover the thirty thousand dollars. It was a tall order growing taller by the minute, and a nagging doubt that I could achieve it was gnawing at me, giving me no peace.

I had no idea how I'd tackle a deadly gunman like Wingo if and when I caught up to him, but that was just another bridge I'd have to cross when I got to it. As for the Apaches, I determined to ride careful and take my chances.

Always being of a mind to wed and bed pretty Sally Coleman, I'd saved my money and forgone the silver hatbands and conchoed saddles much loved by Texas punchers, so there was nothing about me that glittered and would catch the eye of a scouting Apache. My range clothes were much faded and muddy from the trail and the black horse I rode merged into the background of brown grass and deep-shadowed hills.

At noon I sheltered for a while in a thick grove of shin oak and mesquite growing at the base of an outcropping of red sandstone that jutted up like the prow of a ship from the slope of a low hill. Enough rain had collected in a natural basin in the rock for me to fill my coffeepot and among the trees I found dry wood to start a small fire. I trusted to the oak branches to scatter what little smoke the fire made and I eased the girth on the black and let him graze on a patch of good grass behind the rock where he'd be hidden.

Later, as I smoked and drank scalding hot coffee, I looked from the sheltering trees, my eyes searching beyond the teeming deluge to the west, where the Staked Plains stretched away forever, their vast distances now lost behind an iron gray curtain of rain and low cloud.

My mind fell to remembering my first trip up the trail, when I'd seen the last of the buffalo on those plains, and the last of the free, wild Comanche.

The Comanche had come out of that barren vastness one late afternoon under a burning scarlet sky and for a while they'd ridden alongside us, keeping pace, so we were maybe just a couple of hundred yards apart. Simon Prather yelled for us to keep our rifles handy and to bunch the herd and when I looked into his eyes I saw nothing but worry.

The Comanche were strung out over a quarter of a mile, fifty or so warriors in the lead, proud lords of the plains with fine hands unsullied by manual labor. The warriors hunted and made war, knew only the lance and the bow; all else was left to the women. Unlike other plains Indians the Comanche wore no feathers, their long hair hanging loose over their shoulders or bound up in red-ribbon braids.

Behind the warriors the young women, some in beaded buckskin, others in skirts and embroidered Spanish shirts, rode paint ponies that dragged travois, the thin pine poles hissing like snakes through the long blue grama grass.

Next came the old people, wearily trudging on foot. The Comanche had no respect for the aged, figuring that a man who lived long enough to have gray hair and a big belly had not been a gallant enough warrior. On the plains, the truly brave died young. Old men were not listened to in council and in lean times were abandoned to starvation and the wolves. Old women, well past childbearing age and beyond their strength, fared no better. They were useless mouths to feed and as expendable as the men.

Last came the slaves, overburdened and abused, staggering through the dust bent over from their heavy loads, Mexican mostly but with a sprinkling of white and black faces, all of them considered by the Comanche less than human and treated as such.

Finally, as the day was just shading into night, five of the warriors swung out of line and rode up to Mr. Prather. They were ready for war, the bottom halves of their faces from the eyes down painted black. The Comanche made it clear by sign language and a smattering of Spanish that they wanted a dozen cows, but in the end Simon gave them six young calves he would have shot anyway since they couldn't keep up with the herd, a side of bacon, salt and some lye soap.

The Indians also wanted whiskey and ten dollars, but this they did not get.

At full dark we kept the herd close and stood to arms. I took up my rifle and waited by a wheel of the chuck wagon, listening to the dim drums throbbing in the distance of the night and the rise and fall of the wolf wail of the warriors.

The Comanche hit us at dawn, but since there was a dozen of us punchers, all well-armed and determined, they were content to trade rifle shots at long range and no execution was done on either side.

Through it all, Simon Prather walked among us, exhorting us to be steadfast in our time of peril and to keep our faces turned to the enemy.

In the end, the Indians did drop one old cow that Mr. Prather let them have, telling us that it didn't make no never mind because they would stop to butcher and eat the cow and not follow us. And indeed, that turned out to be the case.

Now, as I looked out on their bleak vastness, the Staked Plains were empty of life. The long shadows of the buffalo were gone and with them those of the Comanche and neither had left a mark on the land.

I finished my coffee, threw the dregs on the fire and swung into the saddle.

By midafternoon I was riding back along the trail we'd made in the spring, crossing the divide between the Red and the Wichita. This was hilly country, the black soil heavy with salt, and I let my horse graze on a clump of salt weed for a spell before urging him on again.

I found wagon tracks in the mud a few minutes later.

The tracks were heading due south, and I figured they were of a four-wheel wagon drawn by two oxen. Judging by the way the iron wheel rims had dug deep into the mud, it was heavily laden.

Teamsters sometimes traveled this route, carrying supplies to Fort Worth and other places, but they always cut across the Western Trail, heading west, not south.

I swung out of the saddle and checked the footprints by the tracks, trailing the black behind me. The wagon was not far ahead because, despite the rain, the prints were still fresh.

One set was small and neat, obviously made by a woman, the others those of a booted man.

Bullwhackers don't ride on the wagon, but walk alongside the oxen with a whip to urge them on, and these two were no exception.

What a man and a woman were doing in this country in the middle of an Apache uprising I could not guess. But something, maybe the way the man's prints now and then suddenly veered away from the wagon and slipped and slid all over the place, told me these were pilgrims and the husband, if that was what he was, seemed to be either staggering sick or staggering drunk.

If there were Apaches close, they would have seen those tracks and would know there was a woman with the wagon, a valuable prize they would use to while away a few pleasant hours before they killed her.

I swung into the saddle and followed the tracks. Ahead of me they led into a narrow valley between shallow hills before disappearing into gray distance and rain.

Heavy drops hammering on my hat and slicker, I reined in the black and looked around. The surrounding hills seemed empty of life, but that was no guarantee the Apaches weren't around. It's when you don't see them you worry, and right now I saw nothing but the rain on the hills and the lowering blackness of the sky, lit up now and then by the flash of lightning.

The past weeks had taught me caution, and I eased my Winchester from the boot and laid it across the saddle horn.

A few yards ahead of me a covey of scaled quail, soaked and unable or unwilling to fly, ran from one mesquite bush to another, rattling the plants' stick arms with their small bodies. Then the land fell silent again but for the hiss of the rain.

I leaned over, patted the black's neck,

and urged him forward. He tossed his head, his bit ringing like a bell in the quiet, took off at a canter, then settled back into an easy, distance-eating lope.

My eyes constantly scanning the hills and surrounding stands of oak and mesquite, I rode into the mouth of the valley. A quick glance at the sky told me there were at least four hours until nightfall. Until then, me and the two people who were walking with the wagon would be out in the open and dangerously exposed.

I slowed the black to a walk and rode alert in the saddle, my nose lifted, testing the breeze, but smelled only wet grass and rain and the dank, menacing odor of the dead silence.

Five minutes later, as I cleared the valley and rode into a mesquite-studded flat, I found the wagon.

I reined up when I was still a hundred yards away and stood in the stirrups and studied the wagon, the two people beside it and the lay of the land, not wishing to blunder into trouble.

My first glance told me this was a tumbleweed outfit and my second confirmed it. The wagon was old, the planks warped, the whole sorry wreck held together with baling wire, biscuit tin patches and string.

Off to one side two huge oxen trailed a broken wagon tongue as they grazed, still hitched together. A young girl in a hooded cloak stood by the front of the wagon, looking down helplessly at the shattered, raw stump of the tongue.

A small, bearded man, a jug in his hand, had his face upturned to the rain and sky, his arms spread, yelling words I couldn't hear.

My first instinct was to shy clear of this pair and their troubles, but there are some things a man can't ride around, and I knew deep within myself that this was one of them.

I kneed the black forward and rode to the wagon, the teeming rain running in sheets off the shoulders of my slicker.

The girl stepped toward me as I drew closer and I reined up and touched the brim of my hat. "Ma'am," I said, my voice suddenly unsteady.

Even in a pounding rain, her black curls plastered to her forehead under the hood of her cloak, this girl was breathtakingly beautiful. She possessed a dark, flashing kind of beauty and I thought — treacherously, I admit — that it made Sally Coleman's blue-eyed, yellow-haired prettiness seem insipid by comparison.

144

The girl's eyes were huge and brown, framed by long lashes and her mouth was small but full-lipped and ripe in her heart-shaped face. That was a mouth made for kissing and I had the urge to swing out of the saddle and plant a smacker on her.

Of course I did no such thing, staying right where I was as I said: "I figure you've got yourself in a tolerable amount of trouble, ma'am."

The girl nodded, and from what I could see of her gray wool dress under the cloak, she was slender and mighty shapely. "The wagon tongue just snapped." She turned and pointed to where the wagon's front wheels were almost up to their axles in mud. "We got bogged down and when Pa whipped up the oxen to pull us out, the tongue just broke."

I saw tears start in the girl's eyes, and being young and ardent and of a chivalrous nature, I swung out of the saddle and stepped close behind her.

"Don't you fret none, ma'am," I said. "I'll see what I can do for your wagon."

The girl blinked back tears. "You'd do that for us?"

I shrugged. "Name's Dusty Hannah and since there's no one else around, I guess I got it to do."

At that, the man stepped from behind the wagon, saw me and let out a cheer, then yelled:

Oh! Young Lochinvar is come out of
  the west,
Through all the wide Border his steed
  was the best,
And save his good broadsword he
  weapons had none,
He rode all unarmed and he rode all
  alone.
So faithful in love and so dauntless in war,
There never was knight like the young
  Lochinvar.

The man stopped and blinked at me like an owl. "Well, young Lochinvar, are you come to save us or rob us?" He extended the jug. "Here, take a drink."

I shook my head at him. "I don't care for any right now," I said.

The man shrugged. "Suit yourself. More for me."

Then he put the jug to his mouth and drank deeply, his prominent Adam's apple bobbing.

"My name is Lila Tryon and that's my father, Ned." The girl's eyes searched my face, as though trying to find the understanding she hoped for. "He . . . he's not been well."

Ned Tryon had the same dark brown eyes as his daughter, but what was beautiful in her was weak in him. They were the vague eyes of a dreamer, the eyes of a man unsuited to survive in the hard, unforgiving land that lay around us.

I stepped over to the wagon tongue and Lila came over and stood beside me. "Can it be fixed?"

I nodded. "If you have a hammer and nails in the wagon."

"We do," Lila said. "And there's some sturdy oak wood if you need that."

I stood there looking at the tongue for a while, then turned to the girl and asked: "Where are you and your pa headed?"

She eased her wet hood away from her face and gave me a dazzling smile that made my heart jump. "We've come all the way from Missouri. We had a farm there" — her eyes slid to her father — "but it didn't work out. Then Pa's brother died and left us his ranch down south of the Clear Fork of the Brazos, just a few miles east of Beals Creek."

I nodded. "Know that country well. It's right close to my home ranch, the SP Connected."

"Pa says his brother wrote to him once and described the place, a strong stone cabin on a hundred and sixty acres, all of it good pastureland cut through by creeks."

"I suppose you could keep enough cows on it to get by," I said, "though it will take a strong back and some mighty hard work."

Lila shook her head. "Oh, no, not cattle. Pa plans to farm the place."

"That's cow country, ma'am," I said, my patience fraying fast, unable to believe what I was hearing. "The soil is too thin and rocky for farming. Besides," I added, then instantly regretted it, "we don't take kindly to sodbusters down there."

"Then you'll just have to get used to us, won't you, Mr. Hannah?" Lila snapped, annoyance flaring in her eyes.

That little gal had spirit and I let it go. "You go ahead and do what you must, ma'am," I said. "But you'll fare no better at farming in Texas than you did in Missouri and maybe a lot worse."

Ned Tryon lurched toward us. "Ah," he said, "the lovers' first quarrel and all because of the poor, downtrodden farmer." Tryon tilted back his head and yelled at the uncaring sky:

Bowed by the weight of centuries he
  leans,
Upon his hoe and gazes at the ground,
The emptiness of ages in his face,
And on his back the burden of the
  world.

Tryon spat between his feet, then blinked
his bleary eyes at me. "You're so right, you
know, gallant young Lochinvar. Farming is
a life for a hog. It's not for me, a poet, an
artist . . . a philosopher."

Lila rushed to her pa and took him by
his thin shoulders. "Pa, you promised. You
told me this time we'll make it. Back in
Missouri you said this was the fresh start
we needed."

The man pushed his daughter away
roughly. "As a farmer, never!" His eyes
wild, Ned Tryon clutched the jug to his
chest. "That was your ma's dream, Lila,
never mine and in the end it killed her. Remember the endless poverty and me trying
to wrest a living from land that grew only
rock and weeds? Remember your ma
looking at the catalogs, her eyes bright,
wishful for all the nice things I could never
buy her? Remember how she just faded
away, worn down by hard work and harder
disappointments?" He lurched back to-

ward the wagon. "For God's sake, leave me be, child, and let me drink myself into blessed release."

Lila bent her head and I heard her sob. I was of a mind to say something hard to her father, but he had put a thief in his mouth to steal his tongue and I might as well stand in a storm and chastise the wind.

I stood there, awkward and lost, looking at Lila, trying to find the right words. They didn't come to me, so in the end I said: "I guess I better get to fixing that wagon tongue."

The girl nodded, her tearstained eyes made wetter by the rain. "I'll find you the wood and a hammer."

Lila stepped to the back of the wagon and I followed. She rummaged under the canvas tarp and I got a chance to see what they were hauling. All of it — an organ, a dresser, a rocking chair, china cups and plates and a tarnished silver tea service — was suited to a lace-and-lilac parlor in Missouri but not the rawboned cow country south of the Red.

A plow was tied to the side of the wagon, its steel blade bright, the handles not honed to a honey color by sweat and toil, but still raw and pine yellow. This plow had not seen much work and had rested in a barn more often than it had dug furrows in the soil.

Lila handed me wood, nails and a hammer and I unhitched the oxen from the yoke and brought the broken end of the tongue back to the wagon.

Thunder rolled across the sky and the lashing rain grew heavier as I set about making the repair. I'm no great shakes as a carpenter, but after I splinted the tongue with the wood Lila had given me, I straightened up and figured I had done a fair to middling job.

My work wasn't pretty, but the tongue held when I hitched up the team again, and that was what mattered.

Ned Tryon had found the oblivion he'd sought, lying unconscious under the meager shelter of a mesquite bush. Lila took the jug from his hands and asked me to help her father into the back of the wagon.

The man was barely capable of walking and I had to carry him most of the way. I laid him in the wagon and Lila covered him up with the tarp.

"Dusty," she said when the job was done, "Pa didn't mean all those things he said. Since Ma died he . . . he just hasn't been himself."

Well me, I let that go. I was in wild country with a girl, a drunk and a slow-moving ox wagon and there were Apaches in the hills. Right about then I didn't feel much like talking, so all I said was: "Let's get this wagon rolling."

For all her fragile beauty, Lila was no blushing prairie flower. When I whipped the team into motion and set to pushing on a wheel, she got on another and pushed right along with me, her shoes and the bottom of her dress deep in the mud.

The straining oxen pulled the wagon free and I let them rest for a spell and gathered up my horse. I handed the reins to Lila. "You ride him," I said. "I'll guide the team."

I didn't want the wagon to get bogged down again and the girl must have understood, because she made no objection. Lila hiked up her dress, showing a powerful amount of pretty leg, and swung into the saddle.

She touched the straw bonnet tied to the saddle horn. "Is this for your best girl?"

I nodded. "Uh-huh. Her name's Sally Coleman and her pa owns a spread right close to the SP Connected."

Lila flashed her white smile. "Is she pretty?"

Again I nodded. "As a field of bluebonnets in spring."

The girl frowned, then sniffed. "I never thought bluebonnets were particularly pretty flowers."

I saw where this conversation was headed and changed the subject. "Lila," I said quickly, "come dark we'll have to find a place where we can hole up for the night. The Apaches are out and we could be in a hell of a fix."

The girl kneed the black alongside me as I walked beside the plodding oxen. She glanced down at me and said: "They told us all that at Doan's Crossing. But the Apaches won't bother us. We mean them no harm."

I shook my head at her. "Lila, to the Apache, everyone is an enemy. That's why they've survived so long. There's no word for *friend* in the Apache language. If they want to call somebody *friend,* and that's a mighty rare occurrence, they use the Spanish word *amigo.* To them, you're either an Apache or you ain't, and if you ain't, then you're an enemy."

I flicked the bullwhip over the backs of the oxen. "You may mean the Apaches no harm, but they mean you plenty."

I wanted to tell her they'd go out of their

153

way to capture a pretty woman, but I didn't because for the first time I saw uncertainty in Lila's eyes.

"Dusty," she said, "do you think we're in danger?"

"I do," I replied, deciding not to spare her the truth. "In a heap of danger, and with this wagon and your pa, we're fast running out of room on the dance floor."

Lila opened her mouth to say something, changed her mind and looked around at the rain-shrouded landscape. "Are they out there?" she asked finally, waving her hand at the surrounding hills.

"Could be," I said.

And a few moments later, as thunder crashed above us, I smelled the smoke.

Chapter 10

The smoke smell was fleeting and uncertain, scattered by the rain and the gusting wind.

It could mean that there was a farm or ranch nearby — but it could mean something else entirely and much less to my liking.

Ahead of us the trail curved around a low, rocky hogback, its narrow rifts and gullies choked with mesquite and scrub oak. Wildflowers, goldenrod and primroses mostly, peeped shyly from the wet grass between the hill and us, and off to the left cottonwoods spread their branches beside a fast-running wash.

I halted the oxen and studied the ridge of the hogback.

There, I saw it, a thin smear of smoke rising into the air, very faint and soon shredded apart by the breeze.

Lila kneed the black alongside me. "Dusty, what do you see?"

"Smoke," I replied, "over yonder beyond the ridge of the hill."

"Is it a town?" the girl asked, something akin to hope in her eyes.

I shook my head. "No, there's no town there." I didn't want to scare her, so I said: "But there are small ranches scattered among these hills. It could be smoke from a cabin." I looked up at her. "Climb down, Lila. I'm going to take me a look-see."

The girl swung gracefully out of the saddle and handed me the reins. I glanced at the rocks crowning the ridge of the hogback. Even if the smoke turned out to be a wildfire sparked by the lightning that now and then forked from the sky, there could be a sheltered place up there to spend the night out of the wind and rain and away from the prying eyes of any passing Apache.

I swung into the saddle and slid the Winchester from the boot. Only then did I ride toward the ridge, my eyes restlessly scanning the land around me. The slope of the hogback was less steep than it had seemed from a distance and I was soon among the rocks, here and there stunted cedar and post oak writhing like the tormented damned between them.

Riding even more warily now, the Winchester across the saddle horn, I cleared the rocks and rode to the top of the grassy slope on the other side.

Now I saw what had caused the smoke and it brought me no comfort.

Below, too narrow to be called a valley, a gulch divided the hogback from another low hill beyond. A stream ran along the bottom of the gulch, rocks scattered along its sandy banks and on the slope opposite grew mesquite and a scattering of post oak and cottonwood.

A dugout cabin had been carved into the hill and to its right lay a ramshackle pole corral and small sod barn.

All this I saw in an instant, but what riveted my attention was the man who was suspended by his feet from the low branch of one of the cottonwoods growing by the creek.

A fire still glowed a dull crimson under his head, and a thin tendril of smoke rose from the dying coals. The body swayed slightly in the wind, the branch creaking, and whoever the man was, he had died hard and painfully slow.

I studied the land around me and only when I decided no one was there did I ride down the hill. The Apaches had been here until very recently, too recently for my liking, and I sensed danger, the hairs on the back of my neck standing on end.

Lila was still with the wagon, and vulnerable, but I had to take a chance on her not being seen. Later we could bring the wagon here, going on the assumption that lightning never strikes twice in the same place and that the Apaches would have moved on.

It was a gamble, but since the cards were stacked against me, it was a gamble I knew I had to take. It was better to spend the night here than out in the open.

With a surprised jolt of recognition, I discovered I knew the man whose brains had been slowly roasted over the fire. Even though his mouth was horribly twisted by his last, agonized scream, there was no mistaking the freckles and what was left of the bright red hair of Shorty Cummings.

Shorty had once been a puncher for Simon Prather and I recalled that he'd pulled his weight and did his job without complaint. But the lure of easy money had attracted the little man to the outlaw life and he'd soon hooked up with a couple of hard cases out of El Paso. The last I'd heard, the trio had robbed a bank down on the Peg Leg Crossing country and shot their way out of town, a stray bullet killing a ten-year-old girl as they made their escape.

Riding slow and careful, I circled around Shorty's body and headed toward the dugout, the rain-lashed hills around me waiting in patient silence for what was to come. A dead man lay on his back a few feet away from the door and another hung, head down, over the top rail of the corral.

The Apaches had caught all three out in the open and quickly killed the two El Paso hard cases. I reckon Shorty must have been born under a dark star because he had been the one unlucky enough to be captured alive.

I rode back to where the little man's body hung. The fire was now dead, extinguished by the rain and by Shorty's brains, which had run out after the heat cracked his skull wide open.

It had been a terrible way to die, and I vowed right there and then that no matter what happened, I wouldn't let the Apaches take me alive. Or Lila either.

I found my knife and cut Shorty loose and he fell to the ground with an ungainly thump, legs and arms splayed, ugly and undignified in death. I swung out of the saddle and dragged the man into a clump of long, bluestem grass beside the creek where he'd be hidden from sight. That done, one by one I looped my rope around the feet of the other two outlaws and dragged them behind my horse and laid them beside Shorty.

There was no time for a burying, and I figured this way Lila would not see the bodies and be disturbed by them.

After stretching out the last outlaw, I straightened up and worked a crick out of the small of my back. I swung into the saddle and rode to the ridge of the hog-back. Lila was down there, looking for me, her open hand shielding her eyes from the teeming rain. I waved to her, indicating that she should bring up the wagon. The girl cracked her whip and soon the ox team was plodding toward me, heads low as they leaned into the yoke and labored up the slope.

Scouting around, I found a clearing among the rocks and waved Lila toward it. The oxen reached the ridge and headed into the clearing where Lila halted them.

"What did you find?" she asked, looking up at me with eyes that were wide and just a tad frightened.

"There's a dugout cabin on the hill opposite this one and a barn where we can put up my horse and the oxen."

"People?"

I shook my head at her. "No people," I

lied. "Whoever lived here probably moved out when the Apache scare began." I smiled, trying to reassure her. "Lila, we can spend the night in the cabin if the place is halfway decent. At least we'll be out of the rain."

Doubt clouded Lila's eyes and for a moment I thought she knew I was lying to her. But to my relief she said: "I was just thinking about Pa. This journey has been hard on him and he's not as young as he used to be."

Well, I let that go. If, as I suspected, Ned Tryon was always as drunk as a hoe-down fiddler, no wonder he was aging so fast.

Lila took my silence as agreement because she glanced up at the darkening sky and said: "He'll be all right when we get to the new place. There's still time to put in a crop."

"Maybe so," I muttered, not wanting to pursue the matter further. Then, more brusquely than I intended: "I'm going to check out the cabin. Bring the wagon down, but be careful. The slope is slippery from the rain."

Without waiting for a reply I swung the black around and headed back down the hill.

My brief conversation with Lila had disturbed me deeply. Pinning all her hope for the future on her drunken father was bucking a cold deck. Ned was too far gone in drink and dreams to make it as a farmer. Changing locations would not change the man, and soon the two of them would be running again, leaving one defeat only to chase another.

I hadn't been lying to her when I told her the thin soil of the Brazos country wasn't good for farming. But that was something she'd have to find out for herself, and the thought saddened me.

I was just eighteen that spring, yet as I swung out of the saddle and stepped wearily toward the dugout, I felt years older than both Lila and her pa and, in a way I couldn't fully understand, responsible for both of them.

But I vowed that responsibility would end come morning. They would have to make their own way as I would have to make mine, or else I'd have no chance of catching up with Lafe Wingo and saving the SP Connected from ruin.

Though, as I opened the door of the dugout and stepped inside, the unbidden thought came to me that my chances of getting back the thirty thousand dollars were mighty thin — and all the time getting thinner.

To my surprise, the inside of the dugout was clean and well kept. The dirt floor had been recently swept and the blankets on the three bunks had been pulled up and squared away.

A rusty potbellied stove, long gone cold, stood at one end of the dugout and there was a table with a couple of roughly made benches drawn up to it.

The Apaches must have taken what supplies Shorty and the others had, because the place had been picked clean. Only a scattering of tin cups and a small wooden box remained on the table. When I opened the box I found a couple of dollars in nickels and dimes, a timetable for the Katy Flier and a page torn from a tally book with a sketch of a steep grade where Shorty and the others had hoped to stop the train.

It seemed the outlaws had planned to graduate from robbing banks to robbing trains — that is, until the Apaches had put the final period on the last sentence of the last chapter of their lives.

Looking around me at the cramped, spare cabin, I figured the hunted, wretched existence of the three men lay about me like an open book. The only thing was, there wasn't much to read. Like so many others who rode the owlhoot trail, the three had died too young and too violently and the greater part of the story of their lives must forever remain unwritten.

Oddly depressed, rainwater dripping from my slicker onto the dirt floor, I stood for a few moments in a joyless silence that whispered of other men's lives, then opened the door and stepped outside.

Lila stood beside the wagon and I motioned her into the cabin. But she hesitated at the doorway and asked: "Dusty, what about Pa? We can't leave him in the wagon."

Oh yes, we can, I thought, but said: "I'll help him inside." I felt the soaking wet shoulders of her cloak. "You better get out of those wet clothes and later I'll build a fire to dry them."

Lila took a step back from me, her eyes shocked. "You want me to sit there stark naked?"

"Wrap yourself in a blanket," I said. Then, lying through my teeth, trying to make myself sound a lot more worldly than I was, I added: "Hell, I've seen a naked woman before."

"Have you now, Mr. Hannah?" Lila

asked, her left eyebrow arching. "Well, you haven't seen this one." She thought things over for a spell, then said: "I suppose you're talking about that Sally Coleman person."

"Maybe," I said, defiant as all get out, but beginning to wish fervently I'd never mentioned naked women in the first place.

"You're quite the rake, aren't you, Mr. Hannah?" Lila asked, frosting over like a corral post in winter.

I had no answer for that, so I retreated into confusion, mumbling: "I'll go see to the livestock."

As I walked away, I felt Lila's eyes burning into my back. She was very young, little more than a girl, yet she had an assurance and poise that constantly kept me off balance. Sometimes it's difficult to understand a woman, and this was one of those times.

Was Lila jealous of Sally Coleman?

I shook my head, dismissing the thought. Lila was pretty enough to have her pick of men. Why would she be interested in a forty-a-month puncher like me who couldn't even grow a man's mustache? It just didn't make any sense.

Besides, I would wed Sally very soon. Sally, born and bred on the range, knew and accepted the narrow limitations of the puncher's life, so the whole thing just wasn't worth thinking about.

But as I stepped to the wagon, the face I kept seeing in my mind's eye was Lila's, not Sally's, and that bothered me considerable.

Ned Tryon was sound asleep in the back of the wagon, his mouth open, trickling saliva, the whiskey fumes vile on his breath. I let him stay where he was and unhitched the oxen.

I didn't have much experience with oxen, but when I turned them loose, the big animals immediately started to graze, so I figured they weren't much bothered by the rain and I let them be.

The black I led into the barn, which was small but dry and warm. I unsaddled him and rubbed him down with a piece of sacking. The droppings told me there had been three horses there, no doubt taken by the Apaches, and the saddles were gone, too.

There was no hay but I found a sack of oats and I poured a generous amount into a bucket.

After that, I spent some time pulling up grass for the horse and laid an armful in front of him and only then did I go back to the wagon for Ned.

The man was still unconscious and I half dragged, half carried him into the cabin. I dropped him, none too gently, onto one of the bunks, then turned my attention to Lila.

Her clothes hung on a string the outlaws had tied from one of the cabin walls to the other, probably for this very purpose, and Lila sat at the table, a blanket drawn around her.

I figured she'd planned to do this all along, but had made all that fuss about being naked just to see me suffer.

She rose from the table and said: "I'll take Pa's boots off."

Lila stepped to the bunk and pulled off one of her pa's boots, then the other. But not before the blanket slipped from her shoulders and I caught a fleeting glimpse of a small, firm breast, creamy white, tipped with pink.

My breath catching in my throat, blood rising to my cheeks, I suddenly felt shabby and awkward in my faded blue shirt and down-at-the-heel boots and stepped quickly to the stove, muttering over my shoulder: "I'll see about lighting a fire."

"Yes, you do that, Dusty."

The husky tone of Lila's voice surprised me and made me turn. She was standing there, the blanket once again firmly in place, smiling at me, a bemused expression on her face I couldn't read.

"Getting cold in here," I said, the breath once again balling up in my throat. Had she let the blanket slip on purpose?

No, that couldn't be. And yet . . .

"We have some bacon and flour in the wagon," Lila said, interrupting my thoughts, and her smile was gone.

I nodded. "I'll get it after I get the fire going."

"What about the Apaches?"

"I figure they've moved on," I replied. "I'll keep the fire small and trust to the rain and wind to scatter the smoke."

"You're so wise, Dusty," Lila said, smiling again, just a faint tugging at the corners of her beautiful mouth.

"I try to be," I said, trying to regain control of the situation. "Now there's got to be wood around here somewheres."

There was a small stack of oak and cottonwood branches beside the stove and with them some pages torn from a woman's corset catalog.

I fed paper and wood into the stove and within a few minutes had a fair blaze growing. Thankfully the wood was very dry and didn't send up much smoke.

I'd told Lila that the Apaches were gone, but with Indians there were no certainties, just guesses. They were mighty notional by times and might just decide to ride back this way.

I filled the coffeepot at the creek and later fried up some bacon, adding thin strips of my own salt pork. I made a batch of pan bread, stirring flour and salt into the fat, then dished up the meal.

Lila crossed the room and tried to wake up her pa, but the man just thrashed and groaned in his stupor, and waved her away.

She came back to the table and I poured coffee for us both, my hand unsteady on the pot, the scented, woman closeness of her and the sight of her dark loveliness filling my reeling brain like a growing thing.

After we ate, Lila talked and I listened. Mostly, she spun sugarcoated dreams about how she and her pa would make their farm a success and how he would give up his drinking.

"All he needs is another chance in life, Dusty," she said, touching the back of my hand with her fingertips, her slender arm exposed to the shoulder. "We tried to make it on one hardscrabble farm after another, but it just never seemed to work out for us. Then, after Ma died, Pa started to drink heavier and everything fell apart quicker than usual."

Her eyes searched mine, pleading for something I knew I could not give. "You think we can make it this time, don't you, Dusty?"

I went part of the way, unwilling to surrender more. "Lila, that's hard country down on the Brazos. Maybe you can make it, maybe you can't. But believe me, it won't be easy."

The girl nodded, reading more into what I'd said than was intended. "Thank you, Dusty. I needed to hear that, especially from you."

She touched my hand, and again I found it hard to breathe.

Later, after Lila was bedded down on one of the bunks, I took up my Winchester and scouted around outside.

The rain had stopped for now. A waning moon rode high in the sky, hiding her face behind a hazy halo of silver, dark lilac and pale blue, and the air smelled of grass and the tang of distant thunder. The shadowed hills were still as things asleep and the fragile night silence crowded around me like broken glass.

I climbed to the ridge of the hogback

and looked down at the trail below, seeing nothing but a wall of darkness.

Then I heard a muffled step behind me.

Chapter 11

I turned as the Apache came at me fast as a panther, a knife upraised in his right fist. As he closed I swung the butt of the Winchester, trying for his head. The Indian saw it coming, dodged at the last moment and the rifle hit only the hard muscle of his left shoulder. The impact was enough to stagger the man, but he recovered quickly and jumped at me again.

Around us were only jagged rock and the dark canopy of the sky and I realized with a sickening certainty that soon, very soon, a man must die here tonight, and maybe two.

I grappled with the Apache, my left hand on his wrist, desperately keeping his knife away from me. Now, our feet shuffling on the wet grass, I felt his wiry strength and it scared me. This man was taller than me and he was as strong, and maybe stronger, than I was.

We moved very close to each other, the warrior's belly pushed against my own. He was bending me backward with the sheer, brute strength of his arms and shoulders, and his merciless black eyes glinted in triumph.

I let myself fall on my back and the Apache landed on top of me. His knife hand broke free and he raised it to strike. I twisted my body and arched upward, my bared teeth lunging for his throat. I bit down hard on the left side of his neck and tasted smoky blood as his knife came down. The blade raked along the outside of my shoulder, burning like a red-hot iron, and I heaved with all my strength to my right, throwing the Apache off me.

The man rose, his knife poised. I circled to my left, keeping the Indian in front of me and feinted with the rifle butt. But the warrior was not fooled and he just stood there watching for an opening, the blood from the deep bite wound on his neck running down the shoulder and front of his yellow shirt.

I didn't know how many Apaches were out there. If I fired the rifle I could bring a passel of them down on top of me and right now that was the last thing I wanted.

But the Winchester was the only weapon I had; the folding knife in my pocket was useless in a fight like this.

I smelled the musky, feral odor of the Apache and my own rank sweat as we circled each other. My mouth was dry and my hurtling heartbeats hammered in my ears like muffled drums.

The Apache crouched a little, feinted with the knife, then switched to an underhand motion and slashed upward, trying to gut me. I hit his upcoming forearm hard with the barrel of the rifle and heard bone crack. The warrior cried out and the knife slipped from his nerveless fingers.

I moved in and smashed a powerful right to the man's chin, then another. The Apache reeled back a step, steadied himself, then dove for the knife. But my swinging boot crashed into his face when he was still in the air and that hurt him. He rolled on his back and slammed up against one of the rocks, the wind coming out of him in a sharp gasp.

Snarling, the Apache lay still for a few moments, then sprang to his feet. He came at me, his clawed fingers wide, seeking my eyes.

As he came in, I threw another right, but my fist glanced across his cheekbone and the Apache shrugged it off. We closed, his fingers still reaching for my eyes. As we wrestled, snarling like wild animals, our faces only inches apart, I felt the warrior's strength weakening.

The terrible, raw wound in his neck where I'd torn at him was streaming bright scarlet and it looked to me that I'd chewed through a vein that carried his lifeblood.

The Apache seemed to realize this too and knew he had to finish the fight soon. He took a half-step closer to me, his right foot swinging, trying to kick my legs out from under me.

I stepped away from him, threw a hook that missed and left myself wide-open for his right hand. The Apache's thumb, with its long, hard nail, dug into my eye, trying to blind me and I felt a sudden gush of blood on my cheek. I reached up with my left and grabbed his forearm. The broken bone crunched under my fingers and I squeezed harder. The warrior screamed and tried to jerk his arm away but I held on, grinding my fingers deeper.

The Indian again cried out, his face shocked and white from pain, and tore free of me. I didn't let him get set but swung the rifle again. This time the butt caught him squarely on the side of the head and he crashed violently into a rock and crumpled to the ground.

I staggered back, gasping for breath, unwilling to move, waiting for the man to get back to his feet. From a great distance away I heard thunder rumble and off to the west sheet lightning flashed above the Staked Plains.

Slowly the Apache rose. He was splashed in blood and sweat and his nose and arm were shattered, but there was no quit in him. Wary now, he shuffled toward me, his silent moccasined feet slowly sliding through the wet grass.

I didn't have the strength left to meet him, so I stood where I was and waited for him to come to me.

The Apache ran at me, trying to grasp me with his left hand. But I took a single step toward him and grabbed his broken arm again. I turned my side to the Apache and hammered the arm onto my upraised knee. One, two, three times.

Screaming, the warrior pulled the arm out of my grasp. He swung his leg and knocked my feet out from under me and I thudded onto my back, hitting hard rock. Winded, with my rifle lying three feet away, I lay there, desperately trying to catch my breath.

I moved my hand to support myself as I struggled to get to my feet. I shifted my hand again and my fingers touched the handle of the Apache's knife. I grabbed it and held it ready.

The man, snarling his fury, tried for the rifle. He dived for the Winchester and I threw myself on him. The arc of the knife blade glinted in the moonlight as I swung it high and plunged it deep into his back. I heard the warrior's gasp of pain and rammed the knife into him again and again. The Apache's legs kicked convulsively and he rattled deep in his throat, then lay still.

I rolled off the man and lay on my back, my mouth open, gasping for air.

After a while I stumbled to my feet, teeth bared, panting, looking down at the man I'd killed. I'd battled this warrior with fangs and claws and I had won, and by right of conquest his head and weapons were mine.

No longer completely sane, crazed by the sudden, shocking violence of the fight, I kneeled, grabbed a handful of the Apache's long, greasy hair and scalped him.

Jumping to my feet again, I brandished the dripping scalp high, tilted back my head and let a savage Rebel yell tear from my throat. It was a barbaric, angry shriek, half wail, half scream, heard on hundreds of battlefields during the War Between the States. But the yell had much more ancient and darker roots, stretching back across the echoing centuries to the war cry of the wild, blue-stained Celtic sword warriors from whom my ancestors had sprung.

If there were Apaches around, I wanted them to know by that victorious scream that I'd killed one of them, that I'd torn out his throat with my teeth. I wanted them to suffer as I had suffered, wanted them to know fear as I'd known fear.

Finally, blood from the scalp running down my arm, I slowly returned to sanity.

Suddenly drained, I dropped the filthy scalp on the Apache's back, picked up my rifle and staggered down the slope. At the creek I fell flat on the bank and splashed cold water onto my face and arms, washing away as much blood as I could.

Lila met me at the door of the cabin, awakened by my dreadful howling. She took one look at me and shrank back in horror, stiff with shock, her eyes wide and fearful, face as white as someone dead. I ignored the girl, brushed past her and collapsed onto a bunk.

Then merciful sleep took me and I knew no more.

I woke slowly to a gray dawn.

Shivering, I put on my hat and stepped to the stove. The fire had gone out during the night and I made it up again and soon had a small blaze going.

Lila and her pa were still asleep, so without disturbing them, I picked up the coffeepot and my rifle and stepped outside.

The rain had stopped but surly gray clouds hung low in the sky and the gullies and clefts of the surrounding hills were deep in shadow. The air smelled clean and fresh, like a woman's newly washed hair, and a whispering wind teased the buffalo grass, the shy wildflowers nodding their approval.

I kneeled by the creek and began to fill the coffeepot, wary, my eyes searching the ridge. Nothing moved, but that in itself brought me little comfort. Apaches didn't believe in making themselves obvious. There could be a dozen of them up there. Or none. Fickle fate was dealing the hand and I'd have to gamble that the Apaches had moved on and that the ridge and scattered rocks were as empty of life as they seemed.

Such thoughts do little to reassure a

man, and after I filled the pot and rose to my feet I reckon I was a slump-shouldered study in uncertainty, feeling a lot older but not much wiser than my eighteen years.

The fight with the Apache had left me with a numb ache all over my body and my shoulder burned where his knife had grazed me. I remembered the fight like a man remembers a bad dream, hazy, terrifying and confused, without rhyme or reason.

I had scalped the warrior and held my bloody trophy aloft and like a madman I'd howled my triumph to the uncaring night.

That I recalled, but the why or wherefore of it escaped me. For a brief spell I'd been more animal than human, possessed by a blind, killing rage that had transformed me into something savage, something primitive and dangerous. I fervently wished that as long as I lived I'd never feel the like again.

All the soft thoughts, the lace-and-lavender thoughts I'd once had of pretty Sally Coleman were fast receding from me, being replaced by something darker, harder, more violent. As I stood there in the newborn morning, I felt my carefree youth slip-slide away, the sappy love songs I'd once sung forever stilled on my lips, circumstances thrusting a bleak maturity on me I'd never sought.

I glanced up at the lowering sky and saw only its uniform grayness, the clouds heavy with rain, without light.

Now I must get back to the cabin, yet there remained one last thing to do.

Quickly I walked to the wagon and searched under the tarp. Within moments I found what I was seeking, a half-full jug of whiskey and two more full ones.

One by one, a vague anger building in me, I smashed the jugs on the iron tire of a wagon wheel, smelling the sharp, smoky tang of the whiskey, and tossed away the broken shards.

Only then did I step into the cabin and put coffee on the stove to boil.

Ned Tryon was the first to wake.

The man rolled out of his bunk and fell on the floor, staying there for several minutes on his hands and knees, his head hanging between his arms. The thump woke Lila and she stirred, looking with shocked eyes at her pa. She made to rise, but I held up my hand, stopping her.

"Let him be," I said.

Warned by the tone of my voice, Lila stayed where she was, gathering her blanket around her against the morning chill, eyes moving from me to her pa and back again.

Ned finally rose to his feet and stumbled toward me, trying to form words through the thick cotton lining his mouth.

"Whiskey," he gasped finally.

I shook my head at him and held up the coffeepot. "There's no whiskey. Have some of this."

"Damn you, I don't want coffee. I need whiskey."

He staggered to the door and lurched outside and I followed him.

It didn't take Ned long to figure out what had happened. He stood by the wagon, looked down unbelievingly at the broken jugs around his feet, then turned his shocked, bloodshot eyes to me.

"All of them?" he asked.

"All of them," I answered, not a shred of pity in me.

"Damn you, Hannah," the man whispered, his eyes ugly. "Damn you to hell."

After the harrowing events of the night, I decided right there and then that I'd had just about all I could take. I stepped quickly to Ned, grabbed him by the front of his shirt and dragged him behind the wagon away from the door. I slammed him hard against the side so the whole rig shook and, anger flaring in me, said: "Mister, when you get to where you're going, you can get as drunk as a pig as often as you want. It won't bother me none. But until we're clear of this country and the Apaches, you'll stay sober as a watched preacher."

Ned swore and tried to struggle out of my grasp, but I slammed him against the wagon again. "Listen to me," I said, my face just inches from his own. "The only way we're going to make it out of here alive, the only way Lila will make it out alive, is for you to stay the hell away from whiskey."

I pulled him closer to me, anger scorching my insides like scalding coffee. "Now, personally I don't give a tinker's damn about you, but I do care a whole lot about Lila. You risk her life by getting drunk again and I swear to God I'll gun you."

Ned Tryon's smile was thin. "Yet from this earth, and grave, and dust, the Lord shall raise me up, I trust."

I nodded. "My friend, that's between you and your Maker. But get this straight. One more drunk and I'll put a bullet into you, Lila's pa or no."

"Hard talk in one so young," Ned said.

"Mister," I said, "I've had to grow up fast and recently it seems the hard talk has come natural to me."

Ned stood there blinking like an owl, thinking things through as much as his muddled brain would allow. Finally he nodded. "So be it. I'll have that coffee now."

I didn't give the man any credit for his decision, since he wasn't in much of a position to do otherwise.

I left Ned and stepped back into the cabin. Lila was already up and dressed, and when her pa came inside, she kept looking from one of us to the other. I guess she felt the tension stretching between us because she made no attempt at conversation as we sat at the table and drank coffee.

Only when I refilled my cup and rolled a smoke did Lila speak to me.

"What happened last night?" she asked. Some of the horror that had showed in her eyes when I came off the ridge was still there, a reminder that this girl was unused to the West and the sudden violence that came along with it.

"I was jumped by an Apache," I said. I motioned with my head to the ridge. "Up there."

"Is he . . . is he . . . ?"

"He's dead. I'm alive," I said, ending it. I rose. "I'll go hitch the oxen. Better get ready."

I stepped outside and hitched up the oxen, a task that was easier than I'd expected. A horse or mule team offered a lot more trouble, being much less placid animals and by times difficult to handle.

So far the rain was holding off, and when I saddled the black I tied my slicker over the blanket roll. Sally Coleman's bonnet was in a sorry state and getting sorrier. It had already lost a flower from the brim and the straw was starting to shred here and there.

Shaking my head at yet another unfolding tragedy, I led the black out of the barn and back to the cabin.

Last night I'd thought to ride on and leave Lila and her pa behind. But now I knew I couldn't do it. I was well and truly trapped. Me, I was all that stood between Lila and the Apaches and what they did to a woman, and to haul my freight now would be a lowdown thing.

I made the decision but didn't feel particularly brave or honorable, like that Lochinvar knight Ned kept wagging his chin about. All I knew was I had it to do and there could be no stepping away from it . . . not if I wanted to live with myself after.

When I went into the cabin, Lila handed me a plate of bacon, salt pork and pan bread; suddenly hungry, I wolfed it down.

Ned didn't eat, but sat at the table, his head in trembling hands, battling whatever demons were tormenting him.

Despite myself, I felt a sudden pang of sympathy for the man. Sometimes the best remedy for wrongs is just to forget them, and I tried to do that now.

"Ned," I said, "we got to get moving."

The man looked up at me with faraway eyes and nodded. He rose to his feet and stumbled outside.

Lila watched him go, then asked: "What happened between you two out there?"

I shrugged. "I got rid of your pa's whiskey."

The girl studied me, judging my motives. "He'll be better off without it," she said finally. Then, after a heartbeat's pause: "Thank you, Dusty."

I smiled at her. "I'm starting to think that recently every person I meet is a problem in search of a solution. I found the solution, is all. At least for now."

Ten minutes later we crested the rise and were once more among the rocks. Lila riding the black while me and her pa walked beside the oxen.

At the top we paused and I looked down at the long miles stretching away before us, the Staked Plains to the west lost behind a gray morning haze.

Without saying a word to Lila I left the wagon and went back to the place where I'd fought the Apache. The man's body was gone but written in charcoal on a flat rock near where he'd fallen were the crudely scratched Spanish words:

MATANZAS CON SUS DENTES

I knew enough of the language to translate. It said: Kills with His Teeth.

The Apaches had given me a name and were letting me know that I was a marked man. All they wanted to do now was capture me alive. After that, using all the devilish ingenuity they could muster, they'd test me to see if I was the great warrior I seemed.

I knew that test would be much worse than anything Shorty Cummings had suffered and I would scream and shriek my way into eternity.

A sudden chill in my belly, I walked back to the wagon. Lila raised an eyebrow, but didn't offer a question. For that, I was glad, fearing that my tongue would stick to the roof of my dry mouth.

When Lila did speak, her words did little to allay my fear.

"Dusty," she said, pointing south, "look over there. It's more smoke."

I followed her pointing finger to the low hills and mesquite flats stretching away from us. In the distance I watched the smoke rise, then break, then rise again, black puffs drifting one after another into the lead-colored sky.

Fascinated, fearful, I couldn't tear my gaze away from it. "Lila, that's talking smoke. Apache smoke."

"What are they talking about?" the girl asked, her dark eyes huge.

"Us," I said.

Chapter 12

We were halfway down the slope when the rain began, not the downpour I'd expected but a soft drizzle, lacing across the landscape as fine as spun silver.

As soon as we reached the flat and turned south, I remounted the black while Lila took my place beside the oxen and I rode away to scout the trail ahead.

For the most part this was open country, a grama and buffalo grass plain with low hills rising here and there, their slopes dotted with mesquite and post oak.

I startled a small herd of grazing antelope and they bounded away from me over the crest of a hill and were soon lost to sight. Several times I spotted longhorn steers, strays from the spring herds, but they were every bit as wild as the antelope and kept their distance.

When I reached a shallow valley between a couple of low, flat-topped rises, I reined in the black and slid my Winchester from the boot.

My ears straining for the slightest sound, I sat still in the saddle, scanning the valley ahead and the surrounding slopes.

Nothing stirred.

The drizzle continued to fall silently on the grass and far above me the gray clouds were starting to thin and far to the west I saw a patch of blue sky.

I turned in the saddle, looking for the wagon. It was about a mile behind me, the oxen plodding through the long grass, and I could make out the tiny figures of Lila and her pa.

There was no way around it — the wagon would be here soon and before it arrived I'd have to scout the valley, a likely place for an Apache ambush.

I wheeled the black around the screening rise of the hill to my right and got behind its shallow slope. I rode down into a rocky wash, followed it for a couple of hundred yards, then rode out of it again, finally stopping at a dense thicket of mesquite growing low on the hill.

Rifle in hand I swung out of the saddle and, crouching low, made my way up the rise. I reached the crest and looked around. As far as I could see the land around me seemed empty.

But the Apaches had been here.

A small, charred circle on the grass showed where they'd coaxed a sullen fire out of mesquite root and sent up smoke, probably the talking smoke we'd seen earlier in the morning.

I got down on one knee, my rifle at the ready, but saw only silent hills and rain-washed grass. After a few minutes the pattering drizzle petered out, discouraged by the blossoming sun that felt warm on my back, and around me the color of the grass and hills shaded from dark to light green as the sunlight touched them.

I rose to my feet just as the riders started to come.

A column of cavalry was riding through the valley, a red-and-white guidon fluttering at their head, two pack mules bringing up the rear. The officer in command threw up a hand when he saw me and halted the troop.

I made my way down the hill, under the careful scrutiny of two dozen hard-eyed buffalo soldiers, and stopped beside the officer, an elderly white captain with iron gray hair showing under his battered campaign hat.

"Captain James O'Hearn," the officer said by way of introduction, his voice harsh like he gargled with axle grease. "Ninth Cavalry."

I gave O'Hearn my name and added: "I see you've fared badly, Captain."

The officer nodded. "Had a run-in with Apaches south of here. Lost my scout and a couple of my men are hit hard."

I glanced along the column and saw a Pima draped belly down across his saddle, his long black hair hanging loose, almost touching the top of the grama grass. Two of the soldiers sat slumped in the saddle, one with a bloodstained bandage around his head.

O'Hearn studied me with interest. "What brings you out here, Hannah?"

I nodded toward the approaching wagon. "That. We're headed for the Clear Fork of the Brazos."

The captain watched the wagon creak slowly toward the column, and when he saw Lila walking by the side of the oxen as she finally reached us, he touched the brim of his hat. "Captain James O'Hearn, ma'am. Ninth Cavalry."

Lila dropped an elegant little curtsy, then introduced herself and her father.

Obviously taking pleasure in the sight of a pretty woman in this stark wilderness, O'Hearn smiled and swung stiffly out of the saddle. He turned to his sergeant, a clean-shaven man in a faded blue army shirt, tan canvas pants tucked into his high cavalry boots. "Rest the men for fifteen minutes, Sergeant Wilson."

I watched the troopers dismount, all of them black men in the ragtag uniforms of the frontier army, no two of their sweat-stained campaign hats alike, each shaped to the wearer's individual taste. Most wore the blue shirt and yellow-striped breeches of the horse soldier, but a few affected store-bought pants and all had brightly colored bandanas around their necks.

To a man the men looked worn-out and hollow-eyed, but their weapons were clean and as they searched for wood to boil their coffee, their restless attention was constantly on the hills around them.

These were first-class fighting men who had earned a reputation among the Apaches of being brave and tenacious enemies, no small accolade from Indians who were mighty warriors themselves.

O'Hearn himself looked to be about sixty, but he was lean and hard, honed down to bone and muscle by constant campaigning and the harsh nature of the land itself.

The soldiers shared their coffee with us, and while we drank, O'Hearn paid a great deal of attention to Lila. She was so beautiful that morning that when I looked at her, I felt pain as much as pleasure. Lila had a way of doing that to a man and when I was around her I found it hard to think straight.

It was the captain's voice that brought me back to reality. "Ma'am, I'm returning to Fort Griffin and I'd be happy to escort you and your father there until the Apache renegades are penned up."

Lila flashed her dazzling smile. "Thank you kindly, Captain," she said. "But Pa and I are anxious to reach our farm while there is still time to plant a crop."

O'Hearn shook his hoary head. "Ma'am, I have a daughter your age, and I would tell her the same thing I'm telling you. It's too dangerous for a woman to be out here. The Apaches have split up into a dozen different war bands and they have the whole country between here and the Brazos in turmoil."

He nodded his head to the south. "Yesterday they killed two men at a cabin over on Valley Creek and before that they hit a preacher and his family on the Concho. Killed five people, three of them children."

The officer looked from her pa to Lila. "I urge you, ma'am, to accompany us to the fort where you'll be safe."

Lila was silent for a few moments, obviously weighing possibilities, but then shook her head, a tendril of raven black hair falling over her face. "Captain, Mr. Hannah assures us we can reach our farm in a couple of days. I really do wish to press onward."

The soldier shrugged, a helpless gesture. He turned to Ned. "And you, Mr. Tryon? What do you think?"

Ned looked exhausted and suddenly old. "My daughter has a mind of her own, Captain. I'll do as she says."

O'Hearn studied Ned closely, taking in his haggard appearance and bloodshot eyes and drew his own conclusions. "Then God help you," he said. His shrewd blue eyes turned to me, judging me, sizing me up from the scuffed toes of my boots to the top of my hat. "Now it's all up to you, Mr. Hannah, I think."

I nodded, drawing a breath from deep in my chest. "Once we cross the Brazos we'll be safe. My ranch is down there." I tried a smile. "We'll get it done."

"Well, maybe so," O'Hearn said, unconvinced. He drained his cup and turned to the sergeant. "Mount 'em up, Sergeant Wilson."

The soldiers threw the dregs of the

coffee onto the fire and swung into the saddle.

Captain O'Hearn looked down at Lila and touched his hat brim. "One last time, ma'am, I beg you to reconsider."

"I'll be fine, Captain, but thank you so much for your concern."

The soldier seemed to realize that any further attempt at persuasion was useless. He waved his men forward and the troop clattered past us, their accoutrements jingling loud in the morning silence.

After the soldiers disappeared from sight a deeper silence descended on the valley, and the heat of the sun did little to warm me.

Without a word to Lila, I went back up the hill and retrieved my horse. By the time I caught up with the wagon the day was brightening to noon and the sky was swept clear of clouds. As I surrendered the black to Lila, a hawk circled high above me, then glided off on still wings to the north only to dive with tremendous speed at something crawling in the grass.

A little death had just occurred, but it was one among many, and the sky and the sun and the listening hills seemed none the poorer for it.

We traveled through the growing heat of

the day under a smoldering sun and saw no sign of Apaches. But I knew they were out there sure enough, moving through the vast land that had swallowed them, making no sound, gliding like vengeful ghosts.

I walked beside the oxen, my rifle across my chest, knowing I had no hand in the course of future events, but must wait for whatever happened to come to me.

It was a perilous situation that did little to settle a man's mind and I felt exposed and mighty vulnerable.

That night we made a cold camp in a thicket of mesquite and shared a poor supper of the peppermint balls I'd bought at Doan's store.

Later, after Lila and her pa had sought their blankets, restless, I took up my rifle and scouted around the camp. Above me, in the dark purple heavens, a sickle moon was reaping the stars and a rising wind whispered warnings in my ear in a language I could not understand.

I climbed a small hill above the camp that rose to its crest in a series of narrow benches. Once at the top, I stayed there, listening to the silence that suddenly stirred below me.

Carefully, I descended the other slope of the hill, then froze when I heard a hoof click on a rock. My eyes slowly penetrated the gloom and I saw a huge, shaggy shape walk along the sandy bed of a wash, every now and then stopping to dip its bearded muzzle into a shallow pool where the rain had gathered.

Even in the uncertain moonlight, there was no mistaking the humpbacked shape of an enormous buffalo bull. The animal lifted his head, caught my scent and, his eyes rolling white in panic, he galloped along the wash and disappeared into the darkness.

The bull must have been among the last of his kind and his survival was nothing short of a miracle. Miracles are not for men who believe, but for those who disbelieve. And right then, with all the puncher's inborn superstition, I was willing to believe that the buffalo was a sign Lila and me and her pa would also survive.

Thus reassured, though I knew in my heart of hearts that I was surely clutching at a straw, I returned to the camp where the others were asleep. I caught up my blanket and drew a little ways off, settling my back against a boulder that jutted from the earth among a few post oak. I wrapped the blanket around me and forced myself to stay awake.

I thought about Lila Tryon and the way she looked and the way she looked at me.

Was I falling in love with her?

That was unlikely, on account of how I planned to very soon marry pretty Sally Coleman.

But Sally giggled!

The single memory of that high-pitched, undulating tee-hee giggle cut through all the rest like a knife.

Could I wed a gal with a giggle like that?

Once, it was only a few months ago but seemed like a lifetime, I'd thought her giggle a darlin' thing and when I heard it my breath would ball up in my throat and I'd go weak at the knees.

Now, remembering, I realized it wasn't so cute, but kind of little-girly and immature.

Lila didn't giggle. She had a good, outright, white-toothed laugh that chimed like a silver bell.

Ashamed of myself for my treachery, I put both women out of my mind, forcing myself to concentrate on what was happening around me, and the soft sounds stirring amid the gathering night.

Ned Tryon tossed in his blankets and cried out in his sleep and a coyote yipped in the distance and once I heard, or imagined I heard, a far-off rifle shot.

The wind gusted over the buffalo grass, bending it this way and that, setting the leaves of the post oaks to fluttering. Shivering, I drew my blanket closer around me, worrying over that rifle shot, if that's what it was.

One way or another, I reckoned it was going to be a long night. . . .

I woke with a start as the darkness died around me, probing fingers of dawn light forcing open my eyes.

I stood, stiff and weary, and studied the land around me. The plains and sentinel hills lay still, bathed in brightness from broken clouds that looked like someone had dipped a giant brush in gold paint and stippled them across the vast blue canvas of the sky.

Many people believe the sky is a thing separate from the earth, but it's not — it's part of it. And soon we'd be traveling, not under its arching canopy, but through it, golden light stretching out all around us.

Last night I'd feared to build a fire, but now, wishful for coffee, I gathered a few sticks of dry wood from the hillside, then filled the pot from the wash, where I'd seen the buffalo.

The fire I kept small, just enough to boil the coffee, and when it was done I poured a cup for Lila and brought it to her. The girl woke and smiled at me and I felt my heart thud in my chest. Lila took the coffee gratefully, handling the hot tin cup with care.

I poured coffee for myself, squatted beside her and built a smoke. I thumbed a match into flame and lit the cigarette.

"We should wake Pa," Lila said.

I nodded. "Soon. He had a pretty restless night, crying out in his sleep an' all. I reckon we'll let him rest for a few more minutes."

Lila glanced over at her sleeping father. "He'll be just fine when we reach our farm," she said, a wistfulness touching her voice. She looked at me, almost challenging me to say different. "I know he will."

Me, I let it go. I'd said all I needed to say on the subject of Ned Tryon and I'd no call to speak further. Deflecting any possible questions, I said: "I reckon we'll cross the Brazos tomorrow about twelve miles north of Round Timbers. Before then we'll reach the headwaters of the Little Wichita and then Deepwater Creek." I drew deep on my cigarette. "It's good country down there, plenty of grass and wood."

Lila picked up her cup gingerly, holding it with her thumb and forefinger by the rim. "The farm has been my dream and Pa's dream for months," she said. "I can hardly believe it soon will come true."

I tossed away my cold cigarette butt. "Best we get moving," I said.

Thirty minutes later we took to the trail again, but this time I rode the black, scouting just ahead of the wagon.

The sun was straight above my head and the day was warm when the three riders came.

And there was no mistaking the huge, yellow-haired man who rode grimly at their head, a scoped rifle across the horn of his saddle.

It was Lafe Wingo.

Chapter 13

Wingo rode my paint, and he sat upright in the saddle, heavy-shouldered, his bold blue eyes taking in everything, missing nothing. He wore a soft, thigh-length buckskin shirt decorated with Cheyenne beadwork and gray pants tucked into expensive boots. The tooled gun belt around his waist carried a long-barreled Colt with ivory handles and he affected the elegant mustache and Imperial worn by many Texas gunmen of the period. Wingo wore a silver necklace made of disks decorated with blue stones in the Navaho manner and his thick wrists were adorned with wide, hammered silver bracelets. A gold ring with a green gem glittered on the little finger of his left hand.

He looked well-nourished and sleek, a man used to the best bonded whiskey, fine cigars and beautiful women.

Cold-blooded murder paid well, though I could understand why a man with his expensive tastes would need the thirty thousand dollars he'd been so willing to kill to acquire.

Gold and blood. The two so often went together, all summed up in this one killer.

Lafe Wingo reined up when he was a few yards from me, looked me up and down, and I saw his lips curl as he mentally dismissed me as no danger.

"What the hell are you doing here?" he asked, the challenge in his voice unmistakable. "You're way off your range, ain't you, puncher?"

I wanted badly to kill this man, but he had moved the muzzle of his rifle so it was pointing right at my belly. I could shuck a gun fast, but all Wingo had to do was twitch his trigger finger and I was a dead man. The odds were against me and right now all I could do was bide my time.

Behind Wingo a tall man in a black shirt and cowhide vest sat bent over in the saddle. I couldn't see his face but the bottom half of his shirt was dark with crusted blood and I heard him groan in pain.

Beside the wounded outlaw rode a tall, red-bearded man with thick, untamed eyebrows and penetrating black eyes. He carried a Colt in a cross-draw holster, and unlike Wingo, this man wasn't underestimating me. His careful eyes watched me like a hawk on the prod and right there and then I decided this man could be even more dangerous than Wingo.

The blond gunman was waiting for my answer, so I swallowed my anger and jerked a thumb over my shoulder, playing the green puncher to the hilt. "Name's Dusty Hannah and I'm escorting a wagon down to the Brazos country."

Wingo was suddenly interested. "Wagon? What kind of wagon?"

I shrugged. "Four-wheeled farm wagon hauled by a team of oxen."

Wingo nodded. "They call me Lafe Wingo." He paused, shrewd eyes boring into mine. "Mean anything to you, boy?"

I shook my head at him. "No. Should it?"

The realization came to me then that Wingo, with the hired killer's total disregard for his victims, didn't recognize me. He had shot me at a distance, then up close had kicked me in the ribs, but to him I'd been another faceless, nameless nonentity who'd fallen to his gun.

"My name means much to many people in many places," Wingo said, his gunman's pride wounded. "I guess you've led a sheltered life."

He nodded to the man slumped in the

saddle. "This here is Hank Owens. He's gut-shot and I don't expect him to live." He jutted his chin toward the bearded man. "That's his brother Ezra. We had a run-in with Apaches last night and Hank was gut-shot and Charlie, another brother, was killed."

Alone among Indians, Apaches usually chose not to fight at night, believing that a warrior unfortunate enough to get killed must wander for all eternity in darkness. But the Apache is notional, and he'll fight in the dark if put to it, especially if he senses an advantage.

My life depended on me playing the part of the innocent young puncher, so I looked at Ezra and said: "I'm mighty sorry about your brother, mister."

The man shrugged, his black eyes unreadable. "Charlie was all right. Had him a limp and he talked too much was all."

Hank Owens groaned. He lifted his head and looked at Wingo. "Lafe, you got to get me to a doctor. My belly's on fire."

Wingo turned to the man and smiled. "We got a wagon for you to ride in, Hank. I reckon we can make you right comfortable."

"Where are you headed?" I said, knowing what the answer would be as soon as I asked the question.

"Why, where you're headed, boy. I guess the Brazos country is as good as anyplace else and we may need an extry rifle before we're done," Wingo answered. He smiled, his eyes mean. "That is, if you can hit anything with a rifle."

"I do all right," I said, refusing to be baited. My eyes slid to my saddlebags slung behind Wingo's blanket roll and the man, missing nothing, demanded suspiciously: "You got something stuck in your craw, boy? If you do, spit it out."

I shook my head at him. "No, I was just admiring your paint. Nice pony."

Wingo's suspicions were not laid to rest. "You mind your business, boy," he said. "That is, if you want to keep on breathing."

Lafe Wingo was a trouble-hunting man and right now he held all the aces, so I bit my tongue and said nothing.

Figuring he'd intimidated me enough, the gunman asked: "Where's your wagon?"

"Back along the trail a ways," I answered.

Wingo nodded. "Let's go."

With me leading the way, we rode up on the wagon a few minutes later.

Wingo's eyes immediately moved to Ned

Tryon and, with the skilled gunman's sharp perception, saw him for what he was and dismissed him with a disdainful curl of his lip.

Not so with Lila.

She had removed her cloak and the shameless wind was busily molding her dress to her legs and the womanly curves of her slender body. Her hair was tied back in a pink ribbon and her large, expressive eyes, when she looked at Wingo, revealed an odd mix of alarm and fascination.

For his part, Wingo leaned forward in the saddle and grinned. "Well, well, what have we here?" He brushed his sweeping mustache with the back of his finger and asked, his voice silky: "What's your name, pretty lady?"

Something akin to jealousy flared in me. I didn't want Lila speaking to this man, so before she could answer, I said: "This is Lila Tryon and her pa over there is Ned." Then without really knowing why, I added: "They're farmers."

Wingo reared back in the saddle and let out a loud guffaw, and even Ezra's grim mouth stretched slightly in a grudging smile.

"An' I'm the king o' Prussia," Wingo roared. He nodded toward Ned. "Him, just maybe." His hot, eager eyes moved to Lila. "But little lady, a fine-looking gal like you was never meant to walk a furrow behind a mule's butt."

The blond gunman's insolent, experienced gaze slowly took in Lila from the top of her head to her shoes. I could tell he was undressing her in his mind as he went, stripping her naked garment by garment, anticipating.

And Lila felt it.

Her cheeks flushed and she snapped: "Nevertheless, my father and I are farmers and we can think of nothing we'd rather do than plow our own land."

Wingo nodded, his smile slipped and his face hardened. "I prophesy before we reach the Brazos I'll make you change your mind on that score."

Lila opened her mouth to speak, but Ned surprised me. "You let my daughter be, mister," he said, taking a step closer to Wingo, his fists clenched. "She's young and she doesn't yet understand the ways of the world."

"Then I'll teach her," the gunman said, his eyes ugly. "Same way I teach a horse, with a whip if necessary." Up until then Wingo had ignored Ned, but he turned to him. "And you, from now on keep your trap shut. I don't want to hear nothing from you. Open your mouth again, an' I'll close it permanently with a bullet."

Wingo had laid it on the line and I felt the weight of my Colt as the gun lay heavy at my side, the handle between my elbow and wrist. Hank was out of it, but if put to it, could I draw fast enough to drop both Wingo and Ezra?

No, I decided, that would be a suicide play. From what I'd heard, both gunmen were faster than me, and if we were equals, it would probably mean we'd all three be lying dead on the ground and nothing would be resolved.

I knew that for now I had to bide my time and swallow whatever insults came my way or were directed at Lila and her pa.

As it happened, the tense moment passed when Hank toppled out of the saddle and hit the ground with a thud.

Wingo turned to Ezra. "Get him in the wagon." He nodded at me. "You, boy, go help him."

I swung out of the saddle and helped Ezra carry his groaning brother to the tailgate of the wagon. Wingo dismounted and stepped beside us.

His glance took in Lila's organ and the

dresser and he snapped: "Get that stuff out of there," he said. "This damn wagon will be slow enough without us hauling all that junk."

Lila ran beside us. "Leave it alone," she cried. "It was my ma's furniture, just about all she ever owned."

"Well, your ma ain't here," Wingo snapped. He jerked his head at me. "Boy, toss it all out."

Lila opened her mouth to protest again, but I took her by the arm and turned her to me. "Lila," I said urgently, "let it go. We'll come back for it, trust me."

Wingo grinned. "Sure you will, boy, sure you will. Now do like I told you."

I climbed into the wagon and, as gently as I could, removed the dresser and organ and stood them on the grass beside the trail. Then I helped Ezra get Hank into the wagon.

Lila bit her lip, her face very pale.

I stepped beside her. "It will be all right, Lila," I whispered. "Now isn't the time."

The girl looked at me like I'd just crawled out from under a rock. "You could have stopped this," she said. "You didn't even try."

Wingo, who was standing close by, overheard and laughed. "Oh, he could have tried, little lady. Only thing is, right now he'd be dead." He looked at me, his blue eyes hard. "What's your opinion on that, boy?"

Playing the part of the green puncher again, I shrugged. "I don't see much point in dying over a tinpanny organ."

Wingo nodded. "Boy, you named that tune, sure enough."

He looked down at the grimacing Hank. "How you feeling?"

"I'm hurting bad, Lafe," Hank gasped, his lips very white against the leathery brown of his face and beard. "Just . . . just get me to a doctor."

Wingo smiled, a cruel, uncaring smirk. "You're gut-shot, Hank. There ain't a damn thing a doc can do for you." He motioned to Lila. "See to him."

It was in the girl's mind to refuse, I could tell, but in the end she stepped beside Hank and brushed the man's hair away from his forehead. "You won't let me die, will you, little lady?" the gunman asked, desperation in his eyes.

"I'll do what I can for you," Lila answered.

She walked to my horse and got the canteen from the saddle, poured water into her handkerchief and tenderly dabbed it over Hank's parched lips. "Don't swallow," she said. "But it will help you feel less thirsty."

Hank saw me standing behind Lila. "What the hell are you looking at?" he demanded.

"Nothing," I said.

"Then get the hell away from me," Hank yelled, his fevered eyes wild.

Wingo laughed. "Don't gun the boy just yet, Hank," he said. "We may need him."

He turned to Ezra. "Mount up." And to me: "You too. We got some ground to cover before nightfall."

I swung into the saddle and Ned Tryon whipped the oxen into motion. Lila tied Hank's mount to the rear of the wagon and many times afterward I heard the outlaw moan as the wheels jolted over ruts on the trail and the terrible pain in his belly consumed him.

Wingo rode in the lead, his eyes constantly searching the trail ahead and the surrounding low hills.

I noticed that Ezra always rode behind me, wary and alert. It occurred to me that the man didn't trust me, and the reason became apparent when he suddenly kneed his horse beside mine.

"Haven't I seen you someplace, boy?" he

asked. "Seems to me your face is mighty familiar."

I felt a sudden jolt of unease. Did Ezra Owens see my face as I lay on the ground after Wingo shot me? Did he remember me?

Trying to make light of it, I said: "I've been up the trail a few times, to Dodge mostly. Could be you've seen me there."

Ezra's eyes were thoughtful. "Maybe so." He shook his head. "Nope, I just can't recollect, but it will come back to me by and by."

Right then I realized how fast I was running out of room on the dance floor. If Ezra remembered me, then he'd figure why I was here and after that my life wouldn't be worth a plugged nickel.

If I was to make my move and get back the money, I'd have to do it soon — even if the odds weren't in my favor.

And now I had an even more urgent concern: Lila.

Lafe Wingo was accustomed to taking what he wanted, and he wanted the girl. Soon, very soon, I'd have to stand between them, and that meant a gunfight with two skilled pistoleros, a fight I was not sure I could win.

It was a worrisome thing, and as we rode

through the blazing heat of the day, my churning mind uncovered only more and more problems but no solutions.

Above me, I saw buzzards wheel in the sky, grim messengers of death.

But whose death?

I didn't know it then, but I would have that answer sooner than I expected.

Chapter 14

That night we made camp in a stand of cottonwoods by a wide creek with a couple of feet of milky alkaline water running along its pebbled bottom.

As far as the eye could see, the country around us was flat, dry and sandy with few trees. Here and there clumps of sage and mesquite competed for space with low-growing cactus and the scarred land had still not healed from the passage of the spring herds. This was featureless, unlovely country, indifferent to all human enterprise or desire, a wild place where a man's dreams dried up under the relentless sun and blew away like dust in the wind.

Many had tried to live here and all had failed, leaving the plain to brood alone over its fading memories of the buffalo and the Comanche and a time gone that would never return.

Ned Tryon guided the wagon into the cottonwoods and I helped him unhitch the oxen. We lifted Hank from the back of the wagon and laid him on the ground and the wounded gunman cursed us for our clumsiness, his face stark white from pain and the fear of death.

Wingo, who did not seem to care much for honest labor, told me to gather some dry wood for a fire, since the Apaches, if any were in the vicinity, would be reluctant to attack at night over open ground where there was little cover.

I did as he said and then filled the coffeepot and placed it on the coals to boil.

Later I helped Lila prepare a meal of corn pone and sowbelly, and although she accepted my assistance, we worked in silence, things said and unsaid standing like a barbed wire fence between us.

All this time, I was aware of Ezra's black eyes on me, following my every move. The gunman's suspicions were aroused and I knew he wouldn't let it go until he remembered where he'd seen me.

After we'd eaten and the day died around us, the sickle moon rose in a pale blue sky and a rising wind set the flames of the fire to dancing.

Wingo rose and stepped to his blanket roll, reached inside and found cigars and a bottle of whiskey. The man had an odd smile on his face, cruel and calculating, and I felt uneasy, wondering what was to come next.

I didn't have long to wait.

Wingo squatted by the fire, the bottle held loosely in his hand. He turned and winked at Ezra, then said across the fire to the intently watching Ned, "Hey, Pops, you like whiskey?"

Ned Tryon ran his tongue over his dry lips, fascinated, his eyes on the bottle like a man watches a rattlesnake. He rubbed the back of his mouth with a trembling hand and finally said: "Sure I like whiskey."

Wingo nodded. "Thought you did."

The gunman had read all the signs and pegged Ned for a drunk, and now, his eyes glittering scarlet in the firelight, he asked: "You care for a swig or two?"

Unable to speak, all Ned could do was nod.

"My pa doesn't want your whiskey," Lila flared at Wingo. She rose and placed a protective arm around her father's shoulders. "He's unwell. Leave him alone."

Wingo smiled, his face sadistic. "That right, Pops? You gonna take orders from your daughter and make me drink this here bottle all by my ownself?"

"Let him be, Wingo," I said.

The gunman snapped his head around.

"Puncher, you keep the hell out of this."

"The man has a problem with whiskey," I said. "You'll do him no favor."

"Seems to me, Ned," Ezra said, his voice smooth, "that if a man wants a sup of whiskey, why, that's his own business."

Ned nodded, reckless eyes fixed on the bottle. "My own business, that's right," he mumbled. Ned turned his head to Lila. "Just one sup, daughter. It will steady me."

"Of course it will," Wingo said. "Make a new man of you. Ain't that right, Ezra?"

"Sure enough," Ezra agreed. "Nothing like a drink of good whiskey to steady a man down, make him see things in a better light."

Wingo held up the bottle and shook it, the amber contents sloshing. "Come an' get it, Pops."

Despite Lila's anguished cry of protest, Ned rose unsteadily to his feet. He rubbed his mouth again with an unsteady fist and stepped toward Wingo.

The gunman held up a warning hand. "Not so fast, Pops." He smiled, his yellow wolf's teeth shining like wet piano keys. "You don't think you're gonna get this fine Kentucky whiskey for free, do you?"

Ned stopped. "What do you want?"

"Want? Why, I don't want much."

"Name your price," Ned said.

Wingo turned to Ezra. "Well, this man said it straight up, all honest and true blue as could be. He said, name your price. What should I charge him, Ezra?"

The dark gunman's smile was thin, without humor. "Can you sing, Pops?"

Startled, Ned shook his head.

"He can't sing, Lafe," Ezra said, pretending deep disappointment.

"Well, maybe he can dance." Wingo looked up at Ned. "Well, how about it, Pops? Can you dance? Maybe one of them Missouri jigs I've heard so much about."

Dumbly, Ned Tryon nodded, looking impossibly old and wearied in the revealing firelight.

I'd seen enough. I sprang to my feet, rage simmering in me. "Wingo, give him the bottle or don't, but leave the man his dignity."

Wingo's draw when it came was a blinding blur of motion and I suddenly found myself staring into the business end of a Colt that looked as big as a railroad tunnel.

"Boy" — Wingo smiled, his voice level and conversational — "you got two simple choices: Sit down or die right where you stand."

Ezra was studying me closely. He hadn't drawn his gun, but he was coiled and ready and I knew when it came his draw would be as fast as a striking snake.

Now wasn't the time.

I gulped down my touchy, eighteen-year-old pride like a dry chicken bone and sat, humiliation burning in my cheeks. I caught Lila looking at me and saw something in her eyes, sympathy maybe, and something else . . . contempt? Disappointment? I could not tell.

Wingo holstered his Colt. "Excellent choice, boy."

He turned his attention to Ned. "Now, Pops, where was I afore I was so rudely interrupted? Oh, yeah, now I recollect. Let's see that Missouri sodbuster's jig."

"You'll give me whiskey?" Ned asked, pleading words rustling quiet from his lips like falling leaves.

"Sure," Wingo said. "Hell, that's what whiskey is for, ain't it? To be drunk." Wingo laughed and began to clap his hands, and Ezra joined in with him. Over by the fire, even Hank, hurting and dying slow like he was, grinned.

Ned put his hands on his hips and began to dance. He kicked his feet in a dreadful parody of a country jig, the desperation in his eyes awful to see. Ned Tryon knew how complete was his humiliation, but the lure of whiskey drove him on and his jig became more and more frenzied, his booted feet pounding again and again into the dusty earth, stomping out a demented, detestable dance of the damned.

Wingo and Ezra grinned and clapped faster, quickening the pace, and Ned tried to keep up, sweat beading his forehead, drenching his shirt, his mouth hanging open and slack as he gasped for breath.

"Heee-haaa!" Wingo yelled, clapping even faster, his hands blurring.

Ned danced for five terrible minutes before he faltered to a halt and fell flat on his face. The man lay there for a long while before he looked over to the grinning Wingo. "Whiskey," he pleaded.

The gunman put the bottle to his mouth and drank deeply, then passed it to Ezra. "Nah," he said, wiping his mouth with the back of his hand. "You're a rotten dancer an' you don't deserve no whiskey."

"Please," Ned begged. "Whiskey. For the love of God man, you promised. Give me my whiskey."

Ezra grinned and passed the bottle back to Wingo and the big gunman stood. He stepped beside Ned and said: "You want whiskey, Pops? Here, go get it."

Wingo tilted the bottle and poured its contents into the sand a few inches from Ned's face. Ned tried to intercept the gushing amber cascade with his open mouth, but Wingo grinned and pushed him roughly away with his foot.

When the bottle was empty, Wingo kicked at the damp sand. "There, Pops. There's your whiskey."

Ned made a strangled sound deep in his throat and dived on the wet patch, stuffing the sand into his mouth, sucking at it. His mouth and beard covered in sand, he finally gave up and lay there, sobbing, his thin shoulders heaving.

The whole affair had been set up by Wingo to be a cold, calculated act of cruelty and as I watched Lila lie beside her father, whispering softly to him, my hatred for the gunman grew into a livid fire, consuming me.

I rose to my feet and stepped beside Lila and her pa. Gently I lifted Lila off her father, then raised Ned into a sitting position. The man's eyes were wide-open, but he saw nothing as he stared into the fire like someone already dead.

Beside me, Wingo stretched and yawned. "Well, I've had enough fun for one night.

Now it's time for my blankets." He reached down, grabbed Lila by the wrist and pulled her to her feet. He held the girl close to him, looking down at her tearstained face, his eyes hungry. "Come on, little lady, I don't plan on sleeping alone."

I hit him then.

My right took Wingo square on the chin as he turned to look at me. The man let Lila go, staggered a few steps and crashed heavily on his back. Wingo made no move for his gun, but a triumphant grin spread across his face. "Boy," he said, "now I'm going to tear you apart."

Wingo stood and my heart sank when I realized just how huge he was. He easily made two of me, and by his eager grin and the joy of battle in his eyes, it seemed he was no stranger to rough-and-tumble fistfights.

But my scraps with Wiley back when I lived on his pa's ranch had taught me something. Enough, I fervently hoped, to square the odds.

I put Wiley out of my mind, intent on Wingo, my thoughts concentrated on the big gunman. Wingo circled me, his fists up in the pugilist's manner and it was obvious he'd taken lessons from a professional prizefighter. For such a huge man, he moved well, gracefully balancing on his toes. Yet when he threw his first blow, it was short. I feinted a left, sidestepped and smashed a hard right to his mouth. Wingo roared through mashed lips and spit blood.

The big man took a step back just as I swung a left and my fist met only air.

Wingo danced forward, his fists jabbing, and his greater height and weight forced me back and I took a solid right to my chin that staggered me.

Wingo followed up with a wicked left hook that hit so hard, stars danced in front of my eyes and to my surprise I saw the ground rush up fast to meet me.

I hit the dirt with a thump, tried to rise, and the gunman swung a kick to my head. But I turned away at the last moment and his boot went sailing past my cheek.

Still groggy from the two blows I'd taken, I came up slowly, slipped Wingo's right and slammed a couple of hard punches to his body. Neither punch had any effect on the man and he grinned through bloody lips and bored inside, his fist swinging.

He jabbed a fast right to my ribs, but I countered with my own right and followed up with a wide left hook that caught

Wingo at the corner of his right eye and staggered him.

Blood streamed down Wingo's cheek from the thin tissue above his eye, and he dashed it away with his fist and came after me again.

The gunman had taken several of my best punches. He was bloody but unbowed and still full of fight and I began to fear that he might wear me down simply by his ability to absorb punishment and keep on battling.

I stepped inside Wingo's next punch and slashed at him with quick, telling blows to the body. The man gave ground, then swung a ponderous right that missed me by a mile. I surprised him by not counter-punching. Instead I dove at his waist, dropped my arms to his knees and up-ended him.

Wingo crashed to the ground, but rose fast, lithe as a cat. I was already on my feet and set up, and I drove a right to his chin that made the gunman's head snap back and followed up with a left to the side of his head that split his ear.

Wingo bellowed and rushed me, his arms outspread, hoping to get me in a bear hug. If that happened, I'd be over-come by his enormous strength and he could easily break my spine.

I stepped quickly away and snapped a right to Wingo's mouth, followed by another. Blood spurted, but my punches were weakening as the bigger man wore down my strength, and Wingo just grinned and shrugged them off.

I swung a left hook, hoping to drive him away from me. Too late. My fist bounced harmlessly off the side of Wingo's head and his arms were around me, his hands locking on the small of my back.

Wingo pulled me to him, and slowly forced me backward. A searing white-hot pain stabbed at me and I struggled desperately to break the gunman's hold. But Wingo's strength was enormous and he was grinning wildly as he sought to snap my backbone.

Right then I figured I'd maybe seconds to live and that thought drove me. I suddenly went limp and Wingo roared in triumph and hugged me closer. I judged the distance to the bridge of his nose, suddenly stiffened and hammered my forehead, hard and fast, into the target I'd chosen.

I heard the bone crack and Wingo cursed and let me go, staggering backward, with blood splashed all over his face.

Relentless now, my fear replaced by

anger, I waded after him and swung both fists to his chin. Left. Right.

Wingo went down, tumbling forward, but I met his face with my knee and his head snapped up, his shattered nose spraying a scarlet fountain of blood.

The gunman crashed onto his back and lay there for a few moments and I waited, gasping for breath, my fists ready.

By the fire, I was aware of Ezra watching me, his hand on his gun.

Was he going to make a play if I won this fight?

Beyond caring, I watched Wingo rise slowly to his feet and I moved in quickly. I drove a right and a left into his face, then summed it all up with a terrific right uppercut that jerked Wingo's head backward and the big man went down on his knees.

I circled, wary and waiting, my jaw hanging loose as I battled to breathe.

"Let it go, boy." Ezra's voice cut into my consciousness. "You've whipped him."

I don't know how long I stood there. A minute, maybe longer.

Then Wingo's bloody, battered head slowly came up and his burning eyes met mine. "Now I'm going to kill you, boy," he snarled.

His hand flashed for the gun at his waist, but Ezra stepped in quickly. He grabbed Wingo's gun arm and said: "No, Lafe. We'll cross the Brazos tomorrow and until then we may need his rifle."

"Let me be," Wingo roared, jerking his arm free.

"Lafe!" Ezra yelled urgently. "Damn it, man, think of the money!"

Me, I was ready to make my draw, determined to go down fighting. But I had no need. Somehow Ezra's logic had penetrated the killing fog of Wingo's brain and I could see the man think it through.

"Lafe, we'll cross the Brazos tomorrow," Ezra said, voice soft and reasoning. "By then we'll be clear of the Apaches and you can kill this man." And again: "Think of the money. We've come too far to risk it all now."

It took Wingo a long time to make up his mind. Finally he holstered his Colt. "After we cross the river, I'm dropping you, boy," he said.

Wingo rose to his feet and staggered to the creek under a cold moon. He lay on the bank and splashed water onto his battered face, snuffling and snorting like a butchered pig.

Ezra stepped close to me, his black eyes

in shadow. "Do you believe in God, boy?" he asked.

"I guess I do," I said.

The gunman nodded. "Then I advise you to make your peace with Him, because from this moment on, you're a walking dead man."

Chapter 15

I stepped back to the fire and Lila sat beside me. She had a canteen in her hand and she tenderly began to wipe blood away from my face.

"You're all cut up and bruised," she whispered.

"I'll be all right," I said. "I've been cut up and bruised plenty before."

I looked into her eyes and saw the awakening of something. What was it? Love?

I shook my head, a movement that caused me more than a little pain.

I couldn't have seen love in Lila's eyes, it was impossible. And yet . . .

"You did well, Dusty," she said, interrupting my thoughts. "You stood up for Pa and you stood up for me."

I managed a smile. "And damned near got myself killed for my trouble."

She kissed me then, just a soft, tender meeting of her lips on mine.

"Thank you, Dusty," she whispered. "Thank you for so much."

Gently I pushed her away. "Go see to your pa, Lila," I said. "His mouth and beard are covered in sand."

The girl got up and did as I'd told her and I sat there comparing her in my mind to pretty Sally Coleman.

Did Sally love me?

One time, down by the creek near her pa's ranch, she'd taken one of them motto candies that girls like from a paper sack in her purse and she'd studied the writing for a long time.

"What does it say?" I'd asked.

She'd smiled at me and giggled. "It says, 'I love you,' silly."

Well, Sally looked at that motto for a long time; then she'd just sighed, kind of soft and low, and popped the candy into her mouth.

I'd expected her to give me that candy. It was pink, and I would have tucked it away and treasured it. But she never did.

That didn't tell me much then, but now it planted a seed of doubt in my mind.

Did Sally love me?

The answer was: I didn't know.

Did Lila love me?

I didn't know that either.

Either way, maybe it didn't matter a hill of beans. A day from now I could be a dead man and all the love in the world would not be enough to change that and bring me back again.

The time was fast approaching when I'd have to stand up and be counted. My first duty was to get back Simon Prather's money, but even so I resolved not to let Wingo and Ezra Owens stampede me. I was fated to meet them in a gunfight, but it would be at a time and place of my own choosing, where the advantage, however slight, would be on my side.

But fate is a fickle thing, and in the end the true measure of a man is not fate itself but how he masters it. As events would soon reveal, the fate I was imagining for myself would be very different from the reality: a reality that would be much worse, and much more sudden, bloody and violent, than anything I could visualize.

We took to the trail at dawn under a pale lemon sky banded with scarlet.

Wingo rode point. He was surly and uncommunicative, but the eyes in his battered face blazed with hate when he looked at me. He was setting himself up for a killing, and even for a man like him who loved to kill, my death would mean something special to him.

Lila took her place at the back of the wagon with Hank, who was now far gone, drifting into unconsciousness more and more, and I figured the outlaw must welcome each brief period of oblivion as a blessed respite from pain.

Ned urged on the oxen with his whip, stumbling forward like an automaton. The poetry had fled from the man and all that remained was a dry, empty-eyed husk and, within that, a soundless soul where the music of the verses he'd so loved no longer played.

As always, Ezra rode behind me, wary and alert, a silent, dangerous man ready for anything.

We traveled through the gathering day across that hard land, and yet when I looked around me, I found myself wishing for no other.

Nothing in my life had been easy, but that was the way of Texas. This land did not give freely, and what you wanted from it you took, then fought to keep. Only the strong survived and became part of it, became Texans.

Now, as the smoking sun rose to its highest point and branded the sky, the air I breathed smelled clean, of Texas.

I was young and life surged strong in me

and I dearly wished to remain part of this land. I wanted to live and go on living, but an inner voice told me that this could only be to my disadvantage in the fight to come.

Bass Reeves once said that a man who clings too tenaciously to life will hesitate before going to the gun, maybe hoping for another way, maybe hoping for a miracle.

With men like Lafe Wingo and Ezra Owens, that moment's hesitation was all the edge they needed and their victims, lying pale in dust-blown graves across the West, could testify how wrong it is for a man to put his trust in miracles.

Me, I decided right there and then as we sought a likely spot to camp, best I put my trust in a miracle of steel and walnut made by Sam'l Colt and do my testifying with five rounds of lead.

Sure, maybe I was getting too big for my britches, but remember I was but eighteen and couldn't yet grow a man's mustache. You can't put an old head on young shoulders, and looking back, I realize I should have been a lot more scared than I was, and believe me, even then I was plenty scared.

We were still a couple of hours north of the Brazos, and Wingo decided we should rest for an hour before we made the crossing.

I helped Lila boil coffee and fry up some salt pork, and then while the others ate, she took me aside and slipped off a chain from her neck with a little silver cross on the end.

"Wear this, Dusty," she said. "It will help."

I took the chain from her and put it around my own neck, feeling the warmth of Lila's body still on it. "You don't think I'm going to make it through the day, do you?" I asked.

Lila opened her mouth to speak, found the words dying in her throat and shook her head, her eyes misting.

I tapped the Colt at my waist. "I'm pretty good with this thing, you know."

The girl looked over my shoulder at Wingo and Ezra as they sat hunched over a hatful of fire. "Dusty," she whispered, her lips very close to my ear, "shoot them in the back. Destroy them any way you can. You can't stand up to those gunmen in a fair fight. They'll kill you for sure."

I was neither shocked nor surprised, because I'd given some thought to that very idea and had pretty soon rejected it.

"If I killed those men like that, I'd maybe go on living, Lila," I said. "But it wouldn't really be living, because every single day of my life I would remember and die a little death."

"Dusty, those aren't men. They're animals," Lila said. "You've killed animals before and they don't lay heavy on your conscience."

I nodded. "I've killed my share of deer, but deer aren't men." I held her close to me. "Lila, out here there's a code — a code that dates all the way back to the days when gentlemen settled quarrels with a duel, and it demands that you meet your enemy honorably and face-to-face. Now maybe it's an outdated code, but where Western men gather to talk, they still judge the actions of others by that code."

I saw the puzzled look in Lila's eyes, her complete lack of understanding of the West and Westerners, and I found myself groping for the right words. "I was raised hard, but even so, I was taught to believe in that code and I can't turn my back on it now."

"Then you're a fool," Lila snapped, breaking away from me.

I watched her walk back to the fire, my heart heavy. Was she right and was I wrong?

I shook my head. No matter what happened, I didn't want to be known as the man who shot Lafe Wingo and Ezra Owens in the back. There would be no living with myself after that, and there would be no living with others, men who would be quick to judge and slow to forgive and forget.

I had to draw the line somewhere, and I drew it now. Killing a man in fair fight was one thing — cold-blooded murder was quite another, and I'd have no part of it.

Killing from ambush was Lafe Wingo's way. It wasn't Dusty Hannah's way.

After an hour, we headed south once more, and this time Wingo told me to ride alongside of him.

Around us, the flat land was thick with mesquite, tasajillo, yucca and skunkbush. Heat hazed the pale blue sky above us. The sun's brightness was subdued, like it was shining behind a steamed-up window. But the day was hot, and sweat stained the front of my shirt, turning the faded blue a darker color.

I rode beside Wingo in silence for a few minutes, feeling the man's hate like the heat of a campfire. Recent events had taught me to live with awareness, to notice and sense what I had not noticed and sensed before. My more innocent days, the days when I saw other men as human beings and not potential enemies, were long behind me, maybe never to return.

In most men, hate springs from fear or envy, but not in Wingo, since I knew he neither envied nor feared me. His hatred sprang from his own need for self-approval and from his humbled gunman's pride.

I knew, as he did, that he could not let me live to spread talk that I'd whipped him with my fists. His reputation was at stake and he couldn't let it founder on the sharp rocks of idle frontier gossip.

Finally Wingo eased himself in the saddle and, looking straight ahead, asked: "What you thinking, boy?"

I shrugged. "Not much. About the Apaches maybe."

Wingo turned and looked at me, his battered mouth twisting in a sneer. "You got maybe an hour or so to live, and that's all you're thinking about, Apaches?"

"It doesn't pay a man to dwell on uncertain things," I said. "Maybe you'll be the one to die."

Wingo let out with a roaring laugh, then winced as one of the cuts on his bottom lip opened up. "Boy, this is how it's going to be," he said, choosing his words carefully, each one tolling like a funeral bell. "As soon as we clear the Brazos, I'm not going to call you out and I'm not going to let you draw down on me. You may be talking to the little lady. You might be eating your beans and bacon. Hell, you might be on your knees saying your prayers. But no matter what you're doing, all at once I'm just going to draw and put a bullet in your belly."

No matter how I studied on it, Wingo's warning was pretty much a conversation stopper, but finally I managed: "Thanks for the kind words. I'll be ready."

Wingo laughed again, and I was uncomfortably mindful that Ezra was riding close behind me. If I tried to shoot Wingo, I'd be a dead man. Ezra would see to that.

"Boy," Wingo said, "I've killed more men than they say, and a few women besides. I've taken much pleasure in each of them, but nothing is going to give me more enjoyment than putting a bullet into you."

To my surprise, the big gunman reached out and draped his arm around my shoulder. "Until then," he said, smiling, "let's you and me be real good amigos. Hell, boy, you whipped me real easy and you just a scrawny little feller an' all. Ain't nobody ever done that to me before, and I mean nobody." He turned in the saddle. "Ain't that right, Ezra?"

Behind me, Owens nodded. "Sure enough, Lafe."

"See," Wingo said. "I always speak the truth about what I've done and what I'm gonna do."

His thick arm lay heavy on my shoulder, and I had a mind to throw caution to the wind, brush it off and cuss him for a cheap tinhorn. But I never got the chance.

A bullet furrowed the air above my head — and a split second later I heard the sharp, venomous crack of a rifle.

Chapter 16

The Apaches boiled out of the flat, feature-less land like wraiths, two dozen of them, well-mounted, firing and yelling as they came.

All hell was breaking loose fast — too fast. I slid my Winchester out of the boot, turned in the saddle and cranked off a few quick shots. Beside me, Wingo was doing the same. It's no easy task to sight on a target through a scope off the back of a rearing horse, but Wingo made it look easy.

One Apache suddenly threw up his arms and toppled off his paint pony and another pulled up and slumped over his horse's neck, hit hard.

Ned Tryon yelled something I couldn't hear and whipped up the oxen. The huge animals lumbered into a shambling trot, but no matter how they strained against the yoke, hooves kicking up clouds of dust, their pace was painfully slow.

Wingo wheeled his mount and rode to

the back of the wagon. He reached out his hand and yelled to Lila: "Get up here!"

Ezra was firing steadily, his smoking Colt bellowing, and the Apache charge broke, the warriors splitting up, streaming to the right and left of us.

"What about him?" Lila asked.

"Leave him," Wingo hollered. "He's already a dead man."

"Lafe!" Hank screamed. "For God's sake take me with you!"

The big gunman glanced down at the stricken outlaw, his blue eyes pitiless. "Not a chance, Hank. You're our ticket out of here. They'll be so busy with you, they might forget about the rest of us."

"No!" Lila cried. "You can't leave him here."

"Damn right I can," Wingo yelled. He leaned from the saddle, scooped Lila into his arms and held her close in front of him. The gunman savagely raked the paint with his spurs, drawing long streaks of blood, and was gone in a cloud of dust, the pony's steel shoes winking in the sunlight.

Ezra emptied his gun at the Apaches, then swung his horse around and followed Wingo.

There was no time to be lost. I fired at a big warrior on a bay horse, missed, fired again. My second bullet hit the target because this time the Indian's rifle spun away from him and he crashed heavily to the ground.

I rode toward Ned and kicked my right foot free of the stirrup. "Ned," I yelled, "take a stirrup."

Ned waved me away. "Go," he shouted. "Save yourself and Lila."

I galloped beside the man and reined up hard. The black reared and his hindquarters slammed into the ground, his churning hooves throwing up clods of earth.

"Ned, damn you, take the stirrup," I yelled, fighting the horse as he tried his best to bolt on me.

A bullet plowed into the wagon, a shower of splinters exploding into the air, and another kicked up a startled exclamation point of danger between Ned's feet.

The Apaches were closing on us now from two sides, yelling in triumph, wishful of taking us alive.

I slid the Winchester back into the boot and drew my Colt. As the black reared again and angrily fought the bit, I slammed a couple of fast shots at the Indians nearest us and saw them waver and break.

"Now damn you!" I yelled at Ned.

The man finally realized how desperate things were and his left foot smacked into the stirrup. I spurred the black and, Ned grimly hanging on to the saddle horn, took off after the others. Behind me I heard Hank scream in terror and scream again, shrieking, shattering screeches that scraped my strung-out nerves raw.

After about a hundred yards I turned, looking for pursuers. But the Apaches were milling around the wagon, yipping war cries, intent only on Hank.

I had no regard for killers like Hank Owens, but I couldn't ignore the fact that he was about to die a hideous, agonizing death. Even though gut-shot, his dying would not come quickly or easily. The Apaches knew well how to keep a man alive, the better to prolong the torments they inflicted on him. Hank would last many long, suffering hours, and in the end, he'd curse Lafe Wingo, curse God and curse the day he was born and the father who sired him and the mother who bore him.

His only hope was that he'd die out of his mind, no longer capable of understanding his appalling reality, and so travel beyond the reach of the Apaches.

Wingo had been right though, heartless as it was. His sacrifice of Hank had bought us time. The question was: Had he bought us enough?

As I rode in the dust of Wingo and Ezra Owens, I had no answer to that question.

I've been told that small worries cast big shadows, but what was facing me now was no small worry and uppermost in my mind wasn't Simon Prather's money or Lafe Wingo. It was all Lila, and that surprised me.

I slowed the black to a walk and Ned stepped down. Ahead of us, Wingo and Ezra had done the same, and I saw their heads swivel this way and that as they hunted for any kind of cover.

They found it a few minutes later, an abandoned wagon lying tipped on its side about fifty yards off the trail. Beyond the wagon ran a creek, maybe twenty feet wide with steep banks, a single cottonwood spreading leafy branches over twelve inches or so of sluggish water. Some curly mesquite grew quite close to the creek and here and there catclaw peeped from the buffalo grass.

Wingo and Ezra dismounted and took positions with their rifles at either end of the wagon. As Ned and I got closer, Lila came out from behind the wagon and stepped toward us.

She looked at Ned, the afternoon light harshly revealing the sunken planes of his unshaven cheeks and the dark circles under his sagging eyes.

"Pa," she asked, "are you all right?"

The man nodded. "I just need to rest for a while."

I swung down from the saddle and followed Lila and her pa to the wagon. Then I ground tied the black and slid the rifle from the boot.

"Boy, you keep watch behind us," Wingo yelled. "I don't want them Apaches coming at us across the damned creek."

"They got Hank," I said. I was telling Wingo something he already knew, but I was determined to leave the outlaw at least that three-word epitaph.

"The hell with him," Wingo said, leaving him quite another.

The big gunman seemed to have forgotten about killing me, at least for now. Judging by the tenseness in his jaw and the way his knuckles showed white on the stock of his rifle, I figured the Apaches were his more urgent concern.

I took up a position near the creekbank, keeping the cottonwood to my left, and glanced around. The ashes of a fire lay in a circle near the bank and a battered coffeepot and a man's flat-crowned hat were half-hidden in the grass.

It looked like the teamster who had driven this wagon had been attacked by Apaches only a couple of days before. I had no doubt they'd killed the man, but a scattering of shiny brass cartridge cases around the wagon showed where he'd made a good fight of it.

Just the previous spring, having all the confidence of the young, I figured that life was forever. But now, as the hours ticked slowly toward late afternoon, I had the uneasy feeling that maybe I wasn't as immortal as I'd thought.

Unbidden, the thought came into my mind: Dusty, if Wingo doesn't get you, the Apaches will.

I realized that I was in one hell of a fix and that realization brought me no comfort.

Over by the wagon, Wingo yelled at Lila: "Girl, see if you can find some wood or maybe some dry cow chips. We're going to need coffee."

"Lafe, you think that's wise?" Ezra asked, his face strained, thin mouth pinched. "I mean the smoke."

Wingo slowly shook his head, acting like he was feeling more sorrow than anger.

"Ezra," he said, real slow, "don't you think the Apaches already know exactly where we are?"

A dawning realization crossed the man's face and he gulped. "Yeah, you're right. I guess they do." Ezra's eyes scanned the empty land around him. "I'm jumpy, is all. It's this damned waiting that's getting to me."

"Me too," Wingo said, his tongue running over his cracked lips. "It's like I keep hearing footsteps."

Although Lafe Wingo and Ezra Owens were experienced fighting men and possessed courage of a sort, theirs was the kind of bravery suited to short, explosive moments of action, the now-you-see-it, now-you-don't daring of the typical frontier gunman.

This kind of taut waiting, while a man chewed on his heart and his belly was all balled up in a knot, required a quieter, more enduring courage that neither Ezra nor Wingo seemed to possess.

Did I?

I couldn't even guess. I knew I was scared, so only time and events would provide the answer.

A long-handled shovel lay near the wagon and I used it to dig myself a shallow rifle pit. Then Wingo and Owens took their cue from me and did the same.

The three of us were as prepared as we were ever going to be, and the next move was up to the Apaches.

The day was shading into a cool, blue-shadowed twilight under a burnished sky the color of Black Hills gold when the warriors attacked. They came at us from two directions, one party of eight men charging directly toward me, intent on crossing the creek, the others concentrating on Wingo and Ezra.

Ignoring what was going on behind me, I fixed my attention on the task at hand. I fired at the Apache in the lead. Too fast. A clean miss. Taking a deep breath, I forced myself to slow down and fired at the man again. Another miss. The Apaches were closer now, riding hell-for-leather.

I got up on one knee, levered a round into the chamber, fired, and a man went down. I fired again. Another hit, though this warrior just swung out of the charge, blood staining the front of his shirt, and loped back in the direction he'd come.

Behind me I heard the constant crash of rifles as Wingo and Ezra fired. I jumped out of the trench and gave ground, bullets kicking up dust at my feet. The Apaches reached the creek and began to mill around, bunching together as they slowed their ponies to make the steep descent into the sandy streambed. I threw down the Winchester, shucked my Colt and hammered three fast shots into the clustered horsemen.

Two men went down, one of them screaming, and I emptied the Colt into the rest, as far as I could tell, scoring no other hits.

But it was enough.

No Indians, not even Apaches, will take casualties like that without pulling back to lick their wounds and talk things over. The warriors swung their horses around and loped away. I grabbed the Winchester, sighted on a trailing Apache and pulled the trigger. *Click!* I had hosed the rifle dry.

A bullet fired from somewhere well beyond the creek slammed into the dirt inches from my right bootheel as I fed shells into the Winchester. I looked around for a target, saw nothing and stepped over to the wagon.

The Apaches were gone, but three of them lay stretched out on the ground, short, wiry men in faded Spanish shirts and wide blue and red headbands.

I'd often spoken to old soldiers who'd

fought in the War Between the States and as I stood and surveyed the carnage around me, I recollected one of them saying that the generals on both sides never did learn the folly of attacking entrenched infantry with light cavalry.

The Apaches had made that same mistake, and judging by the number of their dead, I'd say they'd paid dearly for it.

Wingo and Ezra had killed three, and I had downed three and wounded at least one other. The Apaches, always few in number, could ill afford a butcher's bill of that magnitude.

I stepped past Wingo and Ezra, their faces streaked black with powder smoke, and went to Lila who was huddled behind the wagon, her pa's head in her arms.

"Was he hit?" I asked, kneeling beside her.

Ned looked at me and managed a weak smile. "A bullet burned across the back of my head," he said. He reached behind him, probing for the wound and when his hand appeared again it was bloody.

Lila rose to her feet. "Pa, I'll get some water from the creek and bathe your head."

"Better let me do that, Lila," I said. "There are dead men over there."

The girl nodded gratefully, but as I

turned to leave, she stopped me and threw herself into my arms. "Dusty," she whispered, "thank God you're all right."

I tilted up her chin with a forefinger and her lips parted, her eyes suddenly hungry. I kissed her then, hard and long, and when my lips finally left hers I said: "And I'm glad you're all right too." Then with a husky voice, and battling to understand my feelings for her, I added: "I better get that water."

As I walked past Wingo, the man's eyes followed me, a burning, barely subdued rage flushing his face.

The gunman wanted Lila, and he'd kill to get her. But I was prepared to fight to keep her, so as I filled my canteen from the creek, I figured that at least for right now, things were pretty much balanced out on that score.

I handed Lila the canteen and stepped beside Wingo and Owens.

"Shouldn't we ride on out of here, Lafe?" Ezra was asking. "Seems to me we whipped them real good."

Wingo nodded. "We whipped them all right, but they might be back. We stay right where we are until sunup. If we leave now and they catch us out in the open, we're dead men."

Wingo turned to me. "You, boy, rustle us up some grub and see to more coffee. It's going to be a long night."

Wingo was right on that score — because an hour later, just as dark was falling and the first sentinel stars appeared, Hank Owens began to scream.

Chapter 17

Hank's agonized shrieks echoed out of the darkness, screech after shrill screech scarring the tremulous night, spiking into our ears like sharp shards of broken glass.

Lila put her hands to her mouth and her eyes widened in shock and fear.

Ezra Owens had gone very pale, his lips bloodless, and even Wingo looked green around the gills, with his rifle clutched close to his chest and his troubled gaze desperately trying to penetrate the gloom.

There came a fleeting moment of ringing quiet; then Hank screamed again in mortal agony, obviously suffering pain that was beyond pain.

Hearing those dreadful cries, I figured that the Apaches were working on Hank's belly wound, trying to wear us down through mounting terror. Scared men make mistakes, and that was what the Apaches were counting on.

I've learned since that you can't judge the Apache by the standards of white men.

He grows up hard in a hard land and from an early age sees much of death, usually long drawn-out, painful and ugly. In the harsh, unforgiving school of the desert and mountain from whence he springs, the Apache knows that each living creature thrives only by inflicting death on another. The Apache feels nothing in the way of kindness and compassion toward an enemy, because those are women's emotions and show only weakness. Yes, the Apaches were torturing Hank Owens horribly, but it was cold, impersonal, without sadism.

It is the way of the Apache warrior to test, by inflicting great pain, the courage of an enemy. He believes that if an enemy proves strong and brave, his strength and bravery will become part of his own — and his chances of surviving one more day in his pitiless environment become that much better.

It is a harsh way, but even as I listened to Hank's screams, I made no judgments and no condemnations. Why judge and condemn the wolf because he pulls down and savages an elk?

It is the way of the wolf . . . and it is the way of the Apache.

I stepped over to the fire and poured myself coffee, the dying man's screams drowning out even my thoughts. Then I returned to my post.

The cup was hot and I placed it carefully on the side of the wagon and just as carefully, with hands that shook only a little, rolled myself a smoke.

I lit the cigarette and drew my Winchester closer to hand and looked out on the menacing darkness, the scowling sliver of the horned moon touching the grass only here and there with faint, grudging light.

Hank screamed and screamed again, the wild echoes of his rising shrieks reverberating around us before finally dying away, fading like ghastly bugle calls into distance and the haunted night.

Several slow moments of silence passed as I smoked and drank coffee, enjoying the harsh bitterness of both. Lila sat close to my feet, her chin resting on her drawn-up knees, her eyes wide-open but seeing nothing. Beside her, Ned dozed, waking now and then with a surprised jerk of his head.

Ezra Owens, his mouth working, stared into the darkness, a drawn look about him that showed even under his thick beard. The man was confronting some inner demons that he didn't seem to be handling well.

Wingo chewed on the end of his mustache, his restless eyes everywhere, showing the strain of this enforced inaction but, as far as I could tell, mastering his fear.

Hank screamed again.

Cursing, Ezra stepped out from behind the wagon, threw his Winchester to his shoulder and cranked off round after round into the flame-torn night, ejected brass shells tinkling around his feet.

Ezra shot the rifle dry and kept on pulling the trigger, the hammer clicking time after time on an empty chamber.

Finally he lowered the Winchester and walked back behind the wagon. Wingo clapped his hands together in derisory applause. "That was a great help," the big gunman said. "All you did was shoot at phantoms and waste ammunition."

"Maybe so," Ezra said, his face grim. "But Hank is my brother, even though he never amounted to much. I figured I owed it to our ma to do something."

The outlaw slumped against the wagon, then slid to his haunches, holding the rifle between his knees. I glanced at him and noticed an absorbed, calculating look on his face, like he was carefully thinking something through.

I had no idea what Ezra had on his mind, but whatever it was, the not knowing bothered me plenty.

The moon sank lower in the sky and the dark shroud of the night drew itself closer around us. Hank had not screamed for a couple of hours and I figured he'd finally been taken by merciful death.

But I was wrong. The Apaches were not yet done with Hank Owens.

During the darkest part of the night just before the dawn, a lone Apache on a magnificent gray horse galloped past the wagon, something large, flopping and bulky held in his arms.

Wingo snapped off a shot at the warrior and missed. Without slackening his pace, the Apache threw his burden to the ground and was gone, the drum of the gray's hooves fast receding in the distance.

I stepped out behind the wagon and so did Wingo. We walked to the thing lying on the ground and soon saw it for what it was.

It was Hank . . . or what was left of him.

The man's eyes had been gouged out and his naked, ravaged body was covered in blood from the top of his scalped head to his toes.

Hank had died hard and in unbearable

pain — an end I'd wish on no man.

Wingo toed the body, looking for signs of life. There were none. "Just as well," he said. "All I could have done for him is shot him."

And that was when Ezra Owens made his break.

Wingo was riding my paint and he hadn't unsaddled the animal. The saddlebags with Simon Prather's money were still on the horse along with his blanket roll.

All this Ezra knew.

The outlaw suddenly sprang to his feet and ran for the paint. He swung quickly into the saddle and fled, dust spurting from the pony's flying hooves.

Wingo watched Ezra go. He just stood there doing nothing, his smile real small and tight and knowing. Then, before I realized what was happening, he jerked my Winchester from my hands and threw it to his shoulder.

BLAM!

The shot shattered the fragile night into a million separate fragments of sound, the echo bouncing across the flat grassland. In the distance, half obscured by the night shadows, I saw Ezra jerk in the saddle, straighten up to his full height in the stirrups, then topple into the dust.

The paint kept on going, his hooves drumming until I could hear them no longer.

I reckoned Ezra had been at least three hundred yards away when Wingo nailed him, and that in darkness. It was a fine shot by anyone's standards and spoke volumes of the outlaw's skill with a rifle.

Wingo turned to me, still smiling, his eyes hard. "I figured ol' Ezra was going to try that sooner or later." His face took on a thoughtful look. "I guess that just leaves you and me, boy."

"I reckon it does," I said, wondering if I could shuck my Colt before Wingo swung the rifle on me.

But it didn't come to that.

The outlaw merely stood silent for a few moments, shrugged and handed me back the Winchester. "And soon it will only be me. And the girl."

When I look back on it, I knew I should have shot him then and saved myself a world of grief later. But the moment came and went because the Apache on the gray horse rode out of the newborn morning and stopped about a hundred yards from the wagon. As far as I could see, he carried no weapon.

The warrior cupped his hands around

his mouth and cried out: *"Matanzas con Sus Dentes!"*

Kills with His Teeth. It must have been he who had given me that name after my fight with the Apache at the hogback.

"What the hell is he hollering about?" Wingo asked, his face puzzled.

"It means Kills with His Teeth," I answered. "It's a name the Apaches gave me."

Wingo looked at me in surprise. "Hell, for a younker, you sure got around, boy."

I ignored the man, mustered my Spanish and yelled: *"Qué usted desea?"*

"What did you say?" Wingo asked, irritation edging his voice. "I don't speak that damned Messkin lingo."

"I asked him what he wants, but it seems he don't much feel like telling me."

The Apache had given me a name, but I didn't know his. For him, this was powerful medicine that would weaken me if we ever met in a fight.

A few moments passed, the warrior sitting his horse, never for one moment taking his eyes off me. Finally, the Apache raised his arm and pointed in my direction, aiming his forefinger like a gun.

He stayed like that for a long time, in complete silence, then swung the gray around and loped away.

It didn't take a genius to figure out that the Apache had just warned me. He was telling me by his sign that he knew me and had me marked as a mortal enemy, someone he must destroy.

Maybe he was kin of the Apache I'd killed among the rocks, for he sure seemed to be holding a grudge.

Wingo realized that too, because he looked at me, grinning. "Boy," he said, "near as I can tell, you got a powerful lot of enemies and mighty few friends."

I nodded. "Seems that way."

The big gunman slapped me hard on the shoulder. "Well, don't you worry about it none because very soon now it will be all over for you."

"Go to hell," I said, my anger flaring as I pushed him away from me.

Wingo didn't answer. He just took a single step back and went for his gun.

Chapter 18

Ned Tryon came out of nowhere.

As Wingo's Colt swung up, Ned dived for his arm. The old man's forward motion slammed Wingo's gun hand downward and the outlaw triggered a shot into the dirt at his feet.

I palmed my Colt but didn't shoot because suddenly Lila ran between me and Wingo. The outlaw cursed and grabbed the girl, holding her in front of him. Then he directed his attention to Ned Tryon.

"Damn you, you old goat!" he roared, his face twisted in fury. He leveled his gun and pumped a shot into Ned, then another.

My own gun was ready, but if I shot at Wingo, I'd likely hit Lila. The outlaw grabbed his rifle and backed up toward my saddled black, Lila shielding him. I sidestepped to the cover of the wagon, all my attention riveted on Wingo, desperately hoping for a clear shot.

I had already felt the outlaw's strength,

and now he demonstrated it again, effortlessly swinging Lila into the saddle. Keeping the horse between us, Wingo mounted, then hugged the girl close, and I knew he was going to throw a shot at me.

Lila was sobbing uncontrollably, limp as a rag doll in Wingo's arms. I stood there tense and ready. Could I fire and take the risk of hitting her?

Wingo sat the black, grinning at me. His Colt swung up fast and level.

Suddenly Lila came alive.

She turned in the saddle and raked her fingernails down Wingo's face, opening up bloody furrows in the man's cheek from his left eye to his chin.

Wingo roared in pain and fury, his hand jerking to his face and Lila took her chance to squirm away from him. She jumped off the black and landed on all fours on the ground. Wingo, his ruined face streaming blood, cursed and swung his gun on her.

I fired. Too fast.

My bullet clipped the lobe from Wingo's ear and the outlaw roared again, a cry soon dwarfed by the louder roar of his Colt. I felt a sledgehammer blow to my left shoulder and I was jerked around from the impact. That movement saved my life. Wingo's second shot — the one that would have crashed into the center of my chest — whined past harmlessly. I was hit hard, but still strong enough to stay in the fight. I triggered another shot at Wingo, missed as he battled the scared, prancing black and shot again.

But the outlaw had decided not to stick around. He spurred the black and all I could do was waste a couple of bullets firing at his fast-retreating back.

Staggering from pain and shock, scarlet fingers of blood trickling down my left arm from my shoulder, I stumbled toward Lila, who was kneeling beside her pa.

"How is he?" I asked.

Lila looked at me, her face gray. "He's dead, Dusty. He's gone."

The old man's eyes were shut, like he was asleep, and his face was more peaceful than at any time since I'd met him. Whatever his inner torments, he was at rest now.

"He was so strong once," Lila whispered, "a good farmer when he was younger."

"I guess he was once," I said. "The hand of the reaper takes the ears that are hoary, but the voice of the weeper wails manhood in glory."

Lila's eyes searched mine. "Dusty, did you just think that up?"

I shook my head at her. "No, I heard it

once. I don't recollect where."

"It's true," Lila said, her voice breaking on the words. "I will always remember him as he was when Ma was alive, not what he became."

"Ned saved my life," I said. "That's a thing I won't forget."

Suddenly deathly tired, I slumped against the wagon. Lila saw the blood on my shirt and gave a little gasp of alarm.

"Dusty, you've been shot."

I nodded. "Took one of Wingo's bullets in the shoulder."

Her father lay dead beside her, but Lila decided her duty was to the living. She said, her dark eyes concerned: "Unbutton your shirt and let me look."

I did as the girl asked and after she examined the wound her face was pale with shock. "The bullet's still in there, Dusty. It's very deep."

"Figured that," I said.

I dug into the pocket of my pants and brought out my folding knife and opened the blade with my teeth. "Lila, you're going to have to cut the bullet out of there. With this."

Looking back, I don't know what I expected: Lila to faint maybe or shriek and say she couldn't do it. That was what pretty Sally Coleman would have done, I'm sure, since she wasn't big on blood and such.

But Lila surprised me. There was steel in her and she was stronger, a lot stronger, than I had ever imagined.

The girl took the knife, her face frightened but her little chin was set and determined. "This will hurt," she said.

"Figured that," I said, smiling, pretending I was a lot braver than I really was.

Lila nodded. "Now I wish you'd saved some of Pa's whiskey."

"So do I," I said. "Right about now, I'd be ready to swallow the whole jug."

"Not for you, Dusty," the girl said. She wasn't scolding me, just being practical. "To clean the knife blade." She managed a small smile. "God knows where it's been."

I nodded toward the dying fire. "Stick the blade in the reddest part of the coals. Heat will clean it as good as whiskey."

Lila did as she was told, and when she came back to my side after a few moments, the point of the blade glowed a dull cherry red.

The girl pushed aside my wide suspenders and held the knife close to my shoulder. "I'm sorry, Dusty," she whispered. "I'm so sorry."

I didn't get a chance to answer because she immediately plunged the blade into my shoulder and I went rigid, my mouth wide-open, screaming silent screams I heard only in my head.

Lila dug deeper, her eyes intent only on the knife. Pain slammed at me time and time again and sweat trickled down my face. I clenched my teeth and arched my back, each hissing breath coming quick and shallow.

"Be brave, Dusty," Lila whispered, her eyes not seeking mine. "Be brave."

The knife dug deeper . . . deeper still . . . cutting . . . probing . . . grinding on lead and bone.

Jolts of agony cartwheeled through my entire body and my head was reeling, bright bursts of dazzling light exploding like Fourth of July rockets in my brain. I had to make it stop, push Lila's hand away, admit myself to be much less than she was.

"Got it!" Lila yelled. She held up a bloody hand, the bullet held between her forefinger and thumb.

"Thank you," I said. And promptly fainted.

I woke to Lila's face hovering over mine, her brown eyes anxiously searching my own. "How do you feel, Dusty?" she asked.

In truth, I felt weak, drained, so I stepped around her question. "How long have I been out?" I asked.

The girl smiled. "A long time. It's almost noon."

My fingers strayed to my wounded shoulder and touched a thick bandage. Lila smiled. "I used a piece of my shift. I hope you don't mind."

"I'm honored," I said, meaning it.

I glanced around. "Where's . . . I mean . . ."

Lila nodded. "I laid my pa to rest while you were asleep." She nodded toward the cottonwood. "Over there where you'd dug a trench. I made it deeper."

I shook my head at her. "Lila, you should have waited. I'd have helped."

Tears started in the girl's eyes. "Death diminished Pa, made him smaller somehow. His body was small and light. I managed." She attempted a smile. "Besides, you couldn't dig a grave with that shoulder."

Yet again, I marveled at Lila's strength. Once I'd thought her too young and too featherbrained, her ambition to farm her own land just a ramshackle castle she was building in the sky. Now I wasn't so sure.

Something told me this lovely, frail-looking girl had hidden reserves of courage and backbone I couldn't even guess at. I knew then with growing certainty that with her own hands she could and would build a home from what had been only wilderness, as tens of thousands of hardy pioneer women had done before her and would do after.

It came to me then that I could be happy with this woman, content to sit with her quiet and close of an evening after the day's chores were done and look out on the darkening land where our brindled cattle grazed, taking pleasure in it, knowing what lay around us had been tamed by our will and by the strength of our backs.

I reached out with my good arm and pulled Lila close to me and kissed her. It was a kiss with little passion but with much tenderness and she perfectly understood its implications.

"Dusty," she whispered, "when this is all over and you're back at the SP Connected, will you come calling on me?"

"Sure will," I answered. "I'll bring you flowers and them little motto candies all the girls like."

"Will you call on pretty Sally Coleman and bring her flowers and candy?"

I'd walked into that little trap with my eyes wide-open and now I desperately sought a way out of it. "Lila —" I began, having no idea what I would say next, but was saved from having to answer her question by the clatter of hooves on the trail.

Lila helped me get to my feet in time to see a column of about thirty buffalo soldiers come to a dusty, jingling halt near the wagon, their heads turning this way and that as they looked around at the dead Apaches.

What caught my eye was my paint, led by one of the troopers — and the fact that the saddlebags were still there.

The sergeant in charge, a thick-shouldered man with an eye patch and a magnificent set of sideburns, swung his horse out of the column and rode toward us.

"What went on here?" he asked, his black eyes searching mine. He jerked a thumb over his shoulder. "Found this horse wandering and a dead white man back there."

"The horse is mine, Sergeant," I said. "You'll find an SP brand on his flank."

The sergeant turned in the saddle and called a trooper by name. "Check the brand on that paint, hoss," he said.

The soldier did as he was told and yelled

back. "SP, sergeant."

The big noncom nodded and turned back to me. "The brand is as you say." His eyes shrewd, he added: "Now tell me about the dead man back there."

My troubles were none of this soldier's, so in as few words as possible I told him about my troubles with Lafe Wingo, our battle with the Apaches and his killing of Ezra Owens and Ned.

After I finished speaking, the sergeant sat in silence for a few moments, then said: "Young feller, my orders are to pursue and engage hostile Apaches wherever I find them and compel them to surrender or be destroyed. All I can do for you is report what you've told me to the appropriate civilian authority."

I expected nothing more and I nodded my thanks.

"Where are you folks headed?" the sergeant asked, his puzzled eyes on Lila.

"We expect to cross the Brazos at the Clear Fork later today," I said. "Then we'll head south to my home ranch."

"River is low," the soldier said, "so you'll have no difficulty there." He shook his head at me. "But you're heading into a hornet's nest. Victorio and his main band are south of the Brazos and all ain't well in the chicken coop. The Apaches are burning and killing as far east as Abilene and I heard tell a couple of days ago they ambushed and cut up a Ranger patrol on the North Concho. Three Rangers dead and twice that many wounded is what I heard."

"Once we clear the Brazos, it's only a few miles to the SP ranch, Sergeant," I said. "We'll be safe there."

The man nodded. "Well, I sure hope so, for your sake and the little lady's." His restless gaze took in the bandage on my shoulder. "Here, you've been hit."

"Took one of Lafe Wingo's bullets," I said. "Lila cut it out for me."

The sergeant looked at Lila, a dawning respect in his eyes. "I'll get the doc to take a look at it," he said.

"You have a doctor with the column?" I asked, surprised.

"Mule doctor," the soldier replied, smiling. "But he's right good with bullet and knife wounds. Good with the croup too, come to that."

The mule doctor was a tall, lanky corporal with mournful eyes and gentle hands. He unbuttoned my bloodstained shirt and looked the wound over, probing carefully. "Couldn't have done better my ownself," he said finally. "Clean as a whistle." He turned to Lila. "You done real good, ma'am."

Lila smiled and dropped an elegant little curtsy. "There's a first time for everything, Corporal," she said.

The sergeant called the corporal over to him, leaned over from the saddle and whispered something I couldn't hear. The soldier nodded and stepped to one of the pack mules, returning with a folded blue army shirt, which he handed to me.

"It ain't new," the sergeant said. "But it's clean and in a heap better shape than the one you're wearing."

Gratefully I stripped off my own shirt and buttoned into the new one. The color was faded almost to a pale blue, but the shirt was soft and smelled of yellow laundry soap. I slipped the suspenders back over my shoulders and thanked the sergeant for his kindness, but he just waved me off and returned to his men.

The soldiers spent the next hour burying the dead Apaches and then Ezra Owens, carefully segregating the graves.

After a break for coffee, the troopers mounted again and the sergeant rode over to Lila and me. "We got to get moving along," he said. "You folks take care, you hear."

"Plan to, Sergeant," I replied. "And you too. Ride careful."

The soldier nodded. "I'll do that." He touched the brim of his hat to Lila and waved his men forward. And after they were gone, the land around us once again descended into silence and loneliness, the dust of the troops' passing slowly settling back to the dry earth.

The sun was burning white-hot in a lemon sky as Lila and me took our farewell of Ned. I stood beside Lila, my hat in my hands, looking down at the fresh-dug grave, and could find no words.

This man had saved my life and I owed him a debt I could never repay, but decided right there and then that somehow I'd find a way to pay it in full to his daughter.

Lila had gathered some wilted wildflowers; she placed them on the grave. When she rose she looked at me with dry eyes, a little, sad smile on her face. "I think Pa will like it here," she said.

I looked around at the other graves, a heaviness inside me. "One thing, he won't ever pine for company," I said.

Finally, Lila whispered a last prayer then turned and walked with me to the paint.

"Dusty," she said, "we must find the wagon."

"Why?" I asked. "I'm sure the Apaches stripped it good."

"Maybe," Lila said. "But Pa made a little secret compartment in the bed where he stashed two hundred dollars in double eagles. It was seed money, he said, and if I'm to plant a crop I'll need it."

Now wasn't the time to cuss and discuss about farming, so I let it go and said: "Well, let's go see. Maybe we'll get lucky and the money is still there."

It was. Ten gold coins in a small canvas pouch hidden in a tiny box cut into the bed of the wagon, like Lila had said.

Riding double, we took the dusty trail south toward the Brazos, riding under a hot sun, the only sound the plodding of the paint's hooves and the constant hum of bees and the chatter of saw-legged insects in the buffalo grass.

We splashed across the Clear Fork near the old Butterfield stage road just as day was shading into night. The paint was tired from the long trail behind him and the double load he carried, so I decided to hole up somewhere and head for the SP Connected early next morning.

We made a cold camp among some sheltering rocks on the slope of a shallow rise, spreading our blankets on some fine grass that felt as soft as any hotel bed.

Lila came to me in the night and lay beside me and I understood her need and held her close, comforting her as best I could. Gradually, her breathing slowed and she slept.

My wounded shoulder throbbed unmercifully and kept me from sleep. I turned on my back and looked at the sky above, where a million stars glowed brilliant, beautiful, but coldly indifferent to all that happened on the small, dusty planet far beneath them.

Lila stirred in her sleep and gave a little cry and I held her close again, the memory of her mouth on mine a sudden rush of sweet pain. Around us, hidden by darkness, spread the impossibly ancient land, and we two, neither of us past our twentieth birthday, lay quiet in its embrace.

As the night birds called and a coyote barked his hunger to the uncaring stars, I at last fell into an exhausted, dreamless sleep.

I had no idea what tomorrow would bring, and that was just as well.

Had I known I was about to ride into hell, I would have had no rest.

Chapter 19

Lila and me rode across a strife-scorched land, keeping to the divide between Deepwater Creek to our east and Cottonwood Creek to the west. Ahead of us lay the vast sweep of the Colorado and, farther south, the craggy barrier of the Blue Mountains.

Around us was rolling country, pinnacles of gray rock jutting here and there on the slopes of the hills, the grass-covered plains good for horses and cattle.

We rode with a long wind that smelled of rain at our backs, but we were getting close to our destination and I would have no need for my slicker. Just a few miles to the south lay the SP Connected, with its familiar big house, white barns and corrals.

I was coming home, but to a suffering land scarred by conflict.

Twice since we'd crossed the Brazos I'd left Lila with the paint to investigate thin plumes of rising smoke, once finding only the charred timbers of a deserted ranch house. The second time I'd almost stumbled over the bodies of two bearded government surveyors who'd been surprised and shot down outside their tent.

There were plenty of hoofprints of unshod ponies scattered around, and that could only mean Apaches.

As much as I enjoyed the closeness of Lila and the sweet smell of her and how the sunlight got all tangled up in her hair, I let her ride and took a position well ahead, my rifle at the ready.

Despite the gusting wind, the day was hot, the sun high in the upturned blue bowl of the sky. Sweat trickled down inside my shirt and I constantly had to remove my hat and wipe off my brow with the sleeve of my shirt.

Fifty yards or so behind me, Lila seemed cool and comfortable, riding easily, and when I turned to look at her, she waved at me and smiled, her bright eyes holding a promise or an invitation, I couldn't decide which. Anyhow, I only growled and grumbled to myself, knowing full well that girls did that kind of thing just to drive a man crazy.

We were about to fetch up to a low hill crowned with post oak and curly mesquite when I stopped and let Lila catch up to me. My shoulder throbbed unmercifully and waves of tiredness were washing over me, making me feel light-headed and sick.

"The SP is just over the rise," I told Lila. "When we reach the crest, you'll be able to see it."

Lila's eyes lit up. "Oh, Dusty, do you mean it? Are we almost home?"

"Almost," I said, "but I reckon your place is a piece farther to the east, maybe another ten miles or so."

A fleeting sadness crossed Lila's face. "I only wish Pa was here with us," she said.

"Me too," I said, mostly for politeness' sake, since Ned had no inclination to farm. "But don't be getting any big ideas. You're not going to your cabin, where you'll be out there all alone with the Apaches on the rampage. Best you hunker down at the SP for a spell."

Lila opened her mouth to argue, but then seemed to appreciate the logic of my decision. "How long before I can see my place?" she asked.

I shrugged. "Lila, as long as it takes for the army to round up ol' Victorio. A week, a month, a year, with Apaches you never can tell."

"A year!" Lila exclaimed. "I'm not going to wait a year. I'm not even going to wait a month. Dusty, if I've any hope of putting in a crop, I'll have to do it soon."

Well, I didn't see any point in arguing, at least not now when I was so tired. "Suit yourself," I said. "But in the meantime you're going home with me. Ma Prather will enjoy having another woman around and she'll pamper you, trust me."

Lila saw the logic in that too, because all she said was, with a tinge of wistfulness in her voice: "About now I could sure use some pampering."

And so it was that we rode over the crest of the rise and down into the wide and fertile valley that had given birth to, and then sustained, the SP Connected.

I was home, and I was bringing with me Simon Prather's badly needed thirty thousand dollars. It was a good feeling.

The ranch was the usual scattering of barns and corrals, but the bunkhouse was bigger and more spacious than most, though Simon had scrimped on windows, there being only one on each wall of the log building. I knew that only a couple of punchers would be living in the bunkhouse, since Mr. Prather had paid off the hands who'd made the drive to Dodge.

The ranch house had two stories and a tile roof, both levels boasting wide and shady balconies, unusual at that time in

Texas, when even rich ranchers like Charles Goodnight and John D. Chisholm were content to live in what were little more than shacks. Rarer still were the house's three tall chimneys, each made of gray stone, expertly laid by an itinerant German mason.

Simon had built the house as a palace for Ma to live in and he'd spared no expense, hauling the lumber all the way from the coast, and the durable white English paint from an importer in Austin.

Lila was once again sitting in front of me in the saddle, and I heard her sharp little intake of breath as the ranch came in sight.

"Dusty, your ranch is beautiful," she whispered, "like something you see in a storybook."

I laughed. "Lila, the SP Connected isn't mine. I only ride for the brand at forty a month."

"Maybe so, Dusty, but you'll have a place of your own like this someday," Lila said, her earnest little face turned to mine. "I know you will."

I bent and kissed her then and said, "I hope you're right."

Lila nodded, her chin determined. "I know I'm right."

Ma Prather, her hand shading her eyes

from the afternoon sun, saw us coming from a long way off. She had the Texan's ability to see clearly across vast distances of country, yet without her spectacles she couldn't read the label on a peach can, and that right close-up.

Ma waited until I reined up in front of the house and let Lila hop down from the saddle. Then, stiff and sore, my shoulder throbbing, I swung off the paint my ownself and Ma ran into my arms. I hugged her close, enjoying the plump, solid feel of her and the remembered scent of lavender water and newly baked apple turnovers.

"Ma," I said, after I finally disentangled myself and Ma had dabbed at her eyes a time or two with a tiny lace handkerchief, "this here is Lila Tryon. We met on the trail and her pa was killed yesterday" — I hesitated, suddenly tired beyond belief — "or the day before — the days keep running one into the other."

"Yesterday," Lila said.

"Oh, you poor little thing!" Ma exclaimed. And such was her caring nature, she grabbed Lila in her strong arms and hugged her close. "Child, you look worn-out," she said. "A warm bath for you and then some good, solid food to put some meat on those poor bones."

I stepped to the paint and fetched the saddlebags.

Ma was holding Lila's hand in hers and her little lace handkerchief was mighty busy again.

"Ma," I said, trying to find the words, but discovering there was no easy way around it, "this is the money from the sale of the herd, but I have bad news concerning Mr. Prather. He's —"

Ma surprised me then. "Oh, I know all about it, Dusty," she said. "The sheriff in Sweetwater sent a rider out here a week ago with a wire from a Dr. Wilson in Dodge. The doctor said Simon is recovering just fine and he expects him to ride the rail cars home no later than the fall."

Silently, sad, stoop-shouldered Jim Meldrum stepped beside me and stuck out his hand. "Welcome home, Dusty."

He gave me no smile, as was his way, but I took Meldrum's hand, and after we shook, the puncher turned to Ma. "Miz Prather, if I'm not mistaken, I'd say this boy has a story to tell. And he's hurt."

Alarm flared in Ma's hazel eyes. "Hurt? Dusty, where?"

Meldrum answered for me. "Left shoulder, high up. He favors it some."

Before he hired on with the SP ten years before and hung up his Colts, Meldrum had been a Mississippi gambler and a gun handler of no small reputation. His survival had once depended on noticing little things like a man's stiff shoulder, and his experienced eye had quickly spotted what I'd been so anxious to hide.

"It's nothing, Ma," I said. "It's healing over real good."

Ma Prather looked me up and down real close, quickly taking in my exhausted appearance and the telltale swell of the bandage under my shirt. "Jim," she said, "help Dusty into the house." And to me: "Young man, you're going to bed."

Me, I was suddenly too tuckered out to argue. I handed Meldrum the saddlebags and warned him to take care of them real well; then I followed Ma and Lila into the house.

I woke in a soft bed in a room with flowered paper on the walls, an oil lamp burning pale yellow on the table beside me. Outside, beyond the window, it was growing dark and I reckoned I must have been asleep for five or six hours.

When I turned on the pillow, I found myself looking into the whiskered, whiskey-reddened face of Charlie Fullerton, Ma's personal cook, a trained chef who doubled as the chuck wagon biscuit shooter during spring roundups.

"How you feeling, boy?" Charlie asked. His eyes carefully searched mine as though to find the answer written there.

"Better," I said. I looked down at the fresh bandage on my shoulder. "Who fixed me up?"

"I did," Charlie said. "After you told Ma about Lafe Wingo an' them, I put some stuff on your misery that stung and some that didn't, but you was already asleep so you didn't know the difference." He came closer to me and I could smell the whiskey on him. "You hungry, boy?"

Suddenly I realized I was ravenous.

"Mr. Fullerton," I said, which was how we punchers addressed cooks back then, since they could serve up some mighty miserable chuck if we didn't, "I'd like a thick steak, six fried eggs and maybe twice that number of biscuits. And honey if you got it."

Charlie looked at me suspiciously. "What's the matter, boy, off your feed?"

"No, in fact —"

"How 'bout a couple of steaks, a dozen eggs and half a loaf of fried sourdough?"

"Sounds perfect, Mr. Fullerton." I raised myself into a sitting position. "Have Ma and Lila eaten yet?"

"An hour ago. Now they're drinking tea in the parlor and talking them female pretties. If'n you have a mind to join them, I'll bring in your grub."

Charlie turned to go, but I stopped him. "Mr. Fullerton, have you seen anything of Apaches?"

The cook turned, his face suddenly drawn and concerned. "Dusty, Victorio's main bunch attacked the Jurgunsen place day afore yesstidy. Tom Jurgunsen and his boy, Jacob, was killed, and Miz Jurgunsen took a bullet in the back and ain't expected to live."

Charlie took a step closer to me. "Miz Prather is mighty worried. The Jurgunsen spread is only a few miles north of here, and that's why she has Deke Stockton out scouting around right now. There's only you, Deke, Jim Meldrum and myself to defend this place if'n the Apaches hit us. Deke is a fair hand with a rifle, but Meldrum now, he hasn't picked up a gun in a ten year, says he don't hold with shootin' and killin' no more."

"I think Jim will change his mind right quick if Victorio hits us," I said.

If Ma was worried, she must've figured she'd good cause. She was a woman who didn't scare easy. Back in the old days, she'd stood shoulder to shoulder with her husband a dozen times and used her Sharps rifle to fight off raiding parties of Kiowa and Comanche, to say nothing of rustlers.

But Apaches were a different proposition entirely. Victorio wasn't here to hit and run. He had declared war on the United States and was determined to stay. If he chose to attack the SP, few as we were, Ma, Lila and the rest of us were in a heap of trouble.

After Charlie left, I put on my hat, got dressed in the clean shirt and pants Ma had laid out for me and stomped into my boots. Ma didn't hold with wearing guns in the house, so I slid the Colt out of the holster and stuck it in my waistband at the small of my back.

Stepping quietly, I crept downstairs and saw to my relief that the door to the parlor was closed. I tiptoed past and walked out the front door and into the gathering darkness.

A slight rain pattered around me as I stood quiet and still and listened to the night sounds. High above, the horned moon showed its face only now and again as black clouds scudded past. I was still weak from loss of blood but not near so tired, and whatever concoctions Charlie had put on my wound had helped, because my shoulder wasn't so stiff and didn't hurt as bad.

I stood in the shadows for a while, saw and heard nothing, then walked along the front of the house to the corral, a dozen horses turning to look at me as I passed. Twice I stopped and listened, but heard only the soft fall of the rain and the sigh of the free, unbranded wind.

I stepped over to the bunkhouse but the place was dark, so I turned on my heel and began to make my way back to the house again.

I'd only gone a few yards when I heard a muffled footstep behind me. I turned quickly, drawing the Colt from my waistband.

Jim Meldrum stood there, two well-worn revolvers in shoulder holsters hung on each side of his narrow chest.

The man made no move toward his hardware but gave me one of his rare smiles, his teeth showing white in the darkness under his mustache. "Fast, Dusty. Mighty fast and smooth."

I lowered the Colt, letting out my pent-up breath in a relieved hiss. "Hell, Jim, you scared me out of a year's growth," I said.

Meldrum nodded. "Sorry about that. But Deke Stockton hasn't come in yet, and that's a worrisome thing."

"I thought you'd hung up your guns forever, Jim," I said. I'd never seen Meldrum wear his Colts before, but he looked like he was born to them, as though they were an essential part of him.

The lanky puncher shrugged. "Like you, like Deke, I ride for the brand. I've been thinking things over, and if there's shooting to be done, and killing, I'll do it. I may not like it, but I'll do it."

Like every puncher I ever knew, Meldrum's first loyalty was to the ranch, but you don't buy devotion like that for forty a month. To a man like Meldrum, the ranch was not an area of land, of pastures, rivers and forests, but a principle and a way of life. He believed in that principle and that way of life and held the unshakable opinion that it was worth preserving, worth fighting for and even worth dying for. This was the wellspring of his loyalty and what sustained it through good times and bad. Had Meldrum thought otherwise, he would have been spitting on his own life and mine, rendering them both pointless, useless, without reason or purpose.

"Well, I got to get back to the house," I said finally. "Mr. Fullerton will be powerful mad if I don't show up for my grub."

"One more thing, Dusty," Meldrum said, taking a step closer to me. "A word of warning: Lafe Wingo, the man you were telling us about, won't let go of thirty thousand so easily."

"You know him?"

"I know him. Seen him work one time up in Denver. He's good with a gun, maybe the best there is around."

My fingers strayed to my wounded shoulder. "I can testify to that."

"Just step carefully and keep your eyes open. Wingo will come here, to the SP, depend on it."

"Jim, you'll stand with me if that happens?"

"*When* it happens." Meldrum glanced up at the threatening sky, rain falling on the sharp planes of his hard-boned face. Then he lowered his head and looked at me, his eyes bleak. "I'll stand with the SP Connected, Dusty. But there's something you ought to know: I'm handy with a gun my ownself, but I'm not near good enough to shade Lafe Wingo." His cold gray eyes probed mine, searching deep. "Are you?"

I tried to make light of it and grinned. "I wasn't the last time we met."

Meldrum didn't smile in return. "Then best you get in some practice." His face was drawn, his mouth pinched. "I've a feeling you're going to need it."

The rain was falling harder as I walked back to the house, Meldrum's warning lying heavy on me. I felt tight and strange inside, knowing that the last thing I wanted was to meet Lafe Wingo in another gun-fight.

Now that Ma had the thirty thousand and the ranch could get out from under the bankers, I'd thought the entire affair with all its blood and death was over. But if Meldrum was right, it wasn't over . . . not by a long shot.

It was just beginning.

When I stepped into the parlor, Ma and Lila sat on each side of a burning log fire, each holding a dainty cup and saucer in her hands.

Ma, who had retained much of the frugality of her early, hardscrabble years, had kept every dress she'd ever owned, at least those that weren't too worn-out. Lila was wearing a gown of pale blue gingham that Ma must have bought when she was younger and a lot slimmer, and the girl's black hair was pulled back from her face with a bow of darker blue.

The sight of her made my breath catch in my throat and as I sat on the chair that Ma indicated, I heard my heartbeat hammer in my ears.

Lila Tryon wasn't just pretty like Sally Coleman. She had a dark, flashing beauty that Sally could never match, the kind that made a man look twice . . . and then, all unbelieving, look again.

"Dusty," Ma said, after I'd finally settled into my chair, "Lila tells me she wants to get to her ranch as soon as possible."

Before I could answer, Lila said quietly and insistently: "It's a farm, Mrs. Prather."

Ma smiled at the girl. "Lila, you must call me Ma — everyone else does." Then, revealing her natural prejudices as a cattleman's wife, she added, maybe a little too sweetly: "This is ranching country, my dear."

Lila opened her mouth to speak, but I jumped in quickly to keep the peace. "Ma, I already told Lila she can't go to her . . . place until the Apaches are rounded up."

Ma nodded, brushing a strand of gray hair away from one red apple cheek. "That dreadful Victorio, I'll be so glad when the army finally catches him." She looked at me, her brownish-green eyes troubled. "Dusty, did you hear about Tom Jurgunsen?"

I nodded. "Uh-huh. Mr. Fullerton told me."

As if she hadn't heard, Ma continued. "Tom gone, and his handsome young son, and Betty not expected to live. It's just so terrible."

Hooves sounded outside and Ma glanced toward the window. "That must be Deke. I sent him out to scout around for any sign of Apaches." She rose to her feet and laid her cup and saucer on the table. "I'll go hear what he has to tell me."

I was about to say I'd join her, but the door opened and Charlie walked in, holding a tray heaped high with food. "Ah," Ma said, "and here's Mr. Fullerton just in time." She studied the tray closely, nodded her approval and said: "Eat hearty, Dusty. I'll be back soon."

The food was good and I was hungry and for a while the only sound was the clink of my fork on the plate. Finally, after eating most of two steaks, seven eggs and several slabs of bread, I had to admit defeat. I sighed and placed the tray on the table beside me.

"Did you enjoy that?" Lila asked, one eyebrow arching.

"Sure did."

"I've never seen one man eat so much."

I smiled at her. "What did you eat, Lila?"

"Why, I" — she hesitated — "well, not nearly as much as you did, I can tell you that." Lila looked at me, frowning a little. "Dusty, I meant what I said when I told Ma I want to go to my own place. It's the end of one journey for me, and the beginning of another that I'm anxious to start. I can't stay here dependent on Ma's charity."

"Lila, it's not charity. Ma will love having you here. She never had any children her ownself and she'll treat you like a daughter."

Lila nodded. "She already has. But I still want my own home."

I rose to my feet, needful of a smoke, knowing tobacco in any form was another thing Ma would not tolerate in the house. "I'll go talk to Deke Stockton. If he didn't come across any Apache sign, maybe we can ride out to your place tomorrow."

Lila rose and came into my arms. "Thank you, Dusty. It will mean so much to me."

I kissed her lightly on the cheek, then

stepped outside and walked to the bunk-house, Lila's warm woman smell still lingering in my consciousness.

When I stepped inside, Deke was sitting on a bunk, smoking. I looked around and saw that Jim had already moved in pretty Sally Coleman's very much battered and torn Dodge City bonnet, my blanket roll, yellow slicker and booted Winchester.

This was just as well because I didn't want to sleep in the house anymore. Ma's brand of fussing and her soft feather beds could weaken a man.

Deke looked up as I came inside, letting in a gust of rain and wind, and he waved a limp hand in careless greeting in my direction.

Deke Stockton was a man of about my height and size and maybe ten years older. He was a good hand but pinched and sour, all tight-mouthed and closed in on himself. Yet horses, dogs and little children were attracted to him and he to them, a thing I could never understand.

"Howdy, Deke," I said. "Heard you ride in."

The man nodded. "Getting wet out there."

"I'd say so." I waited a spell, then asked: "See any Apache sign?"

Deke shook his head. "Like I told Miz Prather, I rode as far as Cottonwood Creek, then doubled back to the Deepwater and saw nary a thing. After that, I made a wide loop around the ranch. Apart from an old bull elk I surprised up in the hills north of here, I saw nothing."

"Think Victorio has pulled his freight?" I asked.

Deke shrugged. "Who can tell? You know how it is with Apaches. I could have rode right past a passel of them and never even knowed it." He looked up at me. "Hear tell you had a brush or two with Apaches your ownself."

"Sure did," I said. "And all I want now is to stay well away from them."

Deke rose stiffly to his feet and ground out his cigarette under his heel. "Seems to me that around these parts, that's getting mighty hard to do."

The puncher stepped to the door and opened it wide, looking out morosely at the slanting rain. "I got to see to my horse," he said. "Mind if I borry your slicker?"

"Go right ahead," I said. "I reckon I'll turn in."

I watched Deke shrug into my coat, then step outside.

A few moments later a single rifle shot shattered the evening quiet, its ringing racket clamoring around the corrals and buildings of the SP like the hammer of an angry god on an anvil.

Chapter 20

I grabbed my rifle and rushed outside. Jim Meldrum was running from the barn, a Colt in each hand.

"What happened?" he yelled.

But I made no answer, because Deke Stockton was lying facedown on the ground a few yards away, his hat tumbling past the corral, blown by the wind.

I ran to Deke and turned the man over. His eyes were wide-open, but he was beyond seeing anything. A bullet had crashed into his forehead, about where his hatband began. He must have been dead when he hit the ground.

Meldrum stood beside me, looking down at the dead man. "Apaches?"

I shook my head at him. "Jim, Deke was wearing my slicker."

I rose to my feet in time to see the dawning realization on Meldrum's face. "Lafe Wingo," he whispered.

"And he's still out there," I said.

Ma and Lila were standing on the porch

of the house, looking over at us, their faces pale, bodies stiff with shock.

I turned and stepped quickly toward the barn. "Where are you going?" Meldrum called out after me.

"After Wingo."

"I'll come with you."

"No," I threw over my shoulder. "You stay close to Lila and Ma."

I figured the paint was still worn-out, so I threw my saddle on a lineback dun and left the barn at a lope. Tired as I was, weak as I felt, I had to go after Wingo. He'd killed once and he could already be setting up to kill again.

In the first hour, I rode around the ranch, each time widening my loop across that dark, open country. There were a few cottonwoods growing along the stream-beds and a scattering of post oak, mesquite, pinon and some juniper on the slopes of the low hills, but little else by way of trees.

I passed a couple of small herds of bunched cows, all of them wearing the SP Connected brand, and they seemed to be in good shape. A few already had calves on the ground and the range grass itself looked fair to middling for this early in the summer.

As the rain lessened, I rode under a solitary mountain mahogany on the slope of a shallow saddleback and rolled a cigarette. I looked around, but all I saw was darkness. The night was very quiet and now the rain had gentled, its small sound lost as it fell on the grass.

Cupping my hands to avoid the flare of the match being seen by watchful eyes, I lit the cigarette and sat the dun, smoking for a while.

Nothing stirred.

After five minutes, I stubbed out the cigarette on the side of my bootheel and tossed the dead butt into the wet grass. Then I spurred the dun and once again took to the flat.

I spent another hour backtracking the way I'd come earlier, and finally I doubled back and rode to the rise where Lila had gotten her first glimpse of the ranch.

Swinging out of the saddle, I eased the girth on the dun and let him graze. Below me, I saw only darkness. Meldrum, being no pilgrim in such matters, must have ordered Ma and Lila to douse the house oil lamps.

Finally, as a weird and lonesome coyote called, cursing his endless hunger and his harsh fate, I tightened the girth again and stepped back into the saddle.

A few minutes later I rode into the ranch, wet, tired and mighty dispirited. If it had been Wingo who'd shot Deke Stockton, he'd gotten away clean.

And now the gunman presented a danger more immediate and more deadly than even that of Victorio and his Apaches. Come daylight, Wingo could lie hidden with his sharpshooter's rifle and pick us off one by one, then ride in and take the money — and Lila.

I put up the dun, rubbed him down with a piece of sacking and threw him a handful of oats, then returned to the bunkhouse.

Jim Meldrum was waiting up for me, still wearing his guns. "See anything?"

Too tired and too upset to reply, I just shook my head at him.

Meldrum took it in stride. "Miz Lila stopped by, wanted to know if you'd come back. She's some worried."

Exhausted and out of sorts as I was, foolish thoughts of Lila crowded into my numb brain and I figured I wouldn't be able to sleep until I saw her.

I settled my gun belt around my hips and left the bunkhouse and walked over to the house. Lila was sitting on a rocker on the porch when I got there. She was dressed in a blue robe and the bluer shadows of the night.

When I stepped up onto the porch, she stood and fell into my arms. "Dusty, I was so worried about you."

I held Lila close and kissed her. "I scouted the whole area and saw nothing," I said, after reluctantly taking my lips from hers. Then, to ease her mind: "If it was Wingo, he's long gone."

The rain had stopped and I looked up at a tattered sky, where the moon was rounding up the last straggling clouds. "It's getting late, Lila," I said. "Best you get to bed."

Lila nodded, but her eyes were guarded.

"What's wrong?" I asked.

The girl put her arms around my waist and turned up her face to mine. "Ma and Mr. Fullerton have Deke Stockton laid out in the kitchen. They're washing his body because Ma says a man should be clean when he goes to meet his Maker."

Lila held me closer as though I might push her away. "Dusty, please don't ask me to go in there. Not yet."

I smiled at her, trying to calm her fears with whatever small wisdom I possessed. "Lila, just remember that the body in there isn't Deke Stockton, and it never was.

What was Deke Stockton can't die. It still lives, and it will go on living forever." I shrugged. "At least, that's what I believe."

"Maybe so," Lila said, "but I still don't want to see a dead man lying like that, looking like a column of white-and-blue marble, all covered with soap and water."

I realized further argument was useless. And so it was that Lila and me sat side by side on rockers, holding hands, dozing off and on as the long night gathered around us. Then morning came at last and chased away the shadows and over to the chicken coop Ma's gaudy rooster paused in his proud strutting to get up on his tiptoes and crow a welcome to the reborn day.

Before breakfast we buried Deke Stockton, and Ma said the words, reading from Simon Prather's well-worn Bible.

Deke was laid to rest like many a puncher before him, with little talk and a minimum of ceremony in a six-by-three grave well away from the house.

But back at the corral the restless horses reared and snorted and tossed their heads and kicked up clods of mud and the ranch dogs howled like wolves, their lips pulled back from their teeth. And even the big orange tomcat, a cold and callous rat killer, glided from the underbrush and sat for long minutes, looking over at Deke's grave with unblinking eyes that burned like amber fire.

I felt no grief for Deke Stockton because I hardly knew the man, but the animals mourned his passing and that was something I have no way of explaining.

After breakfast, Lila insisted that she wanted to visit her farm that very day. At first Ma and me tried to talk her out of it, but since there was no sign of Apaches in the area, we finally relented.

Lafe Wingo was very much on my mind, but Jim Meldrum figured if I rode real careful and paid attention to what was going on around me, the gunman would not attempt a play by daylight in open country.

It was a small enough reassurance, but I was determined that no tinhorn killer like Wingo was going to dictate how I led my life.

Lila had a penciled map of her place over by Cottonwood Creek, drawn by her pa's brother, and it would be easy to find.

"Two hours' ride, Lila," I said. "No more than that."

I saddled the lineback for Lila and then the paint. Ma told us we should make a picnic of it, and gave me a basket that I tied behind the dun's saddle.

We headed out under a clear blue sky, all sign of last night's rain gone. The land between the SP Connected and Lila's spread was flat, open grass country, here and there shallow rises crowned with mesquite and juniper breaking up the monotony. The recent rains had turned the prairie green and we rode through masses of bluebonnets and long streaks of yellow mustard that stretched for miles in every direction.

The sun had still not reached the highest point in the sky when we found Lila's place, a stone cabin built beside a narrow stream, which I took to be an offshoot of the Cottonwood itself.

In front of the cabin spread out forty or fifty acres of open meadow with plenty of prime grass and beyond that sandier soil, dotted with mesquite and juniper.

I sat the paint and looked around. If Lila raised a herd here, the cattle could go as far as the creek to drink, then head back to the meadow to graze.

With good management of the available grass and some luck, I figured Lila's acres and the open range around them could easily support a hundred head and maybe more, enough for her to get by year to year if she was careful with her money.

As for Lila, she was turning her head this way and that, her eyes alive with wonder and excitement.

"Dusty, I can't believe I'm actually here," she said. "I'm really on my own place."

I nodded. "You could build a good ranch here, Lila. The grass is good, there's water right close and, from what I can see, the cabin was built to last by someone who knew how."

"Let's go take a look inside," Lila said, spurring the lineback just as vehemently as she'd ignored my remark about ranching.

I followed her to the cabin and we stepped inside. The interior was thick with dust and a pack rat had made a nest in one corner, but Ned Tryon's brother had known a thing or three about building and he hadn't stinted on cost.

The floor was covered in smooth gray flagstones, all of them laid level, and the roof was solid, constructed of thick, weathered beams and good timber. A P.D. Beckwith iron stove, which must have cost all of thirty dollars, stood against one wall, and the table, chairs and bunk were store bought, as were the blue china plates, cups and saucers stacked on a shelf near a side window of the cabin.

All the wood, including a wide gun rack,

had matured to a deep honey color, and the floor was covered by a pair of colorful wool rugs.

The cabin had a warm, welcoming look. It was a down-homey place where a man could kick off his boots of an evening and stretch out his legs by the stone fireplace, knowing his own cows were grazing outside and that all was well with his world.

"Isn't it wonderful, Dusty?" Lila asked. I saw tears begin to start in her eyes and I knew she was thinking of her pa.

"Your pa's brother," I said, "what did he intend to do with the spread?"

"Do with it?" Lila looked puzzled. "Why he was going to live on it. Only, he died before he ever got a chance to enjoy it."

"Did he plan to farm?"

Lila shook her head. "No, he wrote Pa that he was going to raise cattle."

"Then he knew well that this wasn't farmland," I said.

Lila stepped to the window. "Look out there, Dusty. Can you see what I see?"

"Grass," I said.

"I see corn and fruit trees and maybe even pecans," Lila said, her eyes sparkling. "This will be a real farm one day."

"Lila," I said, trying to reason with her, "look at the soil out there. It's thin and it's dry and sandy. It will grow grass, at least most of the year, and maybe post oak, but it won't grow corn and . . . and . . . apples."

Lila looked at me, her face stiff, eyes blazing. "Then I surely must beg to differ, Mr. Hannah."

Well, I knew that every time she called me Mr. Hannah my biscuits were burning, so I backed off a step or two. "I guess time will tell, Lila," I said, backing down even more. I attempted a smile and tried to inject some heartiness into my voice. "Hey, isn't it time we ate?"

Lila's anger disappeared as quickly as it had come. "Yes, and let's eat in here — in my own home, Dusty."

"I'll bring in the basket," I said, and stepped outside.

As I untied the picnic basket from the back of the paint, I glanced around at the surrounding country — in time to see a single flash of light among the juniper and curly mesquite at the crest of a low rise to the south.

The flash was brief, just an instant of sunlight glinting on something reflective, a drop of rain on a leaf maybe . . . or on metal.

Pretending to be unconcerned, I strolled

back to the cabin with the basket, whistling through my teeth. I opened the door and stepped inside.

I dropped the basket on the table and smiled at Lila: "While you're getting the picnic things laid out, I'm going to ride out toward the creek a short ways," I said.

"Whatever for?" Lila asked. She opened the basket. "Ma, or Mr. Fullerton more likely, has done us proud. Fried chicken, fresh bread, a whole apple pie and . . . oh look, Dusty, a bottle of wine."

There's a time for explanations, but now wasn't that time. "It all looks mighty good," I said, "and I'm as hungry as a coyote with a toothache." Then, without any further explanation I opened the door. "Be right back."

"But . . . but . . ."

"Be right back," I said again. I stepped to the paint, swung into the saddle and turned south, in the direction where I'd seen the flash of light.

I was becoming more and more convinced the glare, brief as it was, had been no accident of nature. I believed I'd caught the glint of a gun barrel or a concho, and that could mean Apaches . . . or Lafe Wingo.

Whatever happened next, I knew I must

draw the danger away from the cabin and Lila.

But as it happened, that was a hasty, ill-conceived notion, and it turned out to be one of the biggest mistakes I ever made in my life.

Chapter 21

I knew Lila would be standing at the cabin door, watching me go. I turned and there she was, her hands on her hips, her head tilted to one side in complete bafflement. I waved, and kept on riding.

Me, I never thought of myself as an especially brave man, but at the same time I figured I was no coward. All I knew was that I didn't want Wingo, or the Apaches, trapping Lila and me inside the cabin.

The walls were stout — that was sure — but if a body had a mind to, he could keep us pinned up in there until the contents of the picnic basket ran out and we'd be forced to make a break for it — and then, out in the open, we'd be sitting ducks.

Ma and Jim Meldrum wouldn't come looking for us either, at least not for a few days, thinking Lila and me had stayed on at the cabin to get the place ready.

I figured the path I'd chosen was the right one. Better to meet the danger, whatever it was, head on and get it over with, hopefully to my advantage.

I rode across the meadow, the paint knee-deep in grass and bluebonnets, and the only sound was the buzz of insects and the faint whisper of the wind.

The sun was now straight above me in the sky and the day was hot. When I cleared the meadow I reined in and listened — for what I did not know. I took off my hat and wiped my sweaty brow with the sleeve of my shirt, my eyes scanning everywhere around me.

But the land lay still and nothing moved under the burning sun, the jangle of the paint's bit chiming loud in the quiet as he tossed his head against flies.

To the south lay the vast limestone bedrock of the Edwards Plateau. But even this far north, a few narrow veins of limestone ran under the prairie, now and then jutting dramatically above the flat grassland, the rock carved into fantastic shapes by the action of wind and rain.

The rise where I'd seen the gleam of light lay just ahead of me and I replaced my hat and slid the Winchester from the boot. Riding even more warily, I found, near the foot of the low hill, a narrow patch of brush and scrub oak that offered a chance of concealment.

I swung out of the saddle and pulled the paint into the brush. The hill, if you could call it that, was very shallow, rising no more than forty feet above the plain, studded with mesquite and juniper, brilliant swathes of bluebonnets growing here and there among the grass.

I whispered gently to the horse and led him into the brush. Then I stepped onto the slope, rifle at the ready. Moving carefully from one patch of brush to another, I made my way to the crest and got a big surprise. The top of the hill was only about ten yards wide before it sloped away on all sides to form a ridged horseshoe shape below on the plain, enclosing about ten acres of flat land.

Glancing around, I saw no immediate sign that anyone had been up there. But as I scouted around and kneeled to examine the ground more closely, I noticed a small rock had been displaced, lying on its side, revealing some damp earth where it had once lain.

Somebody had been up here very recently — and I was sure I'd seen the glint of the sun on his rifle.

I stood and looked back at the cabin about a mile behind me. The dun still stood, hip shot, outside the cabin, but I saw no sign of Lila.

From where I was on the crest of the rise I had an excellent vantage point to study the land around me. But I noticed no tell-tale dust or other evidence that anyone or anything was moving out there.

To the south, toward the Edwards Plateau, sky and land merged together in a blue-gray haze, and when I turned to the north, the prairie stretched away from me, green, flat and seemingly empty of life.

Whoever had been up here, Apache or Lafe Wingo, he was gone now.

I squatted on my heels and built a smoke, letting the tensions of the last few minutes slowly ease out of me.

When I finished the cigarette I rose and ground the stub out under my heel.

It was time to return to the cabin. Lila would be getting worried.

I turned my steps back down the hill and hit the ground fast as the blast of a rifle shot thundered across the afternoon quiet.

Instinctively my eyes went to the cabin, in time to see a puff of smoke drift away in the breeze from one of the windows.

Then I heard the paint crashing around in the brush, screaming.

I took the slope of the hill at a fast run, dove for the patch of brush and rolled, coming up fast on one knee, facing the cabin.

Frightened by the sudden gunfire, the dun had trotted away a few steps from the cabin, but was now grazing near the stream. I saw nothing moving behind any of the windows.

The paint was down, kicking, and I stepped beside him. His left front leg had been shattered by the rifle bullet just below the knee and his eyes were rolling white and scared, blood spattering me from his ruined leg. I did what I had to do. I put the muzzle of the Winchester close to his head and pulled the trigger. The paint kicked once and lay still.

He'd been a good cow pony, that paint, and he'd deserved a better fate.

It could only have been Lafe Wingo who fired from the cabin. I reckoned he'd hit the paint's leg at a distance of almost a mile, an expert marksman's shot.

A rising rage burning in me, I ran toward the cabin, stopping now and then to take advantage of whatever meager cover was available. I knew the closer I got, the more vulnerable I became to Wingo's rifle, but the paint's death and my concern for Lila made me throw caution to the wind.

I moved closer to the cabin, my rifle up

and ready. But no bullets came in my direction.

I crawled the last hundred yards to the cabin on my belly, pushing the Winchester out in front of me. The sun was beating down, hot on my back, and once I wriggled through a cloud of bluebonnets, sending up swarms of tiny flies.

When I reached the wall of the cabin, I stepped carefully toward the door. I reached out with the barrel of the Winchester and the door swung open easily.

Moving carefully, I set the rifle down against the stone wall, and slipped the thong off the hammer of my Colt.

It was now or never.

I shucked the revolver and sprang in front of the door, hearing the clamoring hammer of my own heartbeats in my ears.

"Wingo! Get out here!" I yelled.

All I heard in return was a mocking silence.

The cabin was empty.

Cautiously, I stepped inside and looked around, the Colt in my fist, with its hammer back and ready. There was no sign of a struggle and the food from the picnic basket lay spread out, untouched, on a gingham cloth on the table.

On the floor under the window lay a

single empty rifle casing. I picked up the brass shell. It was .50-90 Sharps caliber. Wingo had shown the professional gunman's usual prudence, taking time to reload his rifle after he'd killed the paint.

But why kill the horse and not me? I'd been an open target up there on the hill and Wingo had demonstrated that he had the rifle skill to drop me.

That question was answered when I found something I'd overlooked when I first stepped into the cabin.

Propped up on top of the mantel of the fireplace was a handwritten note, scrawled with pencil on a page torn from a tally book. A single, quick reading of the words told me all I had to know.

BRING THE 30 THOUSAND HERE TO THE CABIN BEFORE NOON TOMORROW OR THE GIRL DIES. P.S. COME ALONE OR I'LL KILL HER FOR DAMN SURE.

I stood there for long moments, staring at that scrap of paper, my own guilt and my dreadful fear for Lila icing my insides.

The girl had trusted me!

Lila had seen me hastily ride away just before Lafe Wingo arrived. Did she think

I'd run out on her to save my own skin and left her to the wolves?

What else could she think?

I figured Wingo had been up on the hill, and he let me see sunlight flash on his rifle or on the silver ornaments he wore. Then he had ridden down the other side and swung wide to approach the cabin from behind. By the time I'd reached the hill and had a good view of the surrounding country he had already made his move.

Wingo was a sure-thing killer who made a living shooting from ambush. He knew how to take advantage of every scrap of cover and had melted into the surrounding low hills and brush like a hungry cougar.

The gunman had outfoxed me every step of the way, and Lila was the one who'd paid for it.

She might have still been outside the cabin when Wingo arrived and he'd surprised her so completely she didn't even get a chance to cry out.

She'd trusted me and I'd betrayed that trust. And that thought was like a stake through my heart.

Me, I've never been what you'd call a drinking man, but now I picked up the bottle of wine, knocked the top off and sat with it on the stoop of the cabin.

It took me an hour to finish the bottle, and when it was empty and I tossed it away, I felt no better. And maybe a lot worse.

Feeling sick and light-headed, I caught up the dun and it took me several attempts, my foot slipping out of the stirrup, before I clambered into the saddle. I rode back to where the paint lay, and retrieved my own saddle and bridle, then swung the dun toward the SP.

As I rode, the afternoon light began to wane, shading slowly into dusk. Above me, a pale lemon sky was streaked with scarlet and out among the shallow, shadowed hills the shameless coyotes were already talking.

Many thoughts crowded into my alcohol-fuddled brain, each one loudly clamoring for attention.

But one called out louder than all the rest.

I would not ask Ma Prather for the thirty thousand dollars. That money, earned hard, was all that stood between the SP Connected and ruin.

I would have to find another way.

If there was another way.

Chapter 22

When I was half a mile from the ranch, I stopped at a small creek, swung out of the saddle, lay flat on my belly and splashed water over my face and neck. I wet my unruly hair and combed it down flat and then remounted the dun.

Thankfully, my brain felt less fuzzy and I'd stopped seeing two of everything.

And that was probably just as well, because as I rode into the SP, Jim Meldrum was standing outside the bunkhouse, the eager, impatient way he watched me come telling me he had news.

When I reined up, Meldrum gave me a grin and a wink and told me pretty Sally Coleman was in the house, talking to Ma.

"She's got something to say to you, Dusty," the puncher said.

"What is it?" I asked.

Meldrum shook his head. "Best you hear that for yourself." He gave me another knowing wink and said, "I'll put up your horse."

Right at that moment, I didn't want to talk to Sally. I didn't want to talk to anybody, even Meldrum when he stopped on his way to the barn and asked: "Where's Lila? Did she stay on at her place?"

"Later, Jim," I said. "After Sally leaves."

"You going to take the bonnet you bought for her?" Meldrum asked, an odd, amused light in his eyes.

I shook my head. "Later for that too."

"Maybe it's just as well," Meldrum threw over his shoulder at me as he walked away, and I heard him chuckle to himself.

Now what had he meant by that remark?

I had no time to ponder the question. There was a smart-looking surrey, with a bay horse in the traces, standing outside the house and I swallowed hard and stepped toward the door.

I wasn't in the mood to be a-courting pretty Sally Coleman, but I had to talk to Ma in private. Better to get it over with.

When I reached the porch I took off my hat and smoothed down my hair and then stepped inside. Charlie Fullerton met me in the hallway and nodded to the parlor's closed door. "In there."

I saw it again! Exactly the same amused expression in Charlie's eyes that I'd seen in Jim Meldrum's.

What was going on? And what did Sally want to tell me?

I hesitated at the door and Charlie smiled and said again: "In there, Dusty."

I nodded, took a deep breath and stepped inside.

Sally was sitting on the same chair that Lila had sat in and one thing was immediately apparent — she was almighty big in the belly.

Standing, one arm on the fireplace mantel, grinning like a possum, stood tall, lanky Ethan Noon, one of the Coleman hands. I'd never cottoned to Noon much. The man had no chin, a huge, bobbing Adam's apple and long yellow buckteeth. Noon had a hee-haw laugh that made him sound like a loco mule and he had a habit of stamping a foot and slapping his thigh when something amused him, which was often.

When I walked into the room, Sally smiled and rose to her feet, her hands extended to me. "Dusty," she said, "how very nice to see you again."

I took Sally's hands and kissed her on the cheek, and over by the fireplace, Noon slapped his thigh and gave his hee-haw laugh.

"Sally has brought us some wonderful

news, Dusty," Ma said, her face revealing nothing. "She and Ethan got married three days ago."

Glancing at Sally's swelling stomach under her dress, I figured the nuptials had been just in the nick of time.

Sally still held on to my hands and her eyes moistened a little. "Oh, Dusty, I'm so sorry. You see, after you left with the herds, I fell head over heels in love with Ethan. It all happened so sudden that I simply couldn't help myself." She looked up at me, her face earnest. "Dusty, can you ever forgive me? I know what a terrible shock and disappointment all this must be to you, but please, please try to understand."

I caught Ma's amused smile, as I said, lying just a little: "Disappointed, yes, but I'm happy for you, Sally." I looked over at Noon. "And you too, Ethan."

Sally giggled and Noon hee-hawed several times and slapped his thigh. "The best man won, Dusty, an' no mistake."

Now normally a challenge like that would have earned Noon my fist to his nonexistent chin, but I was happy to let it go.

Compared to Lila, Sally Coleman looked colorless and washed out, her skin and hair the same shade of white, her eyes more rain cloud gray than blue. In her brown woolen dress she looked dowdy and plain, a corn sack tied in the middle. Gone were the red, blue or green ribbons I'd admired so much and the tightly curled ringlets that bounced on her shoulders. In their place was hair scraped straight back from the face in a severe bun, pinned in place by a long steel spike. She looked like a girl consciously trying to become a mature woman before her time and the only thing that remained of the Sally I'd once known was the giggle, still high-pitched, strident and silly.

Once I'd thought myself madly in love with Sally Coleman. Now I wondered what I'd ever seen in her.

"Well," Ma said, rising to her feet, "this calls for a celebration. I believe I can find a bottle of champagne for us."

"Ma," I said quickly. When she turned to look at me, I shook my head. "We have to talk, urgently."

Ma Prather was a perceptive woman. She knew something must be terribly wrong, something that required her attention and was far more important than Sally Coleman and her marriage.

"Lordy, Sally and Ethan," she said, "I guess we'll have to postpone the champagne. I think Dusty here has pressing range matters to discuss."

Noon disengaged himself from the fireplace, and stood there grinning, all hands, feet and stoop shoulders. "That don't make no never mind, Mrs. P," he said. "Me and Sally have to be moving along anyhow." He glanced over at me, a barb glinting in his muddy eyes. "We like to get to bed really early o' nights."

Sally giggled and Noon hee-hawed, and Ma, sensing my urgency, hustled the pair to the door.

After farewells that took a lot longer than they should have, Sally and Noon climbed into the surrey and soon its bobbing sidelights were heading down the trail in the direction of the Coleman ranch.

"What's happened?" Ma asked, her hand on my arm. "Is it Lila?"

I nodded. "We better go inside and talk and I think Jim Meldrum and Mr. Fullerton should hear this too."

I gave Ma my arm and led her into the parlor and when Meldrum and Charlie arrived I told them how I'd been bushwhacked by Lafe Wingo, and Lila taken. I took out the note Wingo had left and passed it to Ma. "This says it all."

Ma fetched her spectacles and read, her

face paling with every word. I think she read the note several times before she finally laid it aside and said: "We have no choice. We must pay this man. Lila's life is more important than a two-by-twice ranch, so there can be no argument."

I shook my head at her. "Ma, you love this ranch. If you don't pay off the bankers they'll foreclose and you'll lose everything, including the chair you're sitting in and maybe even the clothes off your back."

"He's right, Miz Prather," Meldrum said, his long, melancholy face sadder than ever. "You and Mr. Prather built the SP with your own blood and sweat and then you held it against Kiowa and Comanche and white men who were worse than any of them and tried to take it from you." He rose to his feet and, in an uncharacteristic gesture, crossed the room and placed his hand on Ma's shoulder. "Dusty is right. You love this place and I can't stand by and see you throw it all away."

"Jim," Ma said, her voice very small, "saving a girl's life is not throwing it away."

Meldrum nodded. "I know that, but me and Dusty and Mr. Fullerton will just have to find another way." He looked over at me. "Any ideas?"

I shook my head. "Haven't studied on it, at least not yet."

"I'll study on it some my ownself," Meldrum said. He looked down at Ma again. "Now don't you go fretting none, Miz Prather. We'll get the girl back, safe and sound. There was a time when I was pretty good with a gun, you know."

Ma took the lanky puncher's hand, her eyes tearstained. "Jim, you left all that behind you. You told me you were all through with gunfighting."

"Times change," Meldrum said. "And sometimes, for better or worse, a man has to change right along with them."

Ma's eyes shifted to me. "Dusty, what will you do?"

"Get Lila back, Ma," I said. "Right now, that's all I know."

As to how that was going to happen, I had no idea. And judging by the tight, unhappy expression on Jim Meldrum's face, neither did he.

Despite Ma's final, tearful pleas to take the thirty thousand dollars, Meldrum and me rode out at long before daybreak, the saddlebags draped across the front of my saddle bulging — but with torn-up newspapers, not money.

We rode in silence for an hour; then Meldrum reined up his horse and hooked a long leg over the saddle horn. After he'd lit the cigarette, he eased a crick in his back and said: "Dusty, this is where we part company."

"What do you have in mind?" I asked.

"I'm going to loop around and injun up to the cabin before it gets light," he answered. "I'll stash my horse a ways from the cabin and come up on the place on foot. Maybe, if we're real lucky, when Wingo comes out to parley, if he does, I'll get me a chance to nail him."

I shook my head. "It's thin, mighty thin."

"Got a better idea?"

Meldrum's face under his hat brim was deep in shadow, and only when he drew on his cigarette and the tip glowed brighter did red light touch his beak of a nose and the planes of his high cheekbones.

I sat in silence, thinking things through, then said: "Jim, I've got nothing better. Your plan may not be nickel plated, but right now it's the only plan we have."

"Uh-huh, figured that," the puncher said. He sat his horse and I could feel his eyes on me. "Dusty, you may get lucky and Wingo will leave his rifle behind. He outdrawed you once, and maybe with his gunman's pride an' all he'll figure to do it again." Then, echoing what Bass Reeves had told me: "Just remember this, don't fall down the first time you're hit. Take the hits, stay on your feet and keep shooting back for as long as you're able." I heard Meldrum's low, humorless chuckle. "You may not be fast enough to outdraw ol' Lafe, but maybe you can outlast him."

I nodded, but realizing Meldrum couldn't see my head move in the darkness, said: "I'll remember." Right then I was mighty in need of reassurance, but Jim Meldrum, being a practical man, had not offered any, figuring he'd only be speaking weightless words, like so many dry leaves blowing in the wind.

We sat our horses until Meldrum finished his smoke, then built and smoked another.

Finally he shoved his boot back into the stirrup and touched the brim of his hat. *"Buena suerte, mi amigo."*

"You too, Jim. Good luck."

Meldrum swung his horse away and we parted company. I took the dim trail toward Lila's cabin under a dark, moonless sky with the night crowding around me close and warm as a cloak. The air smelled of grass and wildflowers, and I heard no voices. The night birds had long since ceased to call and even the coyotes had fallen silent.

When I was still a fifteen-minute ride from the cabin, I swung out of the saddle and stepped down in a stand of mixed juniper and mesquite by the side of a dry wash. I unsaddled the dun and watched him roll and then I fetched up to a rock near the wash and set my back to it. It was still shy of daybreak and maybe five hours until noon, so I closed my eyes, determined to catch up on some badly needed sleep.

The breeze whispered through the junipers and set them to rustling and the dun cropped grass, every now and then blowing through his nose. Somewhere an owl hooted, throwing no echo as the human voice does, and then the land closed in on itself again and became quiet.

Drowsily, I thought of Lila and her smile and there was a deep longing in me for her. What was she doing right now, as the clouds peeled back from the moon and the stars began to appear?

She was with Lafe Wingo!

Sleep fled from me, the thought chilling me to the bone. Wingo used and abused women like he did his horses, breaking them to his will with the whip. Was that even now happening to Lila?

I rose to my feet, filled with despair and impotent rage. I looked up and searched the moonlit heavens — and found only the cold, distant and aloof stars.

And no comfort.

Chapter 23

At daybreak I rose and stretched, working the stiffness out of my muscles. Mr. Fullerton had packed me a thick steak sandwich and a bottle of ginger beer and I ate and drank and then built a cigarette.

The scattering of butts around my feet grew in number as the morning progressed, and just before noon I saddled the dun and headed for the cabin.

Around me the wild land was being hammered into submission by the sun. The only living thing I saw was a tiny antelope fawn that limped from the thin shelter of a mesquite bush and hobbled quickly away from me, a wounded, stricken thing destined only for death.

I rode on, strangely disturbed. Maybe the fawn was an animal of ill omen, a warning to turn back. But that was something I could not do, my fate, for good or ill, as preordained and as inevitable as that of the fawn.

When the cabin came in view, Lafe

Wingo's horse was tethered outside, but I saw nothing of him or Lila.

I swung out of the saddle and took up my rifle and the saddlebags, choosing to go the rest of the way on foot, keeping to what little cover I could find.

When I was about a hundred yards from the cabin, I stopped beside a stunted juniper and yelled: "Wingo!"

A few moments of silence passed. Then the cabin door opened a crack and Wingo called out: "Did you bring the money?"

I held the saddlebags high enough so Wingo could see them clear.

"Come on in," the gunman hollered. "And leave the damn Winchester behind."

I propped the rifle against the branches of the juniper and walked slowly toward the cabin. Moving my head as little as possible I glanced around, but saw no sign of Jim Meldrum.

Sweat trickled down my back and my insides were knotted up with fear. I was out in the open and Wingo could gun me from the cabin window if he had a mind to.

But that concern was laid to rest when the big gunman, as brutal and arrogant as ever, stepped outside the cabin, holding Lila close to him.

The girl was deathly pale and a huge red

bruise swelled angrily on her left cheek-bone. Even from where I stood I could see that her eyes were haunted, circled by dark shadows.

I badly wanted to draw down on Wingo right then, but he was partly shielded by Lila and I couldn't take the chance of hitting her.

Wingo waved me forward. "Boy, get close enough to throw them saddlebags and then step back," he said.

I did as he told me and threw the saddlebags at his feet. I reckoned this might be my chance to get him in the clear, but he held Lila even closer as he bent and picked them up.

The gunman said something to Lila I couldn't hear, and the girl undid the rawhide ties of the bags and opened them. Wingo inclined his head and looked inside, and I saw the anger rise scarlet and immediate on his cheeks.

"Boy," he said, turning his cold eyes in my direction, "this was ill done." He threw Lila away from him and she sprawled heavily on the grass.

"I told you I'd kill you, boy, and now I will," Wingo said, his hand close to his gun. "And after you're dead, I'll go get the damned money my ownself."

He smiled, a cruel, vicious sneer. "Want me to tell you what I did to your woman last night, boy? Want me to tell you how much she enjoyed it?"

I knew what Wingo was doing. He was trying to keep me off balance, get me so riled up I couldn't think or shoot straight.

And he might have succeeded, because I was about to go for my gun — but Jim Meldrum chose that moment to make his play.

Rightly or wrongly, Meldrum lived by the unwritten code of the riverboat gambler and Southern gentleman. As the code dictated, he would not shoot at Wingo before calling him out. And he did that now.

The lanky puncher rose quickly out of the grass, his rifle in his hands, and yelled: "Wingo!"

Drawing as he turned, Wingo's gun came up with incredible speed. His shot roared a split second later and Meldrum, hit hard, took a step back, his rifle spinning away from him.

I made my draw as Meldrum went for his holstered Colt. Years without practice had taken its toll. He was slow, way too slow. His gun was still clearing the leather when Wingo shot him again.

Wingo didn't wait to see Meldrum fall.

337

He swung toward me, a triumphant grin stretching his mouth under his sweeping mustache. The Colt in my fist hammered and the gunman jerked as my bullet hit him. Wingo triggered his own gun. A miss. The lead sang past my left ear. I fired again and Wingo, hit a second time, staggered a couple of steps back and slammed against the cabin wall, his eyes wide with shock and disbelief. He had not expected me to be any kind of gunfighter and now I was reading to him from the Book. With growing horror, Wingo must have realized that the error of his ways was being writ loud and clear — in hot lead.

Her face pale and scared, Lila suddenly ran toward me and I yelled: "No, Lila! Go back!"

Wingo fired. Lila took the bullet, cried out, spun around, then fell.

My Colt hammered again. And again. Both bullets found their mark and blood splashed scarlet over the front of Wingo's buckskin shirt. The gunman shrieked his rage and staggered toward me, trying to raise a Colt that suddenly seemed too heavy for him.

"You . . . you . . ." he mumbled, his eyes wild, his lips peeling back from his teeth in a savage snarl.

I felt as cold as ice. I raised my gun to eye level, sighted, and fired.

The bullet crashed into the middle of Wingo's forehead and blew out the back of his skull, an obscene halo of blood and brain erupting scarlet in the air around him.

The gunman rose up on his toes, his eyes rolled back in his head, and then he crashed to the ground on his face.

I holstered my smoking Colt and ran to Lila, dropping on one knee beside her. She'd been hit in the back, high on her left shoulder and the bullet had gone all the way through, coming out just below her collarbone.

"Lila," I said, "can you hear me?"

The girl opened her eyes, and to my surprise, she managed a weak smile. "Carry me into my home, Dusty," she whispered.

I gathered Lila in my arms and carried her inside and laid her gently on the bunk, then sat beside her.

"Lila, I need to get you to the SP," I said, brushing a strand of hair away from her face. "We have to find you a doctor."

She nodded. "But take time first, Dusty," she said. "Take time to bury Jim Meldrum."

"I can do that later," I said. "Jim is dead,

and you're still alive. He would understand that your need comes first."

Lila shook her head. "Bury him, Dusty. Don't leave him to lie out here." She looked at me, her eyes pleading. "Jim died trying to save me. Years from now, I want to know that he lies here, that I did right by him."

"But you're losing blood, Lila," I protested. "We don't have time."

"I'll be all right," the girl said. "Take time, Dusty. Jim was a brave man. Bury him right. Please, Dusty, do it for me."

I rose slowly to my feet, knowing further argument was useless. "I'll do it, Lila. I'll bury him right, the way you say."

There was a question I had to ask, nagging at me like a bad toothache, yet I feared to ask it. But it was not the question I feared — it was the answer.

"Lila," I said, picking my words carefully, like a man chooses stepping-stones across a fast-running brook, "last night, did Wingo do anything. I mean, did he . . . ?"

"Dusty," Lila said, her voice slashing across mine like a knife, "don't ask me that question. As long as you live, never ask me that question again."

I looked into her eyes and saw no anger, only a world of pain and hurt. It was plain that the hurt went deep, deep into Lila's soul, everything that made her a woman scarred and cut about with terrible wounds that would be slow to heal, if they ever did. It was a pain I had never experienced, and thus I could only guess at its intensity, knowing I would always fall far short of the appalling reality.

Me, I looked into Lila's eyes and saw all the answer to my question I'd ever need.

For a fleeting moment, I thought about getting on my horse and running away from all this, from Lila, from the SP Connected, from Texas, never taking a single glance back.

But I knew I would not.

I believed I was falling in love with this woman, and now I had some fast growing up to do. Lila needed a man, now more than ever, not a boy. Was I yet that man?

I could not find it in me to answer that question.

Gently, with much care, I took Lila in my arms and held her close. We clung to each other, neither of us finding any words to say. If I could, I would have turned back time and made things as they once were, but that was impossible. What was done was done, and now I would have to deal with it. To worry over what had happened

341

would not empty tomorrow of its sorrow. It would only empty today of its joy.

Finally, I kissed Lila and rose to my feet.

As I walked to the door, she said: "Do right by him, Dusty."

I nodded, and stepped outside into the bright day.

Like me, Jim Meldrum bore an ancient name and the old fighting Celtic blood ran strong in him. He was a warrior and he would be laid to rest like one.

I laid his body across the saddle of the dun and led the horse to a quiet spot far enough away from the cabin. Gently, I lifted Jim off the horse and stretched him out on the grass.

That done, I rode back to the cabin and roped Wingo's feet. Him I dragged back to the place I'd chosen and then I returned again to the cabin. I found Jim Meldrum's rifle and Wingo's Colt and these I kept with me.

There was a shovel in a small shed behind the cabin, but before I dug graves I had yet one thing more to do. I stepped inside, with Lila's troubled eyes following me, and found what I'd hoped to find, a shallow bowl made of brick-colored Indian earthenware.

Wordlessly, I went back outside again and carried all the things I'd found to the spot where I'd left the bodies.

I dug Jim's grave as deep as I could. Because of the thin, rocky soil, the task took me the best part of two hours. Then I dug Wingo's, shallower, placed next to Jim's to form the base of an inverted T.

Sweating, I took off my shirt, then kneeled beside Wingo's body. Piece by piece, ending with the emerald ring on his finger, I stripped him of his gaudy silver finery, his necklace, the silver bracelets around his wrists. I laid all of it in the earthenware bowl and set it aside.

That done, I took my knife and cut the fancy buckskins off Wingo, leaving him stark naked, his staring eyes looking up at a blue sky he could not see. Then I threw him into his grave.

Jim Meldrum I buried in the ancient way, as befitted a fallen Celtic warrior. I laid him out with his arms — his Colt revolvers, rifle and knife — and I placed the bowl of his enemy's silver on his chest, the better to pay his way as he made his long journey to the netherworld.

Then I covered both graves with the good Texas earth, caught up my horse and returned to the cabin.

Lila, looking very pale, sat up on the bunk as I came in. "Did you do right by him, Dusty?" she asked.

I nodded. "I buried Jim Meldrum as befits a warrior, with his weapons. And I laid a dog at his feet."

"Then I'm satisfied," Lila said, sinking back into her pillow.

I stepped to the bunk, took up Lila in my arms and carried her out to my horse.

All the way back to the SP, she lay like a child in my arms, sleeping, her head on my chest. And as we proceeded on our journey, I kissed her hair, not once but many times.

Ma cried bitter tears for Jim Meldrum when we arrived at the ranch, then tempered her grief by fussing over Lila like a mother hen.

She had me carry Lila to the best room in the house, a spacious bed chamber on the ground level, the windows shaded by the porch and a huge, spreading oak tree where crows gathered in winter.

Ma insisted I get a doctor, if one could be found, but Charlie Fullerton was outraged by the very idea.

"I've treated more bullet wounds than any young whippersnapper of a doctor," he told Ma. "And I ain't never lost a shot-up puncher yet."

"Mr. Fullerton," Ma said, reasonably, "Lila is no puncher. In case you haven't noticed, she's a girl."

"Well," Charlie said, "it makes no never mind. I ain't lost one o' them either."

As it happened, even Ma had to admit that a doctor could not have done better than Charlie. He cleaned Lila's wounds, spread them with one of his mysterious salves and bound them up with a neat bandage.

"It feels better already," Lila said.

I don't know if she meant it, but it pleased Charlie enormously. "Told you so," he said to Ma, grinning. "Ain't nobody knows more than Charlie Fullerton about doctoring."

When Charlie left the room, Ma turned to me and said: "Dusty, go wait in the parlor for a spell. I want to talk to Lila alone."

Ma Prather was with Lila a long time, and when she reappeared, her face was strained and guarded. "She's sleeping now, Dusty," she said.

Charlie brought us coffee and Ma said: "Dusty, I know how you love to smoke. Let's take our coffee outside."

We stepped onto the porch, my spurs chiming, and sat in the same rockers that Lila and me had sat in the night Deke Stockton was killed. Ma was very quiet, sipping her coffee as the day slowly died around us and the sky caught fire.

I rolled a smoke and lit the cigarette, knowing Ma would talk when she felt like it.

Finally, she turned to me and said: "Dusty, that girl is going to need a lot of care." She waved a hand at me. "Oh, I don't mean her shoulder wound — Charlie Fullerton can fix that — I'm talking about her deeper wounds, the ones that are much harder to heal."

Me, I searched around for the right words, failed to find them and kept silent.

Ma and Lila had talked, and being a woman, Ma understood the depth of Lila's pain much more than I ever could.

Ma waited long to hear if I'd speak, but I busied myself by rolling another cigarette.

"Do you love her, Dusty?" she asked finally.

"I guess I do," I said. "No, I really do."

"Then you'll have to stand by her. She'll need that from you more than anything else."

I drew deep on my cigarette, enjoying

the harsh, bitter bite of the smoke. "Ma, I was thinking about that very thing earlier. I decided Lila needs a grown man, not a boy."

"Dusty, you're all the man you'll ever be," Ma said. "And a darned good one if you ask me."

"Do you really think that, Ma?" I asked.

Ma nodded. "If you were my own son, I'd tell you the same." She reached out and laid the tips of her fingers on the back of my hand. "Marry her, Dusty. Raise your children and then grow old with her and never, not even once, turn your back on her." She studied me closely. "Can you do all that?"

"I'd surely like to try."

"Do more than try." Ma hunted around for the right words, as I had done earlier. "Cherish her, Dusty. Never let her think for a single moment as long as you both live that you consider her soiled goods."

I took a deep breath and said: "If I made Lila my wife and any man said such a thing about her, I'd kill him."

"But you, Dusty, what do you think?"

I smiled, a genuine smile, finding no need to force it. "I think, Ma, I'm beginning to grow up."

I'll never know what Ma was going to say

next, because Charlie Fullerton stomped onto the porch and said: "Dinner's ready, an' if'n you don't come in and eat, I'll throw it away."

Half an hour later, as I was finishing my second piece of pie, big John Coleman and a dozen exhausted riders reined up outside the ranch house. The faces of the Coleman punchers were haggard and unshaven, but they looked a grim and determined bunch, led by a Kiowa I'd seen a time or two, a silent, brooding man who made a living as a horse wrangler but also hired out now and then as a scout.

I didn't yet know it as I wiped off my mouth and stepped onto the porch, but I'd soon be joining them all on a headlong ride into hell.

Chapter 24

"My Sally's gone," Coleman told Ma as he sat with us in the parlor. "And young Ethan Noon with her."

"John, whatever has happened?" Ma asked, rising alarm edging her voice.

Coleman turned his exhausted red-rimmed eyes on her. "It happened on the trail home after they left here last night."

"What happened, John?" Ma prompted. Her face had slowly drained of blood. She had guessed at what was to come and I could tell she dreaded every approaching word of it.

"Apaches," Coleman said. "We found Sally and Ethan by their upturned buggy early this morning. Ethan made a good fight of it. We found empty cartridge cases scattered all around his body." Coleman's voice caught in his throat and he struggled with the words. "Near as the Kiowa can piece it together, at the end Ethan threw down his empty rifle, drew his Colt and shot Sally" — his unsteady fingers strayed to his right temple — "here. Ethan kept the last bullet for himself. He shot himself in the mouth."

Hardly able to comprehend what I was hearing, I realized how badly I'd misjudged Ethan Noon. The puncher had sand and he'd proved it in the last few violent and terrifying moments of his life.

Coleman was a huge man, big in the chest and shoulders, with a full beard and an easygoing way about him. But now he looked shrunken somehow, and suddenly very old.

"Mr. Coleman, I'm right sorry about Sally," I said. "And Ethan."

The big rancher nodded. "Thank you, Dusty. I know you and Sally were close since you was both just younkers."

The man buried his face in his hands, but still seemed full of talk, the horror of what had happened spiking at him mercilessly. "I figure there were about two dozen Apaches involved in the attack. After we'd taken Sally and Ethan back to the ranch, I rounded up the hands and we took off after them.

"Rode clear to the breaks of Cottonwood Creek and found nothing, then headed south. Finally we saw their dust plain, but they were still a long ways off, and then we lost them. The Kiowa figures they doubled back on us and are headed for the Davis or maybe the Glass mountains. He says the Apaches figure to lose themselves up there among the canyons and rocks.

"I trust that Kiowa. He knows what he's talking about, when he talks."

Coleman took his hands from his face and looked at Ma. "Miz Prather, your ranch was closest, so I figured I'd let the boys eat and maybe exchange horses, and then get right back after them savages again."

Ma nodded. "Mr. Fullerton is feeding the hands in the bunkhouse right now, and of course I'll let you have fresh horses."

Coleman nodded, his eyes bloodshot, his face gray. "Thank you kindly. I surely do appreciate it."

Ma's eyes revealed her growing concern. "John, you're all in. You should rest up for a spell."

The rancher shook his head. "I'll have no rest until I find those Apaches and kill every last one of them."

I rose to my feet. "I'd like to join you, Mr. Coleman. Like you said, Sally and me were close."

"Glad to have you, Dusty," Coleman replied, picking at the plate of food on his lap. "We ride out in half an hour."

I walked to the bunkhouse and readied my gear, then saddled the dun and led him back to the front of the house. Most of Coleman's hands had already eaten and were busy roping fresh mounts from the corral.

I knew most of the men by name, and as I walked past several of them waved a friendly greeting, and one yelled: "Good to have you along, Dusty."

The oil lamps were lit outside the house on each side of the door, casting shifting pools of orange and yellow on the wood floor of the porch, and Ma and Coleman were sitting on the rockers in the shadows, deep in conversation.

I stepped inside and made my way to Lila's room and rapped lightly on the door.

"Come in," Lila called.

She was sitting up in bed when I entered, wearing a pale lavender robe of Ma's, her shoulder all bound up in Charlie's white bandage.

I sat on the edge of the bed and took Lila's hand. "How are you feeling?" I asked.

"Much better. Mr. Fullerton's been feeding me like a horse, says I'm way too skinny."

I looked into Lila's eyes, but they were shadowed and guarded, revealing nothing of how she felt or thought. "I just came in to say so long," I said. "I'm riding out with John Coleman after some Apache renegades."

Lila smiled at me. "Thanks for trying to spare my feelings, but Mr. Fullerton already told me what happened to Sally Coleman and her husband."

"Mr. Fullerton talks too much," I said, then rose to my feet. "Lila, I've got to be moving on."

"Dusty, please take care of yourself," Lila said.

Only after I'd left her room and swung into the saddle of my horse did I remember that I hadn't kissed her. Nor had I asked her to marry me.

It just wasn't the right time, I told myself.

But was that the only reason?

We rode out in moon-splashed darkness under a wild, broken sky, the Kiowa in the lead, most of the tired Coleman riders already nodding in the saddle.

The only sound was the fall of our horses' hooves and the creak of leather, though John Coleman mumbled to himself every now and then, a man being pushed to a breaking point by grief and the desire for revenge.

We headed west for three days and then caught and killed two Apache stragglers in Coyanosa Draw about twenty-five miles west of Fort Stockton. A third warrior was still alive after the shooting stopped and the smoke cleared, and John Coleman said we'd get nothing out of him anyhow and ordered one of his men to kill him.

But he underestimated the persuasive powers of the Kiowa. The Indian told John he'd find out where the remainder of the band was headed and the big rancher shrugged and let him have at it.

As the rest of us made camp and boiled coffee at a shallow runoff between two steep rises covered in creosote bush and tar brush, the Kiowa drew off a ways, dragging the wounded Apache with him. He made his own fire out of sight of us and got to work.

I have to hand it to that Apache — he was tough. Little more than a boy, he kept silent for a long while and it was only as the day shaded into evening and the first stars appeared that he began to scream.

He screamed all night, keeping us from sleep, and just before daybreak the screams suddenly strangled to an agonized stop.

The Kiowa came out of the brush, wiping his bloody knife on his buckskin leggings, and squatted by the fire. As the hands watched, some of them mighty green around the gills, he poured himself a cup of coffee, then rolled a cigarette, lighting it with a brand from the fire. The Kiowa sat, smoking, drinking his coffee, shivering slightly in the morning chill, a man at peace with himself, saying nothing.

Big John, surly from lack of rest, stepped beside the Indian, looked down at him and asked: "Well?"

Without looking up, the Kiowa said: "The Apaches you seek are headed for the Davis Mountains all right, and they'll swing a little to the north to avoid Fort Davis and the Buffalo Soldiers. They plan to link up with Victorio at Wild Horse Draw and then cross the Rio Grande into Mexico. All this the Mescalero boy told me."

"Can we catch them before they get into the mountains?" Coleman asked, his eyes anxiously searching the Kiowa's impassive bronzed face.

The Indian nodded. "We will catch them. It may be today or tomorrow, but we will catch them."

"Hey, Injun, do they know for sure we're after them?" a puncher asked.

The Kiowa nodded, his black eyes flat, revealing nothing. "They know. And they don't fear us."

"They will fear us — by God they will," Coleman roared, slamming his fist into the open palm of his left hand, his face flushed.

The Kiowa shrugged. "They ride to join Victorio. Otherwise the hunters might already have become the hunted."

"I want them all dead," Coleman yelled, ignoring the man. He turned to his hands, taking in each one of them with his sweeping red-eyed glare. "Do you hear that, boys. I want them all dead and I'll give any man who brings me an Apache scalp a fifty-dollar bonus. In gold!"

A cheer went up from the hands, but the Kiowa sat in brooding silence, absorbed by his own thoughts, his eyes open but seeing nothing, looking inward.

I figured the man was having a vision of some kind, but I could not guess if it was good or bad, and had I asked, the Kiowa would not have told me.

It was not yet full daylight when we saddled up and took to the trail, heading due west to keep Fort Davis to our south.

A day's ride took us to the shallow foothills of the Davis peaks, but we saw no sign of Apaches.

The Kiowa rode far ahead of us, scouting the brush-covered hills and shadowed canyons, the rugged, stone pillared mountains a purple silhouette against the pale sky, rising a mile high above the plain.

The Coleman hands were strung out along the trail, men and horses beginning to wear out. There was no talk from the men as they rode and I began to wonder if they'd stick if we didn't come on the Apaches soon.

I reckoned John Coleman had the same thought, because he suddenly turned in the saddle and beckoned to me. I kneed my horse beside the big rancher and was shocked by his appearance. Under his beard, his cheeks were sunken and his skin had taken on an unhealthy gray pallor. Only the eyes were alive, burning with an unholy light, the eyes of a fanatic — or a madman.

"Dusty, listen to me," the rancher said. "There's still a couple of hours until dark and I want this over and done. I want the Apaches who killed my Sally scalped and dead."

"We'll find them, Mr. Coleman," I said,

attempting to humor the man. "They can't be too far ahead of us."

As though he hadn't heard, Coleman went on: "Back at the Rafter C, my Sally lies in the icehouse, wrapped in a sheet, all stiff and white and cold. I can hear her every minute of the day and night, crying out for me to come home and bury her decent." The man's blazing eyes sought mine. "She'll wear a dress that was her mother's. I'll lay her in the ground in it."

The big rancher was teetering along the ragged edge of insanity, though I could sense his inward struggle as he desperately tried not to slip away.

"Go help the Kiowa, Dusty," he said, slapping me on the shoulder. "Find me those Apaches."

I was only too glad to escape those terrible eyes, and I spurred the galloping dun hard as I rode toward the distant figure of the Kiowa.

I caught up with the Indian as he was riding through a narrow canyon, its floor covered in yucca and agarito. On the top of the surrounding hills grew yellow pine and a few black cherry trees. Higher up, the mountain slopes were covered in juniper and pinon and here and there stood stands of slender and stately ponderosa pine, their dark green branches moving restlessly in the wind.

The Kiowa didn't seem surprised to see me. He merely pointed with his bladed hand along the canyon. "They came this way." He nodded toward the soaring mountains. "They intend to cross the peaks and head for Wild Horse Draw."

I looked around me, but saw nothing. "Where are they?" I asked.

The Kiowa gave me a rare, grudging smile and nodded. "Up there."

I looked up, squinting against the harsh sunlight, at the mountain towering above us. It was a steep climb to the crest where granite rocks jutted from the slope like the prows of great iron warships.

As my eyes became accustomed to the glare, I made out a single file of about twenty horsemen winding their way toward the top, an Apache on a gray horse leading them, the rest strung out behind him.

"Hell, they're getting away," I said.

The Kiowa shook his head. "No, because now we stop them."

He slid his Henry from the boot, threw it to his shoulder and levered off three fast shots, the booming echoes bounding among the canyon walls like gigantic boulders being bowled along a stone cavern.

Immediately, the Apaches scattered, men and horses merging so completely into the landscape of the mountain that the slope seemed deserted.

Coleman and his riders charged into the canyon a few moments later.

"Damn it all, did we lose them?" the rancher yelled, glaring at the Kiowa, his frustration evident. "Did we lose them?"

The Indian answered without taking his eyes from the slope. "No, they are up there."

"Will they fight?" Coleman demanded. His gaze turned to me. "Dusty, will they fight?"

"They will fight," the Kiowa replied for me. "They will fight up there, higher up the mountain. The Apache will let us come to them, even though we are few and they are many."

"Hell," the big rancher snorted, "there are thirteen of us."

The Kiowa smiled again, a humorless grimace that didn't reach his eyes. "With Apaches, that may not be enough."

"If you're too yellow to face them, then stay here, damn you!" Coleman flared. "The rest of us will get the job done."

If the Kiowa took offense, he didn't let it show. He turned to Coleman and carefully unbuttoned his shirt, revealing a rawhide string; hanging from it were what looked to me to be a row of withered brown claws. "These are the trigger fingers of the seventeen men I have killed in battle," he told Coleman, his hard-boned face stiff and proud. "I will fight the Apaches."

Coleman looked at the Indian's grisly trophies for long moments, then nodded. "So be it."

He turned in the saddle, addressing his men. "My offer still stands, boys. Fifty dollars in gold for every filthy Apache scalp you lay at my feet." Amid wild cheering, Coleman doffed his hat and waved it above his head. "Now let's go get it done."

Led by the Kiowa, we rode further into the silent canyon.

I slid my Winchester from the scabbard and from far above me I heard a scrub jay call, answered a few moments later by another. And another.

The Kiowa's back stiffened, his eyes constantly scanning the ridges of the canyon. He laid the butt of the Henry on his right thigh, holding the rifle upright and ready as his pony picked its way along the canyon floor.

He had been right. The Apaches weren't about to run. They planned to stay and fight.

Chapter 25

After a couple hundred yards, the canyon widened, giving way to a wide clearing carpeted with grass and wildflowers, a few scrub oak growing around the perimeter. There was evidence that wild cattle had used this place to graze and they'd cut a narrow trail that wound up the slope of the mountain, disappearing into some tumbled boulders a few hundred feet above the level.

We were enclosed on all sides by high, brush-topped ridges, and it was very hot in the clearing. I stood my horse near the shade of an oak and wiped sweat from my hatband and brow.

The Kiowa had swung out of the saddle and was examining the trail up the mountain. He studied the piled-up boulders above us for long moments, nodded to himself, then walked over to Coleman, leading his pony.

"Where are they?" the rancher asked, irritation harsh in his voice. "Damn it, man, where are they?"

The Kiowa pointed beyond the boulders. "Higher."

"Can we get the horses up there?"

"Yes," the Kiowa answered, "but best we go on foot. Men on horseback make large targets."

Coleman didn't argue. He ordered his hands to dismount and leave their horses in the clearing. I swung out of the saddle, eased the girth on the dun, then walked to the bottom of the trail, studying the boulders above me. It seemed a likely ambush spot, but I figured the Kiowa knew what he was doing, and when he took to the slope I stepped after him, Coleman and his men falling in behind us.

Halfway to the boulders, a rabbit bounded out from under my feet and I jumped about three feet in the air in surprise. Behind me I heard a man snigger and even Coleman smiled and said: "Bunny spooked you some, Dusty, huh?"

I turned my head, gave the man a sheepish grin and kept on climbing.

The Apaches had us outnumbered, but when I'd looked around at Coleman's hard-bitten, gun-handy riders, most of whom had fought Indians before, I figured the odds might just about be even.

But all that changed in an instant.

A rifle crashed and the Kiowa, two steps ahead of me, cried out and fell back into my arms. I couldn't catch him, but I broke his fall as he collapsed in a heap at my feet. The Kiowa had taken a bullet square in the chest and he was already dead when he hit the ground.

A volley of rifle fire erupted from the boulders and behind me I heard men curse and yell as they were hit, the rest stampeding back down the trail to the clearing. A bullet kicked up dirt at my feet and another gouged across the stock of my rifle, splintering the walnut.

The Kiowa had been right about the Apaches' willingness to fight, but he had been fatally wrong about where they'd make their stand. The warriors weren't higher up the mountain — they were right here, bringing the battle to us.

I dove into a patch of thick brush and mesquite to my left, a little ways off the cattle trail, shifted the Winchester to my left hand and drew my Colt. The Apaches, scattered among the boulders, were only a dozen yards away and the six-gun would be better for close work.

But after the initial firing died down, nothing moved among the rocks. I glanced down the trail. Three of the Coleman riders were on the ground, one of the men groaning, dark red blood stringing from his mouth as he coughed and tried to crawl back to the safety of the clearing. Finally the man's arms gave way and he fell on his face and lay still.

"Dusty!" Coleman yelled from somewhere below me. "Can you hear me?"

"Yeah!"

"Are you hit?"

"No. But the Kiowa is dead, and three others."

Coleman swore bitterly, then hollered: "We're trapped like rats down here. I'm going to find another way up the mountain before it gets too dark to see." I didn't reply and the rancher hollered again. "Dusty, keep 'em busy for a spell."

Easier said than done, Mr. Coleman!

"I'll do my best," I yelled, suddenly feeling mighty vulnerable and lonely.

The dying sunlight caught the higher ridges of the mountains and the shadows of the ponderosa pines were lengthening. The lost and lonely ravines and canyons were shading into dark blue and the sky above was pale lemon, smeared with wide bands of deep scarlet.

I figured it would be full dark in no more than an hour and I could make my way back down the trail to the clearing — unless Coleman and his surviving men worked their way up the slope and got behind the Apaches.

A few tense minutes ticked by; then a shot from the boulders rattled through the branches of the mesquite bush, inches from my head. I caught a glimpse of something white move among the rocks and thumbed off a fast shot from the Colt. I saw the bullet strike rock and then whine harmlessly away. Another rifle fired from among the boulders, splitting the air above me, then another. I rose up on one knee and hammered four fast shots from the Colt, holstered the six-gun and grabbed the rifle.

I was trapped like a calf in a pen, neither able to climb higher nor make my way down. It was not a situation to reassure a man — a worrisome thing.

Something moved at the top of one of the largest boulders, just a quick blur that came and went. I waited. Gradually a head appeared, then a rifle. The Apache sighted in my direction, triggered a shot that rattled the mesquite bush for a second time, then quickly disappeared.

I raised the Winchester to my shoulder, gambling that the warrior would try another shot from that same position.

Sweat stinging my eyes, I held still, the sights of the rifle steady on the spot where I'd last seen the Apache. Somewhere higher up the mountain an early-waking owl hooted his question over and over, and farther away among the canyons the coyotes were beginning to yap.

Dark hair appeared at the top of the boulder, and with agonizing slowness, the Apache's head and shoulders finally came into view. I watched as the warrior laid his rifle across the rock and I took a deep breath, held it and set my sights on the man's forehead.

Just as the Apache leveled his rifle, I squeezed the trigger. Over the blast of the shot I heard a wild scream, and the head disappeared, splashes of blood suddenly staining the top of the boulder.

And now there were only nineteen left.

I smiled grimly at that thought, finding it little consolation now that our numbers had been reduced to nine by the Apache ambush.

I reloaded the Colt, filling all six chambers, cranked the spent shell from the Winchester and fed another round into the chamber. It was shaping up to be a long night.

Fifteen minutes passed with no firing on either side.

Then the Apaches came at me.

The warriors swarmed from among the boulders and ran toward me, firing as they ran.

I got off one fast shot from the rifle, scored no hit and drew the Colt. The warriors were only a few yards away, bunched together and coming fast, hoping to capture me alive. Going against everything I'd ever been taught about the handling of a six-gun, I spread my legs wide and fanned the Colt dry, the gun almost uncontrollable, roaring and bucking in my hand. But at such close range, the tenderfoot play of the fanned revolver was devastating. Two of my shots went into the ground, another flew wild, but three of the warriors went down, at least two of them hit hard enough that they didn't get up again.

Then the Apaches were tumbling all over me.

I kicked and punched and bit and swore, crashing my fist against a chin here, swinging my boot into a groin there. Then a rifle butt slammed into the back of my head and I knew no more.

I woke to darkness.

It took me a few moments to realize that I was naked, lying on my back, my wrists and ankles bound to stakes driven into the ground.

The rawhide had been wet when I was tied. Now it was dry and had shrunk, the thongs biting into my wrists so that my throbbing hands felt like they were swollen to three times their normal size.

When I looked up, the sky was ablaze with stars and the moon, almost full now, rode high within a circle of its own silver light.

Something stirred to my right and I turned to look. The Apaches sat around a small fire and I smelled meat roasting. One of the warriors raised a chunk of dripping beef to his mouth on a stick, held the meat with his teeth, then cut off a huge piece and began to chew.

But even the tiny movement of my head had been noticed.

One of the warriors rose from the fire and stepped toward me. I saw two things very quickly: The entire lower half of the man's face, from his chin to his eyes, was painted black, among the Apaches a sign of mourning, not war. And I recognized him as the warrior who had sat the gray horse and given me the name *Matanzas con Sus Dentes*.

The Apache squatted on his heels beside me, his eyes shadowed by the darkness. He stayed that way for a long while, and though I couldn't see his eyes, I felt them burning into mine — and I felt their hatred.

Finally I asked: *"Qué usted desea de mi?"*
The Apache surprised me then. In English he answered: "What I want from you is your death."

"Why do you hate me so much?" I asked. Thinking back, it was a pretty dumb question, since the Apache hated just about everybody. But this warrior didn't see it that way.

"You are the one who tore out my brother's throat with your teeth. He and I were" — he raised his hands, forefingers extended, and brought the fingers together — "two from the same womb, born at the same hour. As we grew to manhood, we thought the same thoughts, felt the same things. We were two, but we lived as one."

I'd killed this man's twin brother, and right then I knew I was in deep trouble. And what he said next confirmed it.

"Your dying will be slow and very painful," the Apache said quietly, like he was making polite conversation in Ma

Prather's parlor. "Only a very brave warrior could have killed my brother, but even so, at the end you will scream loud, I think."

The moonlight lay like polished steel on the hard planes of the Apache's face and the thin gash of his mouth. This was not the face of a merciful man, and anyhow, mercy for a captured enemy was a concept totally foreign to him.

"Go to hell," I said, knowing I had nothing to lose by it.

The Apache nodded, saying nothing, no doubt having many times heard this same empty bravado before from men who later died shrieking for mercy or for death.

He rose to his feet and stepped to the fire. When he returned he held a handful of long, jagged cactus spines. He squatted beside me again and slowly, methodically shoved two dozen of the spines just under the skin of my chest and belly, leaving about an inch of each showing.

The pain was an intense, scorching fire, and I bit my lip, determined not to cry out. The torture was only beginning and it could last for two or three days. Could I take it without screaming? I knew the answer to that could only be no.

The Apache turned and uttered something to a warrior sitting by the fire. The man nodded, rose and carried over a thin, burning branch from the fire. The Apache took the brand from the warrior and then, one by one, lit the exposed tips of the spines.

Certain kinds of cactus spines — cholla is one of them — will burn well when dry, flaring up like struck matches.

When the Apache lit a spine, it very quickly flamed its way under my skin, and I smelled my own flesh as it sizzled and burned.

I bore the first two or three, arching my back, heaving against my vicious bonds, and the terrible pain that slammed through me. But after several more spines were lit, I heard someone scream, coming from a long distance away. Then, to my horror, I realized it was me.

Sweat trickled down my forehead as the spines burned and I ground my teeth so hard, my breath hissing, that my jaw began to throb. But that was a little pain against the greater agony of the scorching, flaring spines.

The moon looked down on me and the stars glittered and I heard the wind sigh among the pines. But I was alone with my torment, and all of them — moon, stars, pines and wind — were completely indifferent to my suffering.

The flames from the brand lit another spine, and another. The stink of my own burning flesh was sharp in my nostrils, and no matter how I bucked and strained I could not escape the searing agony of the fire.

Beside me the Apache looked on with cool indifference, like a doctor beside a patient's bed, interested but detached.

He was testing me to see if I was the great warrior he thought I was, and I had the feeling I was failing the test badly.

One thing I wanted to do before the pain became unbearable and I started to uselessly scream and beg for mercy: I wanted to spit in that damned Apache's eye.

I raised my head, trying to gather saliva, but there was none. My mouth was bone dry. Defeated, filled with pain and the greater pain of loss and despair, I let my head thump back onto the ground just as the Apache lit another cactus spine.

Thunder crashed around me and I heard someone scream again.

Chapter 26

The scream was not mine, nor did the thunder come from the sky. I was hearing the cries of dying men and the roar of guns.

The Apache beside me sprang to his feet as John Coleman and his hands charged into the camp. All of them were mounted, having somehow found a way to bring their horses up the slope.

Coleman was in the lead, grim and terrible, his Colt hammering as his horse bucked and kicked, throwing up great clods of dirt. Taken completely by surprise, Apaches were running in every direction and six or seven of them were already stretched out on the ground.

The Coleman punchers were riding through and around the Apache camp, shooting at everything that moved. I raised my head and saw one of the Coleman riders throw up his hands and topple out of the saddle. Then John himself was hit. His horse reared and crashed heavily on top of him.

But, despite the losses among the Coleman riders, the Apaches were in full flight.

A very few had managed to reach their horses and were riding, hell for leather, toward the top of the mountain. Others were fleeing on foot, but these were mercilessly cut down by the vengeful Coleman hands.

Among all the confusion of flying hooves, the screams of the dying and the flash and bang of guns in the flame-streaked darkness, I lifted my head, straining against the rawhide bonds — in time to see an Apache on a gray horse gallop away in the distance before being swallowed by the night.

A Coleman rider with red hair and mustache reined up his horse beside me and swung out of the saddle. The man kneeled beside me, shook his head and whistled through his teeth. "Geez, Dusty," he said, "what the hell did they do to you?"

This was no time for polite conversation. "Cut me loose!" I yelled.

The rider did as I asked, and I scrambled to my feet and, my head swimming, immediately fell down again.

"You best lie there quiet," the hand said. "Man, you're a mess." He touched my chest and when he brought his hand away I saw it was covered in blood and blackened pieces of scorched skin.

"Help me to my feet," I said. "And help me find my damn clothes."

The Coleman hand pulled me upright, and this time I didn't fall.

Men were riding this way and that, some of them still shooting, and a couple of hands were bent over the still, sprawled form of John Coleman.

Helped by the redhead, I found my clothes where the Apaches had dumped them after stripping me. I put on my hat, then my pants and stomped into boots. The shirt I left aside, fearing the rough army wool would rub against the wounds on my chest, and slipped the suspenders over my bare shoulders.

I felt weak and sick, but I had something to do that needed to be done.

"Get me a horse. And a gun," I said to the Coleman hand.

"But, Dusty, you're in no condition to —"

"Hell, man, don't argue," I yelled. "Do as I say."

Me, I have no idea what that puncher saw when he looked at me, his eyes wide and shocked. A wild man, I guess, a raving creature who had just been to hell and back, his chest and shoulders covered in dried blood and scorched and blackened flesh.

Whatever it was, the redheaded puncher didn't think it wise to argue further. He handed me the reins of his horse and gave me his own gun belt and Winchester.

I buckled on the belt, shoved the rifle into the boot, then swung heavily into the saddle. I glanced over at John Coleman. "How is he?" I asked one of the men kneeling beside him. The puncher looked up at me and slowly shook his head, telling me all I needed to know.

I swung my horse around and headed up the slope. Behind me I heard the Coleman hand yell: "Dusty, where are you going?"

Ignoring the man, I rode higher. The moon bathed the side of the mountain in light and a breeze stirred the branches of the pines. I felt stiff and sore and constantly worked the swollen fingers of my right hand, surprised to find they were better than I'd expected.

I topped a low ridge, rode through some dense juniper and followed the dip downward. I climbed higher again, wary now, the Winchester across the saddle horn, and came up on a wide stand of ponderosa pine.

I let the horse take a breather and

scanned the tree line and the higher rocks above the pines. And saw nothing.

If the Apache I sought had come this way, he was well gone, or holed up somewhere.

From where I sat my horse, I was maybe three-quarters of a mile above the flat. Ahead of me the slope gradually grew steeper, rawboned granite rocks and mountain scrub becoming more frequent beyond the tree line, where the pines faded and finally stopped.

Wishful for tobacco, but having none, I kicked the horse into motion and climbed higher. I rode through the ponderosas and in places the passage between the trunks was very narrow and tight, made worse by darkness, because very little moonlight penetrated the thick canopy of the treetops. When I emerged on the other side I was scraped and cut by branches and many of the burn wounds on my chest were oozing trickles of blood.

Ahead of me the slope rose at a much steeper angle, but I spotted what looked like a narrow game trail winding upward toward the swaybacked crest of the mountain. The area on either side of the trail was surrounded by V-shaped rock formations, here and there massive boulders scattered around as though they'd fallen from the pocket of a striding giant.

The moon was drifting lower in the sky, but still spread a thin light, and the breeze, now that I was higher, blew stronger, edged with cold. This I welcomed, because the chill refreshed me and helped clear my head.

I reached the game trail and began the steep climb. But the horse, bred for the range, not mountains, balked, sidestepping on me, tossing his head as he tried to turn back. I fought the horse for a couple of minutes, then decided it was hopeless. All I was doing was draining my already low reserve of strength. I swung out of the saddle.

Where was the Apache? And was he alone?

Those questions crowded into my head, unsettling me as I led the horse back to the tree line and found a patch of bunch grass where he could graze.

I took up my rifle, walked to the trail again and started to climb. The going was hard and I was weak from the torture I'd suffered and from loss of blood. Every so often I had to get down on one knee, battling to catch my breath and gather my strength, my head bowed. Then I climbed again.

The thought never once occurred to me to give up and turn back. The Apache had wronged me and that I could not forgive or forget. The man had a reckoning coming and it wasn't in me to let him escape it.

I passed a small rock formation no taller than a man on a horse, shaped like an inverted V, topped with a scattering of smaller boulders and clumps of scrub grass and black thorn bush.

I'd only taken a few steps past the rock when I heard it: a soft, quick, *whum . . . whum . . . whum . . .*

Turning fast, bringing up the Winchester, I took the blade of the spinning steel tomahawk in my right arm, where the heavy meat of the shoulder muscle meets the biceps.

The wicked little hatchet had been thrown at my back, but I had heard its whispering passage through the air and turned at the last moment. I had saved my life, but the blade was buried inches deep in my arm.

Instantly I lost all feeling in the arm and it flopped uselessly at my side, the Winchester slipping from suddenly nerveless fingers, thudding to the ground at my feet.

Above me I heard a loud whoop of triumph and the Apache jumped from the rock and ran at me, a knife in his upraised hand.

But I was in no shape to fight this battle on his terms.

Desperately, I clawed for the holstered Colt with my left hand, dragging it out of the leather by the hammer and cylinder. The Apache was almost on top of me. I threw the six-gun in the air and grabbed it correctly, thumbing back the hammer as my finger found the trigger.

The Apache closed with me and he slashed viciously downward with his knife. I twisted away at the last moment and the blade raked down my left side, drawing a thin line of blood but doing little damage.

Off balance because of his swing, the Apache stumbled into me and I raised my right boot and shoved him away. The warrior staggered back a couple of steps, his face twisted into a snarl of rage, and came at me again.

I triggered the Colt, feeling the gun awkward in my left hand, and saw the Apache jerk as the bullet slammed into him. Hit hard, the man slowed for just a split second, but it was enough. I fired again and again at point-blank range, every bullet finding its mark in the warrior's body.

The Apache stumbled against me and I pushed him away again. He spun, fell on his face and then rolled over on his back, his black eyes blazing with a mix of hatred, defiance and the lust for revenge.

The warrior raised his head, frantically searching around him, and a hand stretched out for his knife, which had fallen nearby. But he never made it. His teeth bared in an ugly snarl, the breath rattled in his throat and he fell back, his terrible eyes closing for the last time.

I felt no pity for the man and no remorse. I understood what had driven him, because I'd seen the same single-mindedness of purpose, the same desire for revenge, in John Coleman. I did not admire it in Coleman, nor did I in this Apache.

I stepped over the warrior's body and stumbled down the slope, found my horse and rode away from there. I didn't look back.

Chapter 27

"It's too deep, Dusty. Man, it's gone right into the bone."

With my good hand, I grabbed the red-headed puncher by the front of his shirt and pulled the man toward me. "Get it out of there," I said, my teeth gritted against the pain. "Do it!"

I was lying on my back near the fading Apache fire and around me the Coleman hands were gathering their dead.

John Coleman had died without ever regaining consciousness. Including the Kiowa, we had five dead and two wounded — one of them me.

The redheaded puncher peered at the tomahawk buried in my arm. "That ain't Apache," he said. "I think it's Arapaho. Maybe it's Arapaho."

"I don't give a damn what it is. Just get it out of there," I yelled, my patience snapping.

The puncher took a deep breath — I recollect that he had freckles all over his nose and cheeks — grabbed the ax by the handle and yanked. It didn't budge, but wave after wave of agony slammed through me and sweat popped out on my forehead.

"Try it again," I gasped. "For God's sake, pull harder."

The man did as I asked, and this time the tomahawk ripped free, bringing with it chunks of bloody flesh and splinters of bone.

I couldn't stop the wild scream that rose to my lips, and beside me the redhead threw the hatchet aside, dropped to all fours and started to retch. The man finally wiped his mouth with the back of his hand, looked down at me and kept muttering over and over again: "Oh Jesus. Oh sweet Jesus . . ."

It was a prayer, not a cuss, but whether it was for me or for himself, I could not tell.

For me, the next few hours passed in a vague, whirling blur.

The dark landscape changed around me, from night to day, unshaven faces came and went and voices spoke to me, but, taken by a raging fever, I recollect very little of what happened.

I know we took our dead to Fort Davis for burial and that the sprawling post was a beehive of activity as two full regiments of

Buffalo Soldier cavalry got ready to leave in pursuit of Victorio.

I remember a harried young army doctor doing what he could for my arm, and I recall him saying to the Coleman punchers: "If gangrene gets into that arm, he'll need a lot more doctoring . . . and from a better physician than me."

There was some discussion among the hands as to whether or not they should leave me at the fort, but I insisted that I could make the ride back to the SP Connected.

After a deal of cussin' and discussin', most of which I don't remember, the decision was made to take me back to the ranch.

We rode into the SP four days later. I was burning with fever, seeing Apaches everywhere, talking to John Coleman like he was still alive, the dead Kiowa stepping out of a swirling mist, smiling at me, a bloody scalp in his hand, hearing gut-shot men scream and the sky above me cartwheeling, the hot sun spinning, never still for a moment.

As strong hands gently lifted me from the saddle outside the ranch house, I heard one of the Coleman punchers say to Ma Prather: "He's in a bad way, ma'am. Unless somebody cuts that rotten arm off'n him, I don't reckon he'll make it much past the day after tomorrow."

The hell you won't cut off my arm, I yelled. But I must have only thought it, because nobody paid me any mind.

I woke to find myself looking into the whiskery, whiskey-reddened face of Charlie Fullerton, and this second time was no more pleasant than the first.

"How you feeling, boy?" Charlie asked.

"How . . . how long . . ."

"Best part of two weeks. You've been out of your mind, tossing and turning and raving. Been up the trail with Mr. Prather a time or two and refought old battles, lost and won. And you've been calling out for Lila, and saying other things about her as well."

"Mr. Fullerton," I heard Ma say, "that's quite enough."

My arm!

I turned and saw a fat bandage around my shoulder — but the arm was still there!

"Saved it for you, boy," Charlie said, his face beaming. "Dang me, if'n I didn't."

He turned to Ma, who suddenly swam into my line of vision. "Mrs. Prather here, sent a fast rider all the way to Sweetwater for a doctor. When the man arrived, he un-limbered his saw and was all set to cut your arm off."

"Mr. Fullerton stopped him, Dusty," Ma said. She sat on the edge of the bed and took my hand. "For a spell there, we thought we'd lost you."

I turned to Charlie. "But how did . . . ?"

"Well, first off," Charlie said, stopping me as he warmed up to the conversation, "I put the muzzle of my old Remington against that sawbone's head and tole him: 'Mister, you let that boy's arm be. I ain't never shot a medical man yet, but there's a first time for everything.' Well, that doc taken out of here like a buckshot coyote and I went to work."

My head was clearing and I struggled to a sitting position on the bed. "How did you save my arm, Mr. Fullerton?"

"Maggots, boy, maggots, hundreds an' hundreds of them."

Ma shook her head. "It was just horrible, Dusty. I'm glad you were out of your head and didn't know what was happening."

"Maggots?"

"Maggots, boy," Charlie answered. "See, I was a medical orderly during the War Be-tween the States, and I always noticed how the wounds of soldiers who'd lain out in the field for days never got gangrenous. But the wounds of the poor boys laid up in the hospital most always did. So, I ask you, what made the difference?"

I shook my head in bafflement.

"Maggots, boy. Them soldiers who'd been lying hurt between the lines day and night always had maggots in their wounds. Maggots feed on rotten meat, and that's why they cured the gangrene. They ate it, boy, they ate it."

"Mr. Fullerton, that's horrible," Ma said, her nose wrinkling.

"Maybe so, but they saved the boy's arm, and his life."

"Mr. Fullerton," I asked, not really knowing if I wanted the answer, "where did you get the maggots?"

"Easy," Charlie beamed, "rode around until I found me a dead critter and then collected them. I put five hundred on your arm, Dusty, and covered them up with a bandage. Let them do their work for a week, then washed them off. That tommyhawk wound came up clean as a hound's tooth.

"After that, I put on some healing salves of my own invention" — he gave Ma a sidelong look — "the secrets of which I plan to keep to myself, no matter who's doing the coaxing."

Ma sniffed, and Charlie continued: " 'Course, you ain't going to be using the arm for a spell and you'll have a scar big enough to store hay in, but you still got your gun hand an' that's the main thing."

I shook my head at the cook. "No more guns. I've had enough of shooting and killing to last me a lifetime."

Charlie opened his mouth to object, but Ma interrupted him. "Dusty, there's someone outside who's been waiting patiently to see you."

"Lila?"

Ma smiled. "Lila. I'll get her." She gave Charlie a nod. "Let's go, Mr. Fullerton. These two young people need to be alone."

I licked my fingers and was still running them through my hair in a vain attempt to smooth it down when the door opened. Lila stepped inside and quietly closed the door after her.

She was wearing a simple gray dress and her hair was unbound, falling over her shoulders and my heart skipped a beat, me just lying there, thinking her the most beautiful creature I'd ever seen.

Lila crossed the room and sat on the bed. "How do you feel, Dusty?" she asked, her smile something a man would be willing to die for.

"I'm just fine," I said. "And I could ask the same thing of you. How is the shoulder?"

"I'm on the mend, thanks to Mr. Fullerton."

We sat in silence for a few moments. Then Lila said: "Dusty, the day after you got back, Ma and me drove the buckboard over to the Coleman place for Sally's funeral. I hope you don't mind, but I took the straw bonnet you bought for her and put it on her grave."

I nodded. "You did just fine. Sally would have liked that."

Another silence passed between us. Then I said: "Lila, I want to ask you something."

"Ask away, Dusty. I'm listening."

After a few false starts, I finally managed: "Lila, will you marry me?"

Her smile grew wider. "Of course we'll be married. I knew that the first time I ever set eyes on you."

"Soon," I said.

Lila nodded. "Soon as you're able to stand on your own two feet and say I do."

"There's one thing though," I said. "When we're on our own place, I won't be able to walk behind a plow. At least not for a while with this arm."

Lila stiffened. "Mr. Hannah, this is cow country."

So Ma had finally worn her down!

I held Lila close with my good arm, and she whispered. "There's just one thing I want, Dusty."

"Anything."

"Will you clear me a space for a vegetable garden?"

"Of course I will. I'll make you the best vegetable garden this side of El Paso."

Outside the shadows were lengthening, but I saw no shadow of a future parting for Lila and me, now or ever, for as long as we'd live.

I kissed her then, hard and long.

When it was over, Lila rubbed her finger across her top lip.

"What's the matter?" I asked.

"It's your mustache, Dusty. It tickles."

I touched my upper lip with the tips of my fingers and among the fuzz felt stiff, wiry bristles — the beginnings, I fancied, of a fine dragoon mustache. A man's mustache.

I threw back my head and laughed.

Me, I was eighteen years old that summer of 1880.

And my happiness was complete.